AN ANGRY GOD

RUSSELL J. SANDERS

Rattling Good Yarns Press
33490 Date Palm Drive 3065
Cathedral City CA 92235
USA
www.rattlinggoodyarns.com

Cover Design: Rattling Good Yarns Press

Library of Congress Control Number: 2023941001
ISBN: 978-1-955826-47-1

First Edition

For all those devout folks who love and accept, refusing to hate

Autumn
A city in the Midwest

Kevin

So he'd ditched school. No big deal. Kevin knew he'd get away with it. He always did. The trick was to make sure the attendance office only had his stepdad's work phone as a contact. That was easy. He told them his mom worked out of town frequently—she didn't—and that his father oversaw his every move. If he said that with a sweet, sad puppy dog look on his face, he could always pull it off. All he had to do was make sure he filled out the parental contact form, leaving off his mom's work number, and handed it in personally. His mother had never really cared, and his stepdad couldn't be bothered. Even if the attendance clerk called Step's office, he'd blow them off, too busy to deal with something as insignificant as his stepson. But they'd never call because Kevin only ditched when he'd had all he could stomach. And that was not very often. Most of the time, he'd sit, smile, and pretend to take notes. He'd have no use for theorems, *Moby Dick*, the periodic table, the battle of Waterloo, or anything of their other crap in the real world. And if he did, he'd remember it all anyway. That's just the way his brain worked.

Some might say Kevin was too smart for his own good. But he didn't see it that way. His motto was, "Play all the angles and win the game at all costs."

So there he sprawled, in front of the flat screen, catching up on the day's news and smoking a joint. Hand-rolled. Excellent stuff. Just what he needed this fine morning. He'd get rid of the evidence, Febreze the house, and paste a smile on his face long before Mom and Step got home from work. His mom lived at the office, and Step was not much better.

He inhaled deeply and held the smoke in his lungs, as the blue BREAKING NEWS letters filled the screen. The news anchor, Chet Charles, hair all perfect, dark suit with matching tie and silk flower in his lapel, star of Greatwood, Indiana's CBS affiliate Channel 4, monotoned,

"Force Four News has just learned a body was discovered in Fullerton Arboretum an hour ago. Nathan Miller was jogging with his dog when he felt a pull on the leash. Miller apparently tried to get the dog back on the path, but the black lab pulled away, ripping the leash from Miller's hands. When Miller ran after his dog, he found a gruesome sight and immediately dialed 911. Force Four reporter Marlon Gordon is on the scene. Here's what he has to say of this discovery."

The screen cut to Greatwood's heartthrob reporter, muscles bulging in a form-fitting Force Four News polo, park joggers running behind him on the trail, seemingly oblivious to this aforementioned slaughter. The guy, mic in hand, nodded his head—*why do they always do that?*—and began to speak.

"As you said, Chet, a body was discovered. We appear to have a white male, perhaps sixteen to twenty-two, who has been bludgeoned to death. Our cameraman was able to get footage before authorities shooed him away. A warning here—the video is graphic, and parents may want to take caution.

"Out of respect for the victim and his family, we are not showing his face, but I must say, it will be difficult to identify this young man on facial recognition alone. As you can see, his clothing is soaked in blood, appearing as if this attack was in the last few hours.

"The police and crime scene techs are still gathering evidence. It seems, however, this murder, if it is indeed a murder and frankly, I don't see how it could be anything but, is the fourth in a series of murders that have plagued several areas of Greatwood, each time the victim a young man, who was later identified as gay, with sandy brown hair, blue eyes, and a slight build. This latest victim does indeed fit this physical description. As they work the case, police will certainly ascertain whether this particular victim also was gay.

"As we know, our police chief and district attorney's office were reluctant to call these murders hate crimes, yet with this, the fourth young man to be murdered in the same fashion, we expect that designation to be made at the next press conference.

"Certainly, local anti-gay activist Spencer Fellows, founder of the group Family Now, is convinced the murderer is targeting gay men. Just last week, when the third body was discovered, Fellows was quick to release this video statement..."

The familiar Fellows mug, his fake benevolent smile slashed across his face, replaced Marlon Gordon's. He spoke in his *I'm holier than thou* way. "The Lord is indeed angry that we, as a society, are sheltering sinners. And this anger overflows into innocent citizens. If our laws, our moral values, our governing bodies, and our police will not take care of the situation, then, make no mistake, someone will. I'm not advocating the murder of sinners nor lawlessness, but I am saying that the Lord loves a warrior, and whoever is committing these acts will not be turned away from his Heavenly Father."

Again, Kevin saw Marlon's perfect cover model head fill the screen.

"Strong words. They unleashed quite a furor last week. Reverend Sid Kramer, the city's most vocal LGBTQ+ advocate, was quick to release his own statement." Gordon held up a sheaf of papers and read. "Reverend Kramer said, 'Fellows's opinion is just that—an opinion. It is sad that he, a man who purports to be a pillar of Family Now, that local bastion of hate masquerading as a Christian organization, can make such an inflammatory statement. He famously calls himself and his followers 'warriors for Christ.' The Christ I and my friends know doesn't need warriors, for our Christ only preaches love, not hate and certainly not vengeance. I have many friends of all religions, Christians, Jews, Muslims, Buddhists, who feel otherwise. They, like I, feel that no God would ever be happy to see a member of His flock murdered, much less in such a heinous fashion. These murders are being committed by someone who deserves the full force of the justice system. Whether he or she will wind up in the fires of hell is something none of us will ever know. But for now, we need this person caught and locked away.'"

Kevin shook his head as he toked off his joint. That Marlon Gordon is a looker, yes, he is. Too bad he's stuck in this nothing city in his nothing job at that nothing station. I'd bet he's creamin' in his pants right now, hopin' this story shoots him to the major league. He exhaled a long stream of smoke.

"Police have Mr. Miller, the jogger, presumably to take him in for more questioning," Gordon told his viewers. "But officers have agreed to a Force Four News exclusive with Mr. Miller. As you can see, a detective is right here, monitoring our questions so that not too much is revealed about the crime scene." A tall, lanky woman, her hair pulled back into a bun, her dark suit perfectly tailored, stood next to who, Kevin assumed, was Nathan Miller. His face showed a cross between *wow, I'm on TV* and a *deer-in-the-headlights*. "Mr. Miller, what can you tell us about this?"

"I can't tell you much of anything." He spoke hesitantly, his eyes cutting around toward the detective. She was stone-faced. My dog Elvis found the body. It's horrible. The man's face looks like it's been put through a meat grinder. It's sick-making. I—" The detective put her hand on his arm, and he stopped speaking abruptly.

Marlon Gordon's mouth twisted into a tiny frown, righted itself, and then he ventured onward. "Do you jog this path regularly? Anything you've noticed in the past that was suspicious?"

"No. Not like these yahoos out here now, running like nothing else is going on. Here we have a raft of police and crime techs and reporters, and the regulars just keep running, their earbuds cranking out who knows what crap into their ears, their Fitbits strapped to their arms, their water bottles firmly attached to their waistbands. These folks're crazy. I don't know how they do it. Day after day after day. I would be stark staring crazy. Maybe one of *them* did it. You never know what'll happen when the insane get to runnin' around like chickens with their heads cut off." He took a breath, and Gordon jumped in with another question, no doubt hoping to get this guy back on track, so to speak.

"So, Mr. Miller, you've never noticed any unusual activity out here?"

"You mean other than these craz—"

"Other than them, Mr. Miller." Gordon was obviously trying to keep his cool.

"It's just a jogging path. Usually lots of people. This morning, just the regulars. And not many of them when Elvis found the body." An off-camera bark. "Good dog, El," Miller said, and an audible sigh was heard but not seen, no doubt from Marlon Gordon.

Gordon interjected. "Was there any indication there was a body other than your dog breaking away? Did you hear anyone? Did you smell anything unusual?"

"Noth—" The detective pulled on Miller's arm as the camera focused on Marlon Gordon once again.

"Well, viewers, it looks like Mr. Miller has been placed in a squad car. This is standard police procedure. He's not likely a person of interest but he will be taken to the station for further questioning. As we watch the squad car pulling away, we also see an animal control officer loading the witness's dog. No alarm, viewers…in these cases, pets are detained until a family member retrieves them."

Smarmy Chet Charles, back in the studio, appeared on the screen. "Beautiful dog there. Marlon, is there any indication that Mr. Miller was involved in any way?"

In a split screen, Gordon answered, "Chet, before we went live, I spoke to the detective. She told me anything's possible but that for right now, Mr. Miller's story seems credible."

"Was the detective willing to call the assailant a serial killer?"

"No, Chet. In fact, she was reluctant to speak with me at all. It is not likely anyone of authority will rush to judgment on this. That most likely would complicate matters if an alleged assailant goes to trial, and the crimes have not been officially declared serial. Likewise, law enforcement will not call these hate crimes. That is for the district attorney's office to determine. They alone have the discretion of how they want to try a case. But we are getting ahead of ourselves here. The body was only discovered a little over an hour ago. There will be days of investigation before this crime is even tied to the previous three. And, I might add, none of the crimes, so far, have been linked. It is only us armchair detectives calling them serial murders. For now, we all wait. The entire community—the gay community especially—sits on edge. This is Marlon Gordon, Force Four News."

Charles, his face now filling the screen, continued. "Before you go Marlon, did Elvis bark a chorus of 'Hound Dog,' by any chance?"

The screen showed Gordon again, who looked like he was trying to swallow a fuck you. But he simply smiled and said, "No, Chet, no. This is Marlon Gordon, Force Four News."

The shot back on the idiot Charles, he spoke. "There you have it. We have, exclusively, on the phone Dr. Spencer Fellows. Good afternoon, Dr. Fellows. What is your take on this latest crime?"

"Let me say, first, Chet, thank you for calling. We were deep in prayer, my warriors and I, when we heard the news of this latest occurrence. We mourn for the young man's family, knowing the Lord will give them peace if they simply ask. It appears, however, that the young man was a sinner and brought this upon himself. And for that, we cannot mourn."

"Sir, is this not a good time to remind our viewers we need to live our lives with compassion?"

Kevin grinned. He figured Charles didn't give a shit about it all. He just knew his ratings would be in the toilet if he didn't call Fellows out on this.

"When someone, Chet, is leading a lifestyle that corrupts our innocents, spreads disease, and brings abject misery to their families, compassion is not called for. The Lord can forgive some sins, but this one is..."

"We seem to have lost our connection with Dr. Fellows. In other news, things are heating up in Afghanistan. The Taliban—"

Kevin pushed the off button, tossed the remote onto the coffee table, took a drag off the roach, and smiled.

✜✜✜

Kevin punched in the text: Meet me at the Cup. 3:30.

Then he switched off Drew Barrymore's inane chatter, straightened the coffee table, flushed his ashes and roach down the toilet, grabbed the Febreze from under the bathroom sink, and sprayed vigorously throughout the house, including upstairs. You never knew what kind of odor might linger. Mom and Step were almost always out of it, but little brother Markie would pick up on the slightest change in the weather. That little shit was the biggest snitch in the world.

So, for good measure, he sprayed every room a second time.

Speaking of Markie, his bus would be rounding the corner any minute, so Kevin knew he had to grab his jacket and sashay out the door. He locked up and jogged around the corner, where he'd parked the Spyder this morning. That street wasn't on the bus route, so he knew Markie wouldn't see his car and have fodder for any tales he wanted to tell this evening.

Kevin loved the Spyder. With its 414 hp, it could leave any other schmuck in the dust. Step didn't do much right, but when he brought home that car for Kevin, kissing up big time, he managed to bring a smile.

He headed toward the Cup. The official name was The Perfect Cup, but Kevin and his friends just called it "the Cup." They let the posers, like Step, call it by its snooty name. They were only interested in the coffee, not the name.

He slid into a handicapped spot right in front of the door and hung his blue tag on the rearview. That fake tag had cost him a bundle, but it was worth it to get primo parking.

Les was waiting as he came through the door. Kevin made a beeline to his friend, and did that guy hug where they almost touched bodies, then fist bumped each other's backs. Kevin rolled his eyes as he performed the ritual—only because Les expected it.

"Been here long?" he asked his oldest friend.

"Nah, man. Where were ya today? I figured if you could ditch the whole day, I could cut last period, but then I got word there was a pop quiz, so I stuck it out."

"Just couldn't face it, man," Kevin said. "Order yet?"

"Don't worry, I got yours too. I knows what you likes, m' bud." Les loved doing this strange voice which he found funny, and Kevin found a bit annoying. But Kevin humored him because they'd been friends since God was born.

Just then, a voice called out *Les Núñez*. Les went to the counter and retrieved their drinks.

After taking a sip of the hot coffee, Kevin said, "Any buzz at school over the thing at the park?"

"Fullerton? Ain't heard nothin'." Kevin frowned. Les knew proper grammar, but he was prone to butcher the language.

"*Didn't* hear *anything*, Les, *anything*." It was a pet peeve. Kevin didn't care shit about school, but he knew you couldn't get anywhere in this world unless you sounded and acted like you had an education.

"Get off my back, man. I know. I know." Les's words were harsh, but he was smiling. "So what happened?"

"'Nother murder."

"The gay guys?"

"Seems to be. Same MO."

"Gotta be some guy fueled by Fellows's hate." They had talked about that before.

"Prolly." Kevin loved that word, even though it did not pass the good grammar test. He also liked that it sort of defused the conversation somewhat. He didn't want to get too heavy into this murder thing, even though he was the one who brought it up.

"Man," Les said, as he gulped some coffee, then immediately coughed and fanned his tongue. "What does that make? Four, is it?"

"Yeah," Kevin said. "Good coffee, huh?" And he took another sip.

"Sure is, if I don't scald my taste buds off." He got up. "Gonna get some ice."

"You're such a wuss," Kevin called as Les took his coffee to the counter.

When he returned, Les asked, "So same hair color, same body type?"

"Yep. Sandy brown hair, blue eyes, slight build."

"Just like *you* like 'em," Les said, a sly smile on his face.

"Are you saying I'm the killer, you royal shit friend of mine?" Kevin grinned.

"No, no, no. Just sayin'. You need to watch your back, bro, because this guy goes for the same kind you slobber over."

"I'll have you know, Mr. Leslie Arturo Núñez, I may be gay, but I have no type. Man pussy is man pussy."

"Stop! You slam me over my grammar, but you have the biggest potty mouth in town. I'd think potty mouth beats bad grammar any day. But don't fool yourself. You may be content with any trick that turns your way, but you do like the serial's type better than any other."

Kevin smiled. *Potty mouth? Les tries to be bad, but his Catholic upbringing gets in the way.* "Well, I'm discriminating," Kevin said, glad to be steering away—he hoped—from the killings.

"So—you hooked up tonight?"

"Nah, I've got a paper to write on Moby's dick. I figured since I ditched class today, I'd better get the paper in on time, just to keep prune-faced Bayley from getting suspicious about my absence. The last thing I need is for her to go snooping around. Worst English teacher I ever had."

"Yeah, but I bet she's blown away that you can read the book and remember every fuckin' word of it."

Kevin smiled. Good for you, Leslie. I taught you that perfectly good word. "I haven't revealed that trick to her yet."

"Well, I struggled over that damn novel. And it's *Moby Dick*, as you well know, not Moby's dick—although it might have been easier to take if it *had been* gay porn. And you ran through it in one night. I don't know how you do it."

"It's a skill, my friend. That, and my real dad was a Rhodes scholar. I guess I got *his* genes more than Mom's. Too bad he bounced, leaving not a trace, and I got saddled with Step. Then again, Step's a pushover, so I lucked out."

"Not to mention he's loaded. I wish someone had gifted me with that car you abuse. I have to work hard to keep my used Camry in driving condition, or I'm burning shoe leather."

"Oh, boo hoo. Wittle Wessy is so mistweated."

"I'm just sayin.'"

"Speaking of, you wanna cruise? I feel the need for speed."

"Sorry, guy. My mother's working late tonight, and I have to be home to feed my little sister."

"Thank God Markie can feed himself. But I hear you." Kevin paused. "And you're not foolin' me. You're holding out hope that skirt you sniff around like a dog in heat will give it up to you. Then, royally serviced, you'll go home to feed the kid."

Les stood. "Well, it is almost time for cheerleading practice to be over. Someday, bro. Someday. See you tomorrow. Don't do anything I wouldn't do." And, tossing his cup into the garbage, he left.

Kevin sat, nursing what was left of his coffee. He and Les met in the first grade. That was back when Kevin's dad was still in the picture. Les had seen him through every major upheaval in his life. Les knew Kevin was gay before Kevin knew—or at least admitted it to himself. And Les never showed any disapproval whatsoever. He was a great friend.

Smiling and thinking of this one-of-a-kind friendship, his eye shot toward a new customer in line. Sandy hair. Lithe and slender. *I wonder if he has blue eyes?*

Kevin stared, hoping the guy would turn around. At last, after placing his order, the delicious-looking piece of eye candy turned and surveyed the place, looking for a place to sit. By then, the tiny shop was packed. Kevin raised his arm, got the guy's attention, and pointed to the chair Les had left empty.

The guy walked toward him.

"I'm almost through here if you wanna share the table for as long as it takes me to swallow my last few drops." Kevin's voice was smooth, enticing, inviting.

"Sure you don't mind?" Blue Eyes asked. Kevin warmed. Yes, his eyes were blue, the blue of the Mediterranean.

"Kevin." He held out his hand for the guy to shake.

"Mitch." Blue Eyes shook Kevin's hand. It was a firm, warm handshake, and Kevin fought an immediate attraction, the kind that shows up in your jeans.

"What brings you here today, Mitch?" Kevin pasted his most engaging smile on his face, hoping to melt this beautiful stick of butter. Kevin was proud of the fact he was good at the seduction production, as he liked to call this little ritual.

"Uh...could it be I wanted a cup of coffee?" Mitch's question came with a winning smile, so there wasn't a touch of irony.

Kevin smiled. This one would be a challenge. *Good lay? True love? Who knew?*

"You know, I thought that might be the case," Kevin countered.

Might be the start of something. What, Kevin wasn't sure of.

Mitch

He had on a rerun of Big *Bang Theory*. It was distracting him from his studying. He might tell himself the TV was necessary and helpful, but he wasn't fooling anyone. Truth was, he just didn't want to study. Not for Dr. Costner's World Affairs class. He hoped—and thought—he'd paid enough attention in class to ace the test. Fingers crossed. For now, Sheldon and Leonard were a welcome break from Afghanistan, China, the Gaza Strip, and all the other things plaguing the world today. Ah, he loved distraction.

He expelled a tiny laugh. There was a teaser on the TV screen for the *Dr.Ken* show. He couldn't imagine calling Costner "Dr. Steve," though Stephen was his first name. Only on the boob tube were doctors addressed by the familiar. No one would ever address *his* father as Dr. Spence.

He really should get back to studying. He should turn off the set and concentrate. Then, of course, Dr. Ken came on and intro'd the kind of episode that always made Mitch laugh. The catfish. Always goes something like, a poor widow had spent her dead husband's bequest to her and also sold her house to amass money for the poor internet clone she was madly in love with, thinking he was real, but he was really a she—which would at least be a good twist—and a Nigerian she, as well. Of course, Dr. Ken didn't reveal all of this right at the beginning, but that's what those shows always turned out to be. Maybe he'd watch just a little, he told himself.

No! I've got to study.

Suddenly, the breaking news halted his push/pull on study/not study.

"We interrupt our regularly scheduled programming to bring you an update on a story we brought you in the early morning news. Police have positively identified the young man whose body was found in Fullerton

Arboretum this morning. We once again warn you that this is graphic footage."

Mitch had not heard of this before. He'd slept through the morning news. His stomach churned as footage of the victim was apparently broadcast once again.

The familiar face of Marlon Gordon came on. "The victim has been identified as twenty-year-old Callum Slater, a sophomore student at Indiana University-Greatwood. Slater was the newly-elected president of the Campus Pride there and was working toward a Bachelor's degree in Social Work. We're told he had planned to go on for a Master of Social Work degree so he could work counseling gay youth. He was a valued volunteer with the local Gay Youth group at Simpson Center. A spokesman for his family gave us a statement."

Replacing Gordon on the screen was a man, fortyish with graying temples and piercing eyes. A caption read, "Uncle of the victim." The man spoke. "Callum's parents, brothers, sisters, and all the rest of his family are devastated. This was a young man who always put others before himself, whether in his family or his passion, working with gay youth. The world is a poorer place to live now."

The camera showed Marlon Gordon once again. "Thank you, Mr. Slater. We offer our sincere condolences to you and his family. He sounds like a remarkable young man.

"Police are still reluctant to say we have a serial killer in our midst. Nor are they willing to admit that the killer appears to be targeting gay men. But one of our most outspoken community leaders is quick to react to that. We heard from him earlier today."

Mitch watched as his father, Dr. Spencer Fellows, reared his ugly head, and like always when his dad made the news, Mitch could think of nothing else.

He'd spent the last year trying to forget who his dad was—*is*. His mother told of his bloodline a year ago on her deathbed. With her last, labored breaths, she told him the story...

She was a secretary at the counseling group where his father was employed. Fellows was up and coming in a group that extorted outrageous fees from people who had deep pockets and wanted to talk about how their mommies hadn't loved them long before he became the giant figure he is today but filled with his lofty ambitions. Mitch's mom was attractive, innocent, and willing. She was working there because it was a job that paid well. She was naïve and didn't realize the place was just a money gatherer. She really thought they were helping people, especially the dynamic, handsome Dr. Spencer Fellows. Susan Christman was just a young girl trying to make a buck, hoping to save enough of her paltry pay to move out of her parents' home and away from her abusive father. He never touched her. He just ranted and raved and made her life miserable.

When the handsome young doctor started working his charmy smarm on her, Susan saw a way to hasten her departure from home. A marriage to an upwardly mobile young psychologist would guarantee her way out. And since her ugly father had tormented her from the time she'd given up her pacifier, she longed for a safe haven. She hoped the offices of a group of psychologists would be the perfect place to hide—and maybe find that husband she sought. She set her sights on Spencer Fellows, not in a scheming predatory way, but a *hopeful, please help me* way. If this young god with his coal black hair and piercing topaz eyes wanted to woo her, she would give him anything he wanted.

Her naiveté soon turned to stone. She knew exactly the kind of man she was getting involved with, but she felt if she could chain him to her in marriage, she could then go her merry own way, spend his money he was sure to earn, and be independent. After all, Spencer Fellows had dreams of being a public figure, and public figures wanted to avoid the scandal of a messy divorce at all costs.

Problem was, what the young doctor wanted, and what Susan gave backfired on her. She found herself pregnant, and no ladder climber could have that. He put together a hundred-thousand-dollar buyout. Susan never knew where he got that money, but she always remembered his exact words when he offered it: "This is enough to set you up for life. Get rid of that thing inside you, move far away, and leave me alone. Understood?"

Susan told Mitch she nodded, took his money, and did indeed move far away—all the way across town. She knew that was not what he meant, but she had no intention of being bullied. She had plenty on him and would use it if necessary, but she hoped it didn't become necessary.

She put most of the money in a safe deposit box. She knew, she said, that it should be drawing interest, but she didn't want anyone to question where she got such a large amount. She took some and opened an interest-bearing account. Each year, she would take a few thousand more out of the box and add it to her account. The money grew, and she began to invest it.

She also journaled what had happened to her. She placed the journal in her safe deposit box, along with a recording of her final meeting with the good doctor. She told Mitch where to find the key to the box, told him she loved him, and died.

The days following were a whirlwind of grief and burial. Mitch only knew the mother who had raised him, not this scheming young woman who'd birthed him. If her story was true—and Mitch believed every word—his seed had been planted while she was still healing from a viciously abusive upbringing and a misguided plan to make something of herself. She'd more than atoned for any sins of her early womanhood.

Mitch wanted his mother to be honored in death much more than she'd ever been honored in life. And yet he knew he couldn't just flash a lot of cash around, so he arranged for a modest burial, making sure to keep her name out of the newspapers and insisting the funeral home not list anything about her—not even simply posting her name--online. He did not want Fellows to know of her death. She had managed to live under the radar all these years, and until Mitch found a reason to out himself to this father, he wanted to remain unknown. The man believed Mitch was a discarded fetus. Let him continue to think so.

Especially after all the vile things Fellows had said about gays. This man, this monster who provided the sperm to his mother's egg, had developed into far worse than the man his mother had known back then. His hatred of gays had led him to start the abominable organization, Family Now, led by the antichrist himself. He never missed a chance to spread hate like a farmer spreads manure on his crops. Spencer Fellows had made himself rich spewing venom. Family Now may be a non-profit, but make no mistake, its founder and leader took a hefty salary for his *good deeds*. Mitch had found out everything he could about his father, and what he found out, he did not like. So he wanted to stay as far away as possible, from the overt pseudo-Christianity and hatred that his father preaches so loudly and proudly. Mitch would not subject himself to that directly. No, unless he had a reason to out himself to his father, he preferred to remain anonymous.

One thing though, there was definitely someone stalking gay men. And with men like his father spewing their hate, he wasn't surprised. *Most likely, it was one of Daddy's "warriors for Christ."*

Meanwhile, he had to quit thinking about this latest murder and ace this test. He might have a sizable bank account, but it wouldn't last forever unless he became as savvy as his mother and let it grow. And that meant getting the degree she always wanted for him and not spending all she had amassed.

And so, Mitch Christman, born Fellows, switched off the TV and returned to his notes. If World Affairs weren't a required freshman course, he'd blow it off. Still, something good came out of having to listen to Dr. Steve's continual drone: he got to sit across the room from a kid who looked an awful lot like himself. Same build, same hair color, same skin tone. He was a beautiful distraction. He'd tried to introduce himself, but Mitch got all tongue-tied that day as they were leaving class. And, too, another guy was stuck like glue to the eye candy.

This past year he'd been bold around potential lovers, taking the ball and running with it. But this guy, he could tell, was different. All those other times, he was driven by lust. He'd feel his schlong getting hard and know that it was time to make a move. He sometimes felt like a dick. If his meeting guys was always the result of extreme carnal lust, then there had to be something wrong with him. That's not the way relationships work. He knew that. Maybe, he'd thought more than once, he'd inherited the predator side of his mom along with her angel side. Since her death, he just couldn't seem to control himself.

And yes, after he lured them in, he did let a respectable courtship week or so ensue. He wasn't a monster, a total, stalking, demanding predator. He knew how to wine and dine. He was good to them before the eventual sex. But it always led to that, and once it happened, he never felt comfortable afterwards. No relationship, for Mitch, had ever lasted. He didn't know why he was that way. He'd done that even before his mother told him about how she'd lured his father. Maybe not learned behavior.

Maybe ingrained. He did know it scared him sometimes, but like an alcoholic, he felt powerless.

And so, his reluctance with Sandy. That's what he'd begun to call him in his mind. He had no idea what his real name was. There was no attendance taken in the class, and Mitch's mind got so scrambled around the guy, he couldn't even speak to him, much less ask his name.

He just knew him as Sandy, he of the sandy hair and the piercing blue eyes.

He longed for a relationship, not just the usual one-night stand. His dating might be a multi-night ritual, but once he got them in bed, poof! Time to bail.

He banished the thought. His personal shit was something to think about another time. But, first, he had to pass that test.

Distraction, though, once again reared its ugly head. He had to get away from all this. Filled with the World Affairs notes swimming in his head, Mitch made his way to The Perfect Cup, only to run smack into what could be the perfect man. Yeah. Sure. He always did that. Let diarrhea of the mind just run and run whenever he met a cute guy.

Kevin. Beautiful, wild, smart, funny. A naturally muscled physique. He knew that because their conversation progressed. Kevin was supposedly just leaving, but he stayed. Mitch wondered if it was his charm or if Kevin was putting the make on him too.

Kevin told him he avoided the gym at all costs. But, oh, those muscles. He had longish dirty blond hair, just the kind of thing that always turned Mitch on. And his swarthy complexion made a stunning contrast to that light hair. He seemed to be intelligent too—not just a pretty face. In fact, Kevin told him he was the valedictorian of his class. Not too shabby. Mitch liked that. And Mitch felt he could deal with a younger man. After all, Kevin was a senior in high school, and Mitch was a freshman in college, so there wasn't that much age difference.

And as he watched Kevin speed away in that zillion-dollar speed trap, he was impressed. Not because Kevin obviously had dough big time, but because he liked the reckless air he posed as he drove away. He liked a touch of bad boy in his men.

Stop. Those days are behind me. I've had enough of bedding guys and leaving them. So—I'm attracted to the bad boys. I need to concentrate on the good ones. Still, maybe Kevin's a good little boy masquerading as bad.

But enough. He knew they'd see each other again. That was assured. They'd made another coffee date the next day. Now, he had to head home. The damned test lured him in. Costner was a ballbreaker, and he couldn't afford to blow this test.

✠✠✠

Man, oh man, oh man. He'd aced it. He'd live to breathe another day. Dr. Costner was in his rearview mirror, and he might, just might, pass the class. That is, if he did as well on the final as he knew he'd done on this midterm. Now he could kick back and set his sights on his coffee date.

The beautiful Kevin sat at their table as he breezed into the Cup. Kevin had taught him that was what he should call it.

As he pulled open the glass door, he willed himself to put the brakes on. Cool it, Mitch. This might not go anywhere. The last thing you need is some whirlwind romance that just soils your sheets and nothing else any more significant than that.

He sauntered behind Kevin, leaned over, and said quietly, "Boo."

Kevin immediately turned around. "I thought you'd never get here."

"Had to pass my World Affairs test first. It was a bitch, but I aced it."

"Good for you. I need some java. Ready?"

Kevin's dark eyes penetrated, and Mitch wondered again, fleetingly, if Kevin was coming on strong, coming on fast.

They went to the counter together and placed their orders. There were no other customers in the place. So, they waited until the barista filled their orders. Then they sat.

"You drink it black, too?" Kevin asked.

"The only way," Mitch answered. "Strong and dark."

"Is that the way you like your men also?" Kevin asked slyly.

Now that's a bold question, but I'll play along.

"Well, I'm looking at a rich piece of candy here, so I guess that answers your question." Mitch smiled broadly, hoping to show that he was half-kidding with Kevin and half-not. He didn't want the guy to think *he* was coming on to *him*, did he? Maybe. Maybe not. He wasn't sure.

"I like my coffee black but my men with a bit of cream on top." He stared at Mitch, driving his point home. "You know, light brown hair, slender, moonlit eyes." Kevin's eyes undressed Mitch as he leered at him.

Mitch laughed. "Then you'd eat up this guy in my World Affairs class. Just your type." A thought flashed across Mitch's mind. *He didn't show up today. Miss a test? What's up with that?*

"Sorry, but I was listing the qualities of someone closer, not some stranger in a faraway place." Kevin's voice was charming and alluring.

"You talkin' 'bout me?" Mitch said, in a New Jersey *goombah* voice.

"Yeah, youse," Kevin countered.

They laughed, easily and joyfully. Mitch knew. He knew as well as he knew that all the others weren't meant for him. This one was a keeper. He also knew he was crazy, crazy to immediately jump to this. But there was something very different about Kevin. Very different. Move fast, but be cautious, he told himself.

"Well, now we've broken the ice, tell me more about yourself," Mitch declared boldly.

"Not much to tell. You know I'm graduating this year. Top of my class. And I'm not bragging. It all just comes easy to me. My mom's a lawyer, specializing in international law. I tell people she travels all the time, but she doesn't. She's just in her office, twenty-four-seven, it seems."

Mitch saw a fleeting sadness he liked, well, not the sadness but the vulnerability—and then Kevin continued.

"I have one sibling, a charming young fellow named Mark Davis Borland. He's really only a half-brother, progeny of my step. A very high-powered executive. I'd tell you the name of his company, but I'd have to kill you. Very hush, hush, top secret." He smirked.

"So, your stepfather is James Bond?"

"Yeah, that's it." Kevin said, not adding any more to that. "We live in a modest house in River Glen, mostly because Mom's never there, and

Step doesn't care about the house. He's more into clothes, cars, country clubs. You know the outward trappings of wealth. He doesn't give parties, so the house is not visible to his world. As I said, modest."

Modest? In River Glen, Greatwood's haven for the filthy rich? Methinks you're underselling a bit, Kev.

"Markie and I were raised by a live-in nanny until we both outgrew her. She got breast cancer and died and was never replaced. So that's it in a nutshell."

"That's quite a spacious nutshell, my friend."

"And you?"

"Mom's dead. Left me a little money. Not much, but enough to stay afloat until I finish school. Freshman—as you know—at IG. That's about it." There was no way he would be telling Kevin about his father, not now and probably not ever.

"And your dad? What happened to him?"

"Never knew him." *That's not really a lie since I've never met the scum in person.* "Out of the picture long before I ever arrived at this vale of tears." He hoped his fake joking would be enough to quell this strain of inquisition, and it didn't because Kevin didn't pursue it. *Although he did get a strange look of recognition on his face. Did his father cut out on him too?*

"So—I can't believe we talked yesterday about our ol' gay selves. That's something I usually take a while—well, a short while often—to reveal. But you're easy to talk to, Mitch."

"And you, too, Kev. You don't mind if I call you Kev, do you? I feel like we're old friends." *Well, that sounded like a line from some old rom-com. Dork!*

Kevin gave him a salute, a go-ahead to shorten his name. Mitch liked that. It showed a willingness to be open with each other. But not too open. Not the *Spencer Fellows my father reveal* kind of open.

This is a good thing, what's happening here. Kevin seems much older than his—what? Seventeen, eighteen years? Mom always told me I was old beyond my years, and I think she was right. Growing up with a very serious mom and no other relatives surrounding you can make you grow up fast. I'm thinking Kevin could be a good match for me. *Dive in, he told himself.*

"Kev, here's the deal. I gotta lotta experience, mostly just sex. You down with that?"

"Totally. I've played the field a lot m'self, Mitch. Hit a lot of grounders, some homeruns."

"You a baseball fan?"

"God no! I was just tryin' to be cute. Was I? Was I cute?" Kevin grinned, and Mitch laughed at him.

"Why, honeychile, just cute as a bug in a rug," Mitch drawled. Kevin was winning over his heart, and he couldn't believe it was happening so fast. *Heart, take note. Slow this down a bit.*

Mitch looked up to see a Hispanic guy looming over them. "Oh, hi, Les," Kevin said nonchalantly. "Wondered if you were coming in today."

"Uh—you never said anything about the Cup today at school, so I figured somethin' was up. Looks like you snagged a fish on your line," Les said.

"Be quiet, Les, my boy. A good fisherman needs silence when he reels in the big one." Kevin laughed. "Les, Mitch. Mitch, Les."

Mitch shook Les's hand.

"Grab your coffee, and sit a spell, bro," Kevin told Les. "But a short spell 'cause I got me some fileting to do on this catch here." Les shook his head as he sauntered away to the counter.

"Hope it's okay if Les joins us. He's my best friend—since forever."

"No, it's fine, Kevin. I want to get to know you, and—" Mitch grinned, "grillin' a best friend's the best way I know t' start."

"Well, take it easy on me, if you would." Kevin's voice sounded like he was a bit worried.

Les returned with his coffee, pulled a chair from a nearby table, and sat. "Man, I need this brew," he said. He put the cup to his lips when Kevin pulled his hand away. "Don't burn your tongue again, bro," he shouted.

Again, Les shook his head. "I already put ice in it, Mommy." Then Les turned to Mitch. "He's a pain in the butt, but I love 'im." His eyes widened. "Not *love* love him. You know. *Friend* love him."

"So you're not gay?" Mitch asked.

"Not even a li'l bit. Got me the sweetest sweet thing on the cheerleading squad. She's at practice now. That's why I have time to hang with you guys." He looked at Kevin. "But only for a li'l bit, you know?" Kevin nodded, like he was affirming Les's statement.

"You're fine with Kevin being gay?" Mitch knew that some guys were uncomfortable with the idea of homosex, and he was relatively sure Les was okay with it, but he just wanted to make sure.

"Oh, yeah, man, I'm down wid it. Even if I wudn't, Kevin does what Kevin does." He took another sip of coffee.

"Good. Because I plan to woo your best friend here, Les."

"Have at it. Just don't come cryin' to me if he gets to be too hot to handle." He smiled.

"Promise," Mitch said.

"Now," Kevin said to Les. "Isn't it about time you got off to cheerleading practice? You wouldn't want her to run off with the quarterback."

Les looked at his watch—or rather, his bare wrist, for he wore no watch. "You're right, bro. I need to *skee*-daddle." He laughed as he jumped up and made his exit.

"Funny guy," Mitch said.

"Surely is, surely is." Kevin nodded as he repeated himself.

"I'm glad you have a best friend. I've never known that." Mitch was a bit ashamed of what he said, and his tone of voice made him sound pitiful. But it was the truth. He'd spent his life making alliances, not friends. Maybe he was a product of his mother, he often thought, a person who played along to get along.

And maybe Kevin could change all that for him.

Brent

Brent stretched and yawned. There was nothing worse than having nothing to do. Bored, bored, bored, bored. He should have signed up for the morning class. Yeah, that meant setting his alarm, but at least he'd have something to do MWF. He'd turned on the TV, anything to wipe away his ennui. He loved that word. Not the meaning, but the word itself. It seemed so *trapped in an apartment in Paris*. Brent knew he should be out on a day like this, shooting hoops, running, hiking through the woods, but he couldn't bring himself to move his lazy butt.

What's wrong with me? I never used to sit here just waiting for a phone call. Why am I just sitting here like a slob? My cell phone will ring anywhere I am.

Callum'll call when he gets a chance. He was in class 'til nine, the course I refused to sign up for. He probably got stuck in traffic getting home. I know him. He has to get home, put away his stuff, change clothes, and grab a bite before he calls me. He's that kind of guy. Predictable. Totally predictable.

I should be studying for our World Affairs test tomorrow, but I know that crap backward and forwards, so no need. God, I wish we'd taken that Freshmen class when we were really Freshmen. I feel old sitting there with all those babies.

Suddenly, he saw the familiar blue Breaking News screen come on. Finally, some distraction.

Brent stared at the screen. Another murder. Obviously, these are serial murders. Targeting *us*. This was the fourth, and the first three were totally a pattern. They hadn't used the hate crime words, either. Plain as day, that's what they were. A killer doesn't target three gay guys without having a powerful hatred for the gay *lifestyle. When, oh when, are people going to give up that word? We're gay—always been that way. It's not some lifestyle we choose, like finding a club to join.*

And look at this shit—Callum would hate me using that word. This latest fits the pattern like a worn shoe. The film that guy Gordon's showing of the victim is right in line with the other three. The blood, the bludgeoning. It all fits.

Oh shit! Oh, fuck! No. Brent gasped for air. Oh, God, no. He held his chest, desperately trying to breathe. Those shorts. I know those shorts. I teased him about 'em just last week. What self-respecting gay guy has shorts with monkeys on them? I asked him. Tears flowed. He still couldn't catch his breath. He couldn't say his name. And now. There they are. On that piece of bloody meat. On TV. It can't be. Cal.... No. He sniffed. Wiped his nose with the back of his hand. No way. He stood, frantically running around the room, not knowing what he was doing, not caring what he was doing. Grabbing for breaths. Grabbing for clarity.

He turned back toward the TV.

But that's his shirt. His body froze. *Oh my God. Please, please tell me it's not.* He put his hands across his eyes, shielding them from what he was seeing, from what he didn't want to admit. But he quickly took his hands away. He couldn't *not* look. *But he always wears that shirt with those shorts.* He fell back onto the couch, covered his eyes with his hands again. Started whimpering that grew into sobs. He was having some sort of out-of-body experience. He spoke involuntarily. Like his voice was on autopilot. "Oh, shit... oh shit... oh shit. No... no... no. It's... not... him. It's... not him.

"It's... some other guy with the same shorts, the same shirt." The last words flowed like burning lava because he knew. He knew.

He screamed. Bloodcurdling. A scream to shake the rafters. A primal scream.

"It can't be Callum!"

✚✚✚

Robotically, Brent emailed Dr. Costner: "Sorry. Can't be in class tomorrow. Can't go into details. Hope you'll let me make up the test. Urgent. Can't be helped."

His fingers barely functioned as he typed. He wanted to spill out his guts to his teacher. Dr. Costner was a nice man. If Brent could explain, he'd understand fully.

He pushed send. Then broke down. Again.

The police had already been to see him. They'd asked he not tell anyone who the victim was. *The victim.* That brought floods of new tears. *Like he was just a thing. Not a Callum. Not my Callum.*

And the sobs echoed in his little apartment.

The police had come straight from informing Callum's parents. Thinking of them, he was able to stanch his tears for Callum. Brent's heart went out to them. He and Callum had been a thing for four years. Callum's folks had embraced him, Brent, like he was their son as well. They were good, good people who raised a good, good son.

And now he was gone.

Tears once again leaked from his eyes. He knew Callum wouldn't want him to feel this abject grief, but he couldn't help it.

Gone. A concept Brent couldn't, refused, to wrap his mind around. He felt abandoned. In a deep, dark closet. A refrigerated, icy closet.

✛✛✛

It had been hastily thrown together, but Brent sat, in the first row, with Callum's parents in the university auditorium, waiting for the tribute or vigil or service or whatever this thing was to begin.

He'd put on his only suit, straightened his tie in front of the bathroom mirror, and trudged over. His heart skipped when he saw Mr. and Mrs. Slater. He hadn't been able to call them the day before. The grief wouldn't let him.

They each hugged him, and the warmth of their hugs melted the ice in his blood that had been there ever since the police had shown up at his doorstep. Callum's brothers and sisters enveloped him in a group hug, and the love was warmth, like a quilt wrapping his wounded soul.

This thing had been organized by Campus Pride to honor Callum. Brent felt it was weird to gather so soon after his brutal murder, but the guy who called him said their members were so utterly devastated that they had to do something. *Tell me about it*—Brent remembered thinking but not saying.

And then, when he and the Slater family walked up the center aisle to the first row, his heart swelled. Hundreds of students and faculty were there. Brent knew that everyone loved Callum, but he never expected this.

A familiar young woman dressed in black slacks and a blazer came to the mic at center stage.

"Hello, everyone. I'm Melinda, and I worked alongside Callum in Campus Pride. It's rare for a sophomore to be elected president of any campus group. No one in Campus Pride ever thought it would happen, but no one in our group had ever met Callum. He was a force. A gentle, loving force. Old and wise beyond his years. We won't dwell today on how he was ripped from us. That's for another time and for others to ponder. We're here because we all needed a big group hug. And seeing you all here right now is that group hug we sought. And we hope you are feeling the love too. Many, many others will come to the mic to tell Callum stories. We ask only two things: keep it light, keep it gay. And I don't mean that in the 21st century customary way, but that's okay too. For Callum was never, ever ashamed of who he was, and he made us all proud—of him and of ourselves."

Brent watched as countless people paraded across the stage. Some simply told of how much they liked Callum. Some had elaborate stories of "the time he did this" or "the time he did that." He wanted it all to be healing, but he was so angry, so heartbroken, so unhealable. As he sat there, tears streaming down his face, Callum's mother took his hand in hers and gently held it in her lap.

Dr. Costner was the last to speak. Brent had no idea that he and Callum were even close. The teacher kept himself very businesslike in class. And Callum must have respected that, for he had never told Brent that he knew Dr. Costner outside of the class they took together.

Dr. Costner told of a boy he met, many years ago. A boy in a summer camp where he was a counselor. The boy was different. He was unmercifully bullied. The teacher admitted how ashamed he was of his former self because he had allowed that boy to be bullied, had thought it was all part of "boys being boys." He offered no further explanation for his own behavior than to say, "I had been brought up to be the stereotypical and unfortunately not yet discarded archetype, the *manly* man, by a very stern father.

"But one of the other campers took it upon himself to stop the bullying. This boy, this ten-year-old, took the bullied kid under his protective wings. He fought back at the boy's tormentors. And he won. Not by force, but by education. In a gentle, loving way, he schooled the bully out of those tormentors, teaching them that everyone is unique. He said some are like the boy they'd so despised, and some are like them. 'And that's what makes the world go around,' he said. That teacher, that ten-year-old, was Callum Slater, and he not only taught his fellow campers, but he taught his counselor as well. My life was deeply enriched that summer. I'm not sure Callum even realized that Dr. Costner was Counselor Steve or not. He certainly never seemed to let on. But knowing Callum, I realized that my style with my students is to be somewhat aloof. It's served me well in the classroom, but oh, how I wish I had reached out to Callum and let him know how he changed my life."

There was silence when Dr. Costner finished. Then the audience broke into applause, not the raucous ovation you'd give at a rock concert, but applause that affirmed that Dr. Costner's story had touched them, had been something they related to.

Brent stood. He walked up the stairs at the edge of the stage and stood behind the mic.

"I didn't want to talk today. I didn't think I had it in me. But Dr. Costner's story made me realize something. I am today what Callum made me. He was my friend, my teacher, my love, my heart. And I will miss him until the day I die and then some."

Everyone in the room stood. Then. spontaneously, they started singing "Amazing Grace." Brent thought, "I don't know why that's the song they always sing at something like this, but somehow it makes sense. Callum *was* amazing grace." And he joined in. And as he sang, he walked back to Mr. and Mrs. Slater. They let him fall into their arms.

At the end of the song, Melinda took the stage again. "Thank you for this. May you all go now with grace. Whether Christian, Muslim, Hindu, Buddhist, Agnostic, or other, spread Callum's grace throughout this campus and throughout the universe."

Her closing remarks were a bit much, Brent thought, but he knew they were from the heart. And that Callum would have liked them.

Joined together, forever now, he and Callum's folks walked from the auditorium. As he walked them to their car, he saw another of his class members.

He didn't know the guy personally. There was not much personal interaction in Dr. Costner's class.

The guy walked up to him as he closed the car door on Mrs. Slater's side. Brent told her, "See you day after tomorrow." Those words were comforting but heartbreaking because he knew "day after tomorrow" meant "when we bury Callum."

"Hi. I'm Mitch. We're in Costner's class together. What's going on? All these people filing out of the auditorium? Was there an important lecture I missed?"

"A service."

"A service?" Mitch repeated, this time as a question.

"For Callum."

"Callum?"

Brent didn't want to have this conversation right here, right now. He only wanted this guy to go away. But he remembered Melinda's charge to them.

"Callum Slater. He was in our class too. Sandy hair, slight build, blue eyes?"

He saw recognition on this Mitch's face.

"Sandy?" Brent gave him a blank look. "That's what I called him, if that's the guy you mean. Good looking guy. I noticed him. Wanted to jump his bones, if you know what I mean."

How could he say such a thing with Callum barely gone? Brent wanted to punch the guy's lights out. But Callum would not have wanted that.

"Mitch—that's your name, isn't it?"

Mitch nodded.

"Here's the thing. Callum and I were partners, and this service was to honor him." He tried desperately to state that like it was simply a fact and not fill his voice with the anger he was feeling.

"Was?" A puzzled look crossed Mitch's face.

"Yes, Mitch. Callum was murdered. Didn't you see the news?"

"That was your boyfriend? Oh, my God, I'm sorry. So, so sorry. What an ass I am."

"It's okay. You see, Callum was the most understanding person on the planet. He wouldna been offended. You didn't know." Brent swallowed the anger he wanted to express. For Callum. "But now ya know, I hope you'll think twice about tellin' a perfect stranger ya wanted to sleep with his boyfriend. Again, the latter a fact you didn't know." He spit those last words. Then he composed himself once again—something he was practicing more and more. He couldn't believe he'd put all those words together, but somehow they were in Callum's honor, and he felt good about it. For the moment. Then he plunged back into his grief.

"Again, man, I'm really sorry. I'm a fuckwad. Ya need anything? Ya want me to walk with you a bit? I won't talk. Promise. Just thought maybe you'd want some company."

This guy Mitch was really trying to redeem himself. But Brent wasn't having it.

"I'm fine, Mitch. I just wanna be left alone. Okay?"

"Sure," Mitch said.

And Brent walked away.

Brent couldn't believe this shit. This Mitch was offensive, apologetic, caring, and stumbly, almost in the same breath. And gay.

Callum would have liked that. And Callum would not have liked Brent's reaction to Mitch, nor all the *shits* and *fucks* that had crept into his mouth since...

He smiled, thinking of Callum, as he walked under the beautiful autumn trees, their leaves just turning, winter announcing itself before making its way to the campus in the not-too-distant future. Callum was springtime. Perpetual springtime. And that's what made him such a joy. He could turn, as they say, any frown into a smile.

Brent remembered the first time he laid eyes on Callum. There he was, standing out among a group of protestors at one of the first Family

Now rallies. The vile Spencer Fellows spewed, condemning to the pits of fiery hell each and every gay, lesbian, transgender, and whoever else stood under their umbrella.

The relatively tiny group of protestors was making the noise of thousands, valiantly trying to drown Fellows out. They waved rainbow flags and noisemakers and shouted, some holding up banners and signs. Fellows somehow managed to bellow above it all.

And then Callum, no flag, no sign, stepped out of the crowd. He walked toward Fellows. He stood, staring at him, not saying a word. Brent felt like Callum's eyes must be piercing through Spencer Fellows and wounding him deep into his soul.

The cacophony died down. Within seconds, the only sound was coming from Fellows.

"And He shall smite them. He shall send them all to the depths—"

And he was silenced.

By those eyes.

Spencer Fellows, this blowhard trying to make a name for himself, was brought to silence, not by loud protest, but by one boy. One boy. Staring at him. Showing he was unafraid.

And Brent fell in love. He had to know this guy who'd brought Spencer Fellows to his knees.

Fellows walked away. Not to be forever banished from his pulpit of hate. But at least for that one day.

The crowd dispersed. Incredibly, nothing was ever on the news about it. Brent figured Spencer Fellows, at that time, was not as powerful as he was now. Or maybe he was. Maybe he squelched the story of the boy who was his temporary downfall.

At any rate, Brent made it his goal to find this boy. He asked around. He went to every gay gathering in the city. He described the boy to every teen he came in contact with. He queried each and every gay person who would give him the time of day. But months went by, and he still didn't have a clue as to who the boy who silenced Spencer Fellows was.

Then his drama club—he was a sophomore in high school then— took their show to regional one-act play contest. Brent was stage manager. His cast was so keyed up that morning that his hands were full keeping their shit together.

Finally, after they performed, and they were first, he could relax in the theater, kicking back and watching the competition. Number two was a production of *Harvey*, the old comedy about the guy with an imaginary rabbit as his best friend.

The curtains parted and there stood *the boy*. He was the lead in this show. Brent quickly grabbed the program and looked for his name: Callum Slater. He remembered thinking, "Well, Callum Slater, before this day is over, you'll be mine."

When Callum's cast came out to watch the remaining shows, Brent sauntered over to him. He gathered all his sixteen-year-old bravado, and, like a cowboy in a calf roping event, threw his imaginary rope around this beautiful guy he'd been searching for months.

"Man, I've been looking for you for months." Brent felt triumphant. He wasn't that bold. Ever. But this demanded it.

A questioning look came across Callum's face.

"First of all, I'm Brent. I stage managed them—" He pointed to his cast. "Let me say you were awesome, and your show's amazing. I want *us* to win, but I sure hope you take all the other awards." He laughed.

Callum smiled, and Brent knew this guy was everything he'd built him up in his mind to be. "Uh—you still haven't explained what you meant. About looking for me for months?"

Brent felt a blush forming, but he squelched it.

"Oh, sorry, guy. I was at the rally. The one you stopped. With that look. That amazing, Fellows-burning look."

"Oh, that. It was nothin'. Somebody had to do something."

How can this god not recognize his mystical powers?

"What you did was awesome. That guy's an asshole, and you silenced him with a stare." He wanted to add "from those gorgeous moonlight-kissed eyes," but he thought that might be a little much.

"Anybody coulda done it. You. You could do what I did. I just did it. That was all."

"You really don't know you're the all-powerful wizard?" Brent couldn't believe he was being so *not himself*.

"P-shaw, as my grandmother would say. Your beautiful browns could strike the greatest orator dumb."

Brent loved his use of the word *orator*. It set his Callum apart. No other guy he'd ever met would have used that word. He smiled at his thought. He was already thinking of him as *his Callum*.

"So, now that we've established that we're both gods in human clothing, I'm Callum."

"I know. I know." Brent held up the program. "Looked ya up."

"Great. Now, how 'bout your name."

"Brent. Brent, Brent, Brent. I want ya t' remember it."

"Great to meet ya, Brent, Brent, Brent, Brent. Can I call you Brent for short?" Brent was captivated further by Callum's smile.

He blushed. "Sorry. I'm not so good at pickin' up guys. And I hope that's what I'm doin'."

"Too soon to tell, but I will say this, you have a way with ya. After all this is over—" Callum swept his arm across the auditorium—"what say we meet up some time. You got your phone?"

Brent handed him his phone. "Here's mine. Enter your digits, Brent to the fourth power. And I'll enter mine here." He punched in the information and said, "And now, I must join my schoolmates, oh powerful Brent. We got a contest to win."

The rest of the day went. That's all Brent could say about it. His show actually did advance to state competition, but Callum won Best Actor. And that win meant more to Brent than his school's Best Play trophy.

From that day on, it seemed Brent and Callum were a couple. In true Callum wisdom, he ensured they started out slowly—just phone calls for a few weeks. Then they met for coffee at the Cup. But soon, they were going on Friday night, Saturday night, and Sunday night dates—after church, which was really important to Callum—and spending time at each other's houses constantly.

With graduation looming, after two magical years together, it was a given they'd both go to the university there in town, UIG. Brent couldn't even imagine not being with Callum.

Callum did insist they maintain separate residences. He was the sensible one. Two—almost two and a half—years together, and Callum still was not going to "lead him on," as he put it. He wanted to make sure they were together forever before they did anything. And that meant their time together was strictly hugs and kisses and, sometimes, if Brent begged loud and long enough, some mutual handplay. But Callum insisted he was saving himself for marriage, like some virgin girl dreaming of a *Brides Magazine* extravaganza.

That's what Brent would regret most of all. He would cherish every moment he ever spent with Callum, knowing they were truly and forever in love.

But oh, how he wished they'd done the one thing Callum just wouldn't do.

Kevin

Markie bounded into Kevin's room, yelling, "Kev, Kev! Wake up!"

Kevin's plan for Saturday was to sleep way past noon. Shit.

Typical Friday night. As usual, he had a date. Nothing different about that, except this time, it was with Mitch. Earth shatteringly different. He drove. Picked up Mitch in the Spyder and used Step's credit card to blow up the town. Dinner at the swankiest place in Greatwood—which isn't the Manhattan of Indiana by any means—then drinks at a club where Kevin knew neither he nor Mitch would get carded. He spared no expense. Not to impress Mitch, although he hoped he it did, but mostly to stick it to Step. Step groveled for Kev's *luv*, so he never checked Kevin's charges. He just let his accountant pay the bill with no questions. So Kevin loved pulling as much as he could get away with out of Step's giganto bank account.

But he enjoyed the date, even if it was partly to spite his stepfather. He and Mitch even did some crunkin' at Greatwood's one and only hip-hop club. Mitch was pretty impressive on the dance floor. Kevin intended for the evening to end very differently, but not so. He deposited Mitch back at his apartment around two a.m., and then Kevin drove over to O'Halloran Park to hang out, smoke some weed, and see what was shakin'. The first joint was good enough to merit a second one, but there was little to no action. *What's up with that? The park is usually crawling with cruisers on a Friday night.* He guessed they were spooked about the latest murder. Exhaling a huge stream of smoke, he smiled. Happy. And then he headed home and to his bed.

And the little fucker woke him up.

"Get out of here, you little shit." He rolled over, pulled the covers up, and tried to go back to sleep.

But Markie was pulling his shoulder back and forth. "Wake up, Kevin. We're goin' to the movies."

Without opening his eyes, Kevin spat out, "So? Go ahead on and leave me alone."

"You don't understand." Markie punched his words, shrieking them, like that would change Kevin's mind about waking up. "Dad said you'd take me." Then his voice got lower, "Besides the movie is an R, so I need you to get me in."

Kevin opened his eyes reluctantly. "Like you'd understand it anyway, you little piss ant. Find yourself a Disney movie, and take the bus. I'm sleepin'."

"Daddy won't like it. He said you'd take me." Markie crossed his arms and frowned.

"Like I give a fuck what Step wants," Kevin said. "He's not *my* daddy, and I don't have to do what he says. Now, outta here, leave, go away, adios, you hear?"

Kevin pulled the covers up again, this time over his head. Markie must have left, for it felt like he'd nodded off when his phone buzzed.

Not opening his eyes, he untangled himself from the covers and reached for his phone. "Yeah?"

"Kev? You asleep?"

Kevin came to life. "Mitch? Whassup?" He smiled. "Great time last night."

"Yep. Great time. Although I have to admit, I've never been served in a club before. I don't even have a fake ID."

Kevin laughed. "So I busted your cherry, huh? First drink out? Don't tell me that was your first drink ever."

"No. I've had drinks, just not in a club."

"Well, welcome to Kevin's world, bro. When can we do it again? Free tonight?"

"Actually, Kev, I *was* calling about us getting together, but not to go clubbing. This is a bit more sedate."

"Sedate? Do I even know that word?" There was a pause. "Just kidding. Valedictorian, remember? I know the word. Sure do." He was trying to bring a laugh from Mitch, but he heard nothing. "Okay, guy, sorry. What'd you have in mind?"

Kevin heard Mitch expel a breath. "This is a very strange idea for a second date, but I wondered if you'd go with me to a funeral this afternoon?"

Kevin said nothing. Funerals were absolutely not his thing. But he did want to see Mitch again. "Who died? I hope it wasn't your grandmother." *Why did I say that?* "Sorry, just my lame humor."

"You heard about the guy who was murdered?"

Uh-oh. Kevin did not want to hear any more about that.

"Uh—yeah," he said uncertainly, afraid to enter uncharted choppy waters.

"Well, the guy was in my World Affairs class. Callum Slater. I didn't know him. But apparently just about everyone on campus did. I met his partner yesterday."

"His lover?"

"Outdated term, but yeah. Nice guy. Anyway, this morning on the news, they said Slater's funeral is this afternoon, and I thought it would be a nice gesture to go. Surely his parents would appreciate as many people there as can get there, and from what Brent, that's Slater's partner, tells me, he deserves a great sendoff. I know it's crazy. Goin' to a stranger's funeral. But it's just something I wanna do. Somehow—" he paused a moment—"it's something I *need* to do."

Kevin heard something in Mitch's voice. Something he wasn't telling him. But if going to a funeral he certainly didn't want to attend would get him out of a movie date with the little monster and get him back together with Mitch, then he was for it.

"Sure, Mitch. I'll hang with ya. Got nothin' better to do. What time?"

"The thing's at three, Mueller's Funerals. Know where that is?"

"I think I do. But don't worry. Spyder's got GPS. So—show up at your place about two-fifteen, just to pad the gettin' there time?"

"Sounds great. I'll be waiting outside."

"Perfect. I'll be in my best *Kevin go to funeral* attire."

Mitch chuckled. "Curb your humor after we get there, okay? Probably not a joking occasion."

"I hear ya. See ya later." And they ended their call.

Kevin had no sooner finished with Mitch than Step barged into his room.

"Kevin, Mark tells me you're refusing to take him to the movies this afternoon." Step's blue eyes bore into Kevin's sullen stare. "Your brother doesn't ask you for much, you know." He ran his fingers through his lightish-brown hair, now showing gray. This was his gesture that meant he was pissed with Kevin.

"*Half*-brother," Kevin mumbled.

"What's that?"

Kevin knew he'd stepped in it. "Nothin'." Then he quickly made his case. "I can't take him because I have a date—of sorts."

"A date? Who is it this time? Another one of those losers you hang around with? Your mother and I accepted that you're *gay*—" Step said that like he was a leper. "But at least you could find guys who are not beneath you. I could ask around."

The last thing he needed was for Step to pimp him out.

"If you must know, this guy is someone I just met a few days ago. He asked me to go with him to a friend's funeral today." He knew Step wouldn't ask for clarification about the "friend." "I just think it will be a nice thing for me to do. To go with him. To show him support in his grief. To be his rock in this time of need." He laid it on thick. He also bit the inside of his jaw to keep from smiling at his cunning.

He saw Step melt.

"That's a good thing you're doing. I'm sorry I yelled at you. We'll see if Mark has a friend he wants to take with him. Surely, that friend's parents can take them. He'll enjoy going with someone his own age more, anyway."

"Why can't *you* take him?" He knew the answer, but he wanted to hear the shit repeat his mantra once again.

"I have to be at the office." And he left Kevin's room like all was settled.

Kevin took his phone and texted Les.

"Had it out with Step again. Don't know Y he fucks w/ me."

A moment passed, and the ding of reply sounded.

"This time?"

"Wanted me to take the little shit to the movies."

"So?"

"Can't. Bigger fish. Funeral."

"U're shittin me. U? Funeral?"

"Yeah. W/ Mitch."

"Who died?"

"Park guy."

Kevin waited for the ding of Les's return message. But his phone chimed instead.

"My fingers got tired. This is too big. Spill it, Kevin."

Kevin laughed. "Just what I said. The guy in the park. The one who was murdered. Mitch knows the guy's lover. Well, he just met him, really. He wants to go to the funeral to show his respect, and he asked me to go with him."

"And you, Kevin Life of the Party No Funerals Ever, said yes?"

"Look, I'm not as heartless as you think, dude. I can be supportive when I wanna be. And after last night, I wanna be supportive."

"Last night?" There was a sly note in Les's voice. "Did you fuck the new guy?"

"His name's Mitch, and no."

"I know his name's Mitch, and what happened last night then?"

"We just had a good time. Dinner at Albin's—"

"Used Daddy's credit card, huh?"

"He's not my daddy, but yes, Step's platinum card was put to good use."

"And?"

"Drinks at The Rotor."

"Where they think Kevin hung the moon and always serve him and his guests, even if he brings in someone who is obviously ten years old."

"I've never taken someone that young in there. You offend me, bro." His words cut, but he knew Les wouldn't take offense.

"Some of those twinks you hook up with look awful young. But I admit, Mitch looks his age and then some."

"A little booty wigglin'. Mitch can really bust a move, I tell you what?"

"And where did this crunkin' happen? CU46?"

"Yeah."

"So after all that, there was no seeing him for sex? After you took him to a club that literally has that in its name?"

"Takin' it slow. Anyway, he called a little bit ago and proposed today's outing. And since I wanted to see him again, I said I would go."

"This is just not the Kevin I know and love, but good luck. Enjoy the festivities, bro. And dress appropriately, as my mom would tell me. Funerals are serious, dude. Later."

As he put his phone back on the bed table, he got up, stretched, and picked up the TV remote. He could use a bit of noise as he got ready for his hot date.

Wouldn't you know? That ubiquitous voice and face. Marlon Gordon. Doesn't he take Saturdays off?

"Authorities have determined the same weapon was used to kill Callum Slater as was used on the other victims. An anonymous source just confirmed this exclusively to me. This source would not say what the object was or how, amidst all the carnage, crime techs were able to determine a single object was utilized. I have to say, folks, this case is baffling. We have four seemingly identical murders—gay men, similar physical characteristics, brutal and bloody. And yet no one is willing to declare this the work of one person. And puzzling me even further is the fact that the murders are not being called hate crimes. But rest assured, I'm devoting myself to bringing you each bit of information as these cases unfold. Marlon Gordon, Force Four News."

Kevin stared at the screen, mesmerized by Gordon and his tenacity.

Brent

Brent awoke with a start. "Callum, is that you?" he called out before he realized that Callum wouldn't be, couldn't be, answering. The realization started another crying jag. He didn't know how he had that many tears in his body. He'd been sobbing, almost nonstop since Wednesday. There'd been moments. Moments when he thought of Callum and smiled. Thought of Callum and his grace. Thought of Callum and his beautiful soul. And the tears dried. But then another grenade of grief exploded, a bomb that rattled the core of his being, pounding into him he would never see his Callum again.

This day, though, he had to get through. For Callum's parents' sake. For his own sake. For Callum's sake.

He set his feet firmly on the floor. There were no covers to pull back. He'd slept naked, on top of the covers on that cold autumn night, window open. Deep down, he'd hoped he'd feel pain as he slept. Something akin to what Callum must have felt.

But he felt nothing. Nothing physical. It was a wonder he slept. His mind roiled, like it had each night since the news, but he must have cried himself to sleep.

And now he needed to shower, get into the suit he so rarely wore, and head over to the Slaters' house. They had insisted he ride in the limousine with them. His parents had offered to take him, but when he said he was going with Callum's family, his always understanding mom said, "Absolutely. The Slaters need you. We'll meet you at Mueller's. We love you." She hugged him. "We're hurting for you."

He shuddered. He dreaded this ordeal. But he knew that Callum would make it through something like this with loads of grace. He was everyone's rock. And that's how Brent planned to handle it too.

Shaved, showered, dressed, and as prepared as he ever would be, he drove to the Slater house. TV news trucks were camped out, reporters with their microphones, cameramen with their gear. Vultures, all of them.

Marlon Gordon thrust his mic in Brent's face as he walked up the sidewalk, shouting a question at him. Brent just kept walking and went through the front door that opened as soon as he got to it.

"We've been watching for you," Callum's sister said, as Callum's mother rushed to embrace him.

"How are you doing, baby?"

"I'm okay," Brent answered. "How are you guys?"

"We're holding up. Friends from the church have been here night and day. In fact, some of my lady friends are in the kitchen getting ready for the onslaught afterwards." She dabbed a handkerchief to her eyes.

Brent hugged her again.

"I'm fine, dear. I just never thought I'd be burying my beautiful son. But I'm strong." And Brent saw she didn't shed any more tears.

Callum's dad came into the room, dressed in a dark grey suit. "I hope this is okay. I don't have a black suit." He spoke as if he just needed something to say.

"You look fine, darling," Callum's mother said to her husband.

"What time's the limo coming?"

She gave her husband a look like she knew she was repeating something he'd asked about a zillion times, but her voice didn't show any irritation when she answered, "At 2:30, dear."

She had made coffee. Or maybe the church ladies had made coffee. Anyway, Brent thought holding a cup of steaming brew was at least something to do while they waited. As he walked to the sideboard where the coffee service was, he asked, "Anyone else?"

"Thank you, son. I'd like a cup," Mr. Slater said.

"Sure thing," Brent said. "Mrs. Slater?"

"No, dear, I'm fine. And how many times do I have to tell you to call me Margaret?"

"Sorry," Brent said. She'd been telling him that for years, and he never felt it was appropriate, but after this, this thing they were going through together, he knew Mr. and Mrs. Slater would be Margaret and Sam for the rest of his life.

He poured Sam's cup of coffee, took it to him, and came back to pour his own. Then he sat on the sofa, sipping the hot coffee, each sip keeping him from having to say anything.

An hour or so, and three cups of coffee, passed. The silence was broken by a phone ringing in the kitchen. A woman with a lovely smile stuck her head into the doorway.

"I took the liberty of answering your phone, Margaret. You left it on the kitchen island. It's the home. They say they are just around the corner and will arrive shortly."

"Thank you, Bette."

Everyone in the living room rose. Sam Slater said, "Margaret, Brent, you two and I will go in the first car. Kids, you follow in the second car. And be on your best behavior, you hear?"

Brent thought, "Like he needed to tell them that. Those kids loved their brother more than anything. They are not about to act up on this day."

The reporters miraculously had cleared out by the time the two limousines arrived. No doubt they figured they needed to get to Mueller's to intrude on the mourners.

The ride to Mueller's was somber. No one spoke. No one cried. Only the sound of heavy breathing filled the car, the kind of breathing you do when you dread something.

As they pulled into Mueller's drive, Brent saw them.

Fellows and his minions.

Mitch

Mitch didn't see them at first. He marveled at how many cars were in the parking lot. There were almost no spots left. They had to navigate around the TV vans just to find one of the few remaining parking spaces. Kevin cut the engine, and they started the trek to the chapel.

There was a weird silence. It was a beautiful autumn day, but it seemed as if not a breeze stirred, not a single bird chirped. Hundreds of mourners filled the lawn in front of Mueller's chapel.

But as he and Kevin got closer, Mitch saw his father. Fellows and about twenty of his Family Now faithful stood silent, holding signs that shouted louder than their voices ever could. Mitch saw *God Hates Fags, He Will Burn, God Is Angry*, and others that spewed the hatred his father preached. Spencer Fellows was not a preacher but a god to all who bought into his vile, filthy philosophy.

Kevin said, "Looks like the roaches crawled out of the woodwork."

"Yeah," Mitch answered. There was no way he was going to tell Kevin that the king of the roaches was the man who spawned him.

Amazingly, Fellows didn't block anyone's way. The mourners filed past him and his group members. No one confronted him. No one acted as if he even existed.

Mitch was also pleased to see that no reporters crowded around. Their trucks were fully in view, but for once, they must have decided that people needed time to mourn.

Then he spotted the Force Four truck. Marlon Gordon and a cameraman did a live stand-up several yards away from the chapel entrance. *Just stay far, far away, bozo.*

The chapel was packed to overflowing. As more and more people arrived, there was only standing room. He and Kevin luckily squeezed into two seats in the back row, against the wall. All kinds of flowers surrounded a gleamingly polished, reddish-toned wooden casket. A blanket of deep red roses covered it. Mitch stared at it and remembered his mother's service, with its intentionally paltry attendance and few flowers. He wished he could have given his mother a sendoff like this one.

"No open casket?" Kevin whispered into his ear.

Mitch looked at him. There was a smirk on Kevin's face, he thought.

"Oh yeah," Kevin said, like he'd just remembered the circumstances of Callum's death.

Mitch decided the smirk, if it was one, was just Kevin's sick sense of humor. It went way too far, but then again, no one their age had dealt much with death.

A soloist sang a lovely, almost happy song, and then a preacher came forward. He spoke of Callum's short life and accomplishments and how everyone loved the boy. And then he corrected himself, "Man—for Callum Slater was more of a man than most of us are in middle age. He always seemed to have an old soul, a wise soul."

Old soul? Same thing mom used to say about me. But I doubt my soul is even half as good as Callum's must have been.

A few others spoke, but not the Slaters or Brent.

The preacher led them in a prayer. As he spoke loving, comforting, peaceful words, Mitch's mind wandered, and he heard in his mind the prayer that Spencer Fellows would have spoken. He shuddered.

Then six pallbearers appeared, surrounded the casket, picked it up in unison, and carried it up the aisle.

The gravesite was nearby, for Mueller's had their own cemetery. But the crowd mostly dispersed after the service. There was a short prayer at the grave, with Brent, the Slater family, a few people who were probably family and church members, the uncle who'd spoken on TV, and Mitch and Kevin attending.

When it was all over, Brent came to where Mitch and Kevin were standing.

"Thank you for coming. It means the world to me that Callum is appreciated in death as much as in life." His voice wavered at that word *death*. He looked at Mitch. "You didn't even know him, but you seem to have connected with him enough to come see him off."

"Your words moved me the other day. I felt I had to be here," Mitch said, feeling like his words were totally inadequate as he tried to express what he now felt for this remarkable Callum Slater. He took Brent's hands in his and held them a moment. As he did so, he felt Kevin's breath on his neck. "Oh, I'm sorry. This is my friend Kevin. Kev, this is Brent, Callum's partner."

"So sorry for your loss," Kevin said. Mitch thought it didn't sound very convincing, but then again, Kevin didn't really know Callum—never met him.

Mitch

"That's it for today. Before you go, just remember: have a joyful weekend, but keep safe," Dr. Costner told his class.

"Hey."

Mitch zipped his backpack, having stowed away his pen and notebook. He stood when he heard Brent's voice. "Brent. Great to see ya." He leaned in and gave Brent the bro hug. "I noticed you missed class last week. I meant to call, but then you showed back up Tuesday. Again, I shoulda said something to ya then. But I dunno, somehow I thought you might still be"—he groped for a word—"*processing*. How ya holdin' up?"

"It was touch and go the week after the funeral." He flashed a strange, quizzical smile. "That's a word I didn't think I'd be able to say so soon after it all." Mitch put his hand on Brent's shoulder for a moment, and then took it away. "Anyway, you're right. I needed some time. But life goes on, doesn't it? Unless I was going to trash the entire semester—and believe me I thought about it—I had to get back. And routine is healing, you know?"

"I found that out when my mother d..." Mitch's voice trailed away.

"You can say it. Died. Death. Funeral. See? Those words come easy to me now."

Mitch wanted to hug him—not just the guy hug thing, but a full, arms surrounding, pulling in close, feel the warmth and love hug. But he held back. He really didn't know Brent. Didn't know how he'd take it.

"Well, I, for one, am glad you're back. I know it's tough, but like ya said, life goes on."

Brent leaned in, gently pulled him, and hugged him. Mitch was right. Brent needed a hug, and he'd decided to take one. But that was okay. Grief does things to you.

Brent pulled away. "I'm sorry. That was way too much. I just…"

"It's okay. We all need hugs sometimes. I'm glad you feel comfortable with me, guy. I've gotta bounce, but walk with me? You have your car? I'll head your way. We can talk. 'Bout anything. Sometimes talking helps, even if the words are empty nothings."

"I took the city bus." Brent trembled. Then he stood stock still. "Didn't feel like driving. In fact, my car's still at the Slater house. I Ubered back to my place. The to-do at their house after the funeral did me in. I knew if I drove, I'd start thinking about Callum—and the *why*— and I'd probably crash into something. I've been meaning to go pick it up, but I'd have to see Margaret and Sam, and they'd remind me, and all my resolve would melt, and I'd probably crash driving home. I've been a mess. But I'm better now."

So much for gotta bounce. He needs me. "How 'bout I take you over there? They'll both be at work now, right? Kids're most likely back in school. You can get your car and not have to see anyone. You feel like drivin'?"

"I feel like such a chickenshit, Mitch. Callum'd want me to be strong and fearless. I'm getting' there, but there was only one Callum ever in this world, and I'm not him. I love Margaret and Sam dearly—almost as much as I love my own parents—but the last several days've been hell."

"Understandable." Mitch's heart was breaking for Brent. "So—you up to it? We pick up your car, and I'll follow you home to make sure you're safe. You can drive as slow and careful as you want. We'll pretend we own the road. Any horn honkers, anybody who flicks us off can just deal with it. 'Kay?"

Brent smiled. "I'd like that."

They walked silently to Mitch's car, parked in Lot E. Nothing was said, but Mitch felt they'd bonded deeply and nothing needed to be said.

Mitch pushed the unlock button on his key fob and headed to the driver's side. He opened his door, tossed his backpack into the seat behind him, and got in. Brent sat in the passenger seat, already buckled up.

Mitch started the engine. As he pulled to the parking lot entrance, Brent was still silent.

"Dr. Costner seems to've changed. He's never before wished us a happy weekend. That threw me for a loop. Not his MO," Mitch said, trying to keep it light.

"Callum."

"Come again?"

"Callum's why."

"I still don't follow, Brent." He glanced over, smiled at him, tried to make a joke. "Use your words, as my mom would say."

Brent didn't seem to register that Mitch was trying to lighten the mood. "At that service? The one where we met after it was over? Dr. Costner spoke. Seems he had a long-ago connection to Callum. He told of how Callum changed his life when Callum was only ten and Dr. Costner was his camp counselor. It was very moving."

Mitch wanted to hear the entire story, but now was not the time. Brent was talking, and Mitch feared interrupting him. Asking Brent to fill him in on the connection might bring back too much and clam him up.

"So," Brent continued. "Dr. Costner remembered how Callum had changed his life, and he—Dr. Costner—realized he'd reverted somewhat. He had forgotten that Callum taught him that you catch more flies with honey than vinegar, as they say. Seems like the good doctor is trying to make up for lost time."

"I hope you're right. He was always a great teacher, but he could be somewhat of a cold fish."

"I know I'm right," Brent said. "He told me when I was in his office to make up the test I missed the day after they found Ca..." His voice quivered.

I guess he isn't over it as much as he thinks he is. Mitch pulled one of the tissues from his center console. They'd been there ever since he'd had a raging cold the last winter. No. They'd been there since his mom died. But this was the second box of them.

"Need this? It's okay."

Brent took the tissue. He let out a violent burst of tears. Mitch totally knew how that happened. A box and a half of tissues testified to what could happen without any notice.

As quickly as the flood started, it was over. Brent wiped his eyes.

"That's the last time you'll see that."

Mitch knew, just knew, it wasn't the last time Brent would cry. It probably wasn't the last time he'd see Brent cry. But he admired his resolve. From all he'd been told, the resolve was a way to honor Callum.

"Anyway," Brent continued, his voice steeled, "Dr. Costner's been the kindest of my teachers. I guess because of his connection to Callum. The others haven't said a word about my missing a buncha classes, but they've sort of avoided me, like they don't know what to say. I suppose the Campus Pride members have been quick to tell them who I am and why I missed. But Dr. Costner? He's gone out of his way to see that I'm caught up with class notes. I aced that test, by the way. I don't know how, but I did."

"Wow! I'm impressed," Mitch said.

"Go on with yourself! Dr. Costner told me you got a point higher than I did on that bugger. You're the king of the class, my friend."

It's good to hear your mood lighten up.

"We'll rule together, benevolently, of course." He took his right hand off the wheel just long enough to high five with Brent.

"You know, the police won't tell me anything."

Well, so much for lightening up.

"They may not know much. These things probably have stumped them." Mitch gauged his words carefully, wondering just how far he could go.

"All four of 'em have been so torn up that they'd need one of the TV show forensics super-experts like Kasie on *NCIS* to unravel anything."

Brent surprised Mitch with that statement. After all, Callum was one of the *'em's* he was talking about.

"Somebody had to have seen something," Brent continued. "There's no way there could have been joggers on that trail, and they not see anything. Maybe they have no idea what they saw relates to Callum's murder, and maybe the detectives aren't makin' a connection even if they've been told somethin'. But I'm tellin' you, Mitch, somebody knows somethin' that would help us solve this."

Mitch couldn't believe what he was hearing. Brent had gone from shaky, fearful mourner to determined investigator in a heartbeat. And what did he mean by *us*?

"The police, the beat cops, and the detectives surely have questioned anyone near these crime scenes over and over. And the reporters—they are determined to solve this."

"Who? That shit Marlon Gordon? He's only in it for what he can get out of it. You can see it all over his face. He'd implicate his own mother if he thought he could get a few more viewers to up his ratings. You ever wonder why he keeps giving Fellows a soapbox to stand on?"

Mitch hadn't thought much about it, but Brent was making sense. "Fellows hasn't been on any other channels, I've noticed." As Mitch said *Fellows*, he thought *my dad*, but he wasn't about to bring that up.

"Gordon probably has an exclusive deal with that festering turd." Brent wiped his eyes again. "'Scuse my language. Callum hated the way I talk sometimes."

"'S okay. And I wouldn't doubt it a minute. What you say about Gordon and *the good reverend*." He filled that with the syrup of extreme disgust.

"No—I'm convinced no one is even close to finding out who did this."

"So?" Mitch asked.

"So? So we—you and I—could do our own investigating."

Mitch slammed on the brakes, pulled the car to the side of the road. "You and me?"

"I've been thinkin' about this for a long time. Ever since I lost Callum. Holed up alone with your grief, your mind races. I know there's somebody out there who can help me find Callum's killer. I thought I'd have to do it alone—and I was, *am*, prepared to do that. But two people are better than one."

"But why me?"

"I dunno. When Dr. Costner told me we were his top two students, I suddenly realized that your mind must work like mine."

I have no idea how your mind works, and this whole thing is scaring me a little. Messing with a serial killer is not something I ever thought I'd do. I really thought I was not that crazy.

"Sounds dangerous to me. This is a serial killer we're talking about here," Mitch said, editing what he was thinking.

"Serial killer? Not according to the *authorities*." Mitch saw and heard contempt in Brent's statement. "Look—maybe, just maybe, working together, we can uncover somethin' the police can't, won't, haven't."

"But we're not trained for that." Mitch tried to reason with Brent. He himself was afraid of what could happen if they poked around, but he was very afraid for Brent, frightened that Brent would let his grief get the best of him.

"Exactly. Look, Callum lived in a student apartment complex. *We're* students. The kids in his complex will talk to us. We can probably get more out of them than some badge-toting dick."

He was actually making sense, and that scared Mitch even more.

"And what do we do with this info if we find it?"

"Depends. If it has promise, we can turn it over, or we can keep diggin' for more leads."

"After we talk to his neighbors, then who?"

"Campus Pride members, park joggers."

"What if one of 'em is the killer?"

"Mitch, I get it. This is risky. Insane in a way. But ya can't win the lottery if ya don't buy a ticket."

"Say I help ya, will ya stop if I tell ya to?"

"Depends."

Mitch didn't like that answer.

"On what?"

"On how close we are. I'm hopin' we find out enough to turn it over to the police and let them do their job. I promise we will keep all our questionin' in public places. The joggin' trail. Outside doors. Open classrooms. Dorm hallways. That's why I need a partner. If anyone tries anything, it'll be two against one."

"This is crazy, man." Mitch knew he shouldn't agree to this. But Brent was determined. And whatever they found out—likely nothing—would get the police further along to stopping this madness. Maybe. "Okay. But we do nothin' reckless, okay?"

"Okay."

Mitch sighed. "What's the plan?"

"Saturday morning. My place. I'll text you the address. We'll start with Callum's apartment complex. We might wake some people up, but they'll likely be home after partyin' on Friday night."

"You think it's wise to wake up a hungover college student?"

"Probably not, but if we get there about ten-thirty, they should be already comin' out of their stupors."

Brent pointed ahead. "That's my car."

Mitch pulled up behind a beat-up old Camry.

As Brent hopped out of Mitch's car, he said, "See you Saturday."

What have I gotten myself into?

Three blocks away, Mitch remembered his promise to follow Brent home, to make sure he got there safely.

So much for that. Brent was so hep on this idea of his that there was no way he'd think of anything but *on his drive home.*

✝✝✝

Kevin and Les were at the Cup, sitting at a table against a back wall when Mitch scanned the room and headed to them.

"Lookee who's here," Les said. *Was that a snark?* Then he stood. "Gotta run," he said. He pointed his next words to Kevin. "Think about what I said."

"What was that all about?" Mitch said, sitting down.

Kevin pushed a cup across the table to Mitch. "Your preferred order, m' lad. Still hot. Placed it when you texted you were on your way."

Mitch picked up the cup and sipped. "Thanks. I need this." He smiled at Kevin.

In the coupla weeks he'd known him, he'd grown to really like him. The verdict was still out, though. Mitch didn't know if this would turn into something permanent or not. Maybe it was just a fling. He refused to let himself get hot and heavy with Kevin—and he was getting the vibe Kevin wouldn't turn him down if he offered—because he'd been there, done that. And didn't much like himself for it. This might be headed to long term. And that was something totally new to Mitch. He might not have it in him. He didn't want to hurt Kevin. Or himself. That's why he knew he had to take it slow. Mitch had a whirlwind of love 'em and leave 'ems after his Mom passed. He didn't realize it at the time, but now he thought he was trying to fill the void. Mindless sex that kept him from thinking, remembering, feeling. So he wanted to protect them both this time, not just his selfish self. He'd hurt a lot of guys. He wasn't proud of that. He'd hurt himself. He was even less proud of that. Kevin was funny and sweet, and God knows, a looker, but he also had a wild streak. Mitch felt he had to tame Kevin before he could take this relationship any further.

"You don't have to buy me coffee, you know. You're very thoughtful."

"Thoughtful, schmaughtful. Just me kissin' up to ya." He grinned. "Might help me get in your pants, is all." He flashed a wicked, playfully seductive smile.

"It just might. You keep it up, Kev—" he reached over, put his hand on Kevin's hand, and held it there for a moment—"and..." He quickly pulled away. Swiped his nose to try to cover up his sudden retreat. He dropped his gaze, avoiding Kevin's eyes. "I know I'm slow-goin'." Mitch sighed. "But one of these days, I could surprise you."

"Well, you better. I haven't worked this hard for a man since I earned my sex wings."

Mitch looked at him. *I've never heard that before.* Mitch laughed. Because Kevin was funny. Because it broke the tension.

"What? New terminology here? Need to spell it out? Popped my cherry? Got de-flowered? Went round the bend? Was de-virginized?"

Mitch belly-laughed. He liked this bad boy bravad-, but he found himself wondering if it was more than that. *Watch it, Mitch. Take it slow. Be cautious. No matter how he charms you.*

Mitch took another sip of coffee. "You didn't answer my question."

"Question? What question?"

Did he really not remember, or was he avoiding him? "Les told you to think about what he said."

"Oh, that. It was nothin'."

"Whatever," Mitch said, taking another sip. He thought if he acted like he didn't care, Kevin would spill. And sure enough, he was right.

"Les thinks I treat Step bad."

"And do you?" After all, you don't even give the guy the courtesy of using his name.

"He gets what's comin' to him. Step's only in it for himself."

"What's that supposed to mean?"

"Look, he married my mother for whatever reason, and then he decided he'd rule my life." Kevin frowned.

"How's that? All I've seen is that he gave you a car that cost a trillion dollars, and all I've heard is that he pretty much lets you have your own way. So enlighten me. What's up with this attitude you have about him?" Mitch tried to speak gently. He didn't want to offend Kevin, but Step, as Kevin rudely called him, seemed like a hell of a lot better candidate for Father of the Year than his *own* dad.

"Okay, granted Step gives me things." Kevin paused. Pinched his lips. Shook his head from side to side. "He's only tryin' to buy me. And he doesn't try to control my every move, but he would like to if I'd let him. He's even tried to pimp me out."

Mitch's eyes widened at that. *Is this Step a sex trader?*

"I see that look. He's not a trafficker. I'll give him that. Nothing sleazy goin' on," Kevin said. "But he wants to fix me up with a guy—any guy— who fits his idea of what I *should* want, not who *I* want."

"Wait a minute. Your dad—"

"Step. Dad."

"Your stepdad is okay with your being gay, but he wants you to make better choices in your men?" That was incredible to Mitch. And normal. All at the same time. "That's what parents do. No one's ever good enough to date their kid. You should be happy he's okay with your bein' gay." Mitch was beginning to think, in some ways, that year or two he had on Kevin was a lifetime of maturity. *I guess Mom was right with her old soul stuff.*

"Well, he only accepts that fact grudgingly. You shoulda heard him when he found out."

"You came out to him?"

"Came out? More like thrust out. By the little monster, I might add."

Mitch rolled his eyes. If Kevin was really his for life, he'd *have* to cure him of that. He remembered, in high school, when the other kids talked about their younger sibs, they frequently acted like they didn't like them. He never could figure that out. He would have loved having a little brother or sister. So he was not surprised Kevin and his little brother didn't get along. But calling him "little monster" and the like had to go.

"You mean Mark?"

"Yeah, Mark. Total big mouth. One day, I had a guy in my car and we were messin' around. Mark got off the school bus, saw us, and the next thing I knew, he was tellin' Step."

"Come on, Kevin, the man has a name, I presume."

"Okay, okay—Sloan. Pussy name. Anyway, Step—er, Sloan—went totally insane. Would you believe he got Mom home from work long enough to have a parental intervention? She's never home."

"Maybe he was just concerned. Maybe he was worried you weren't sure of what you were doin'. Maybe he just wanted to talk it out. And your Mom? There's safety in numbers."

Kevin looked at Mitch like he was a moron.

"She let *him* do the talkin'. And talk he did. More like yellin'." He paused. "At first." He paused again, like he was thinking about what was to come. "Then it was all this bullshit. 'Your mother and I care about you. Your mother and I want you to make good choices in life. Your mother and I love you.'"

"So, see? My point is made."

"Not so fast. I was almost buyin' his crap—right up to the 'I love you' part. That's when I *knew* it was total, unadulterated bullshit. He didn't care. He's never cared. Neither of 'em care. Sometimes I think my mother hatched this elaborate marriage plan to get me off her hands. Dump me with the new hubby. I swear my mother's never, ever home. She'd sleep at the office if she thought she could get away with it. Step's not home much, but he's there a hell of a lot more than she is. And he spends most of his at home hours bitchin' at me about something or other."

"So he doesn't love you, you say. And yet, you're certainly not Ella of the Cinders, mistreated and forced to do his bidding."

Kevin scrunched his face up. "What the hell are you talkin' about?"

"You're smart. Figure it out. It's a good analogy."

There was a long pause while Kevin thought.

"You mean Cinderella?"

Mitch smiled and nodded.

"Well, if I'm Cinderella, that makes you Prince Charming."

"I wondered when you'd come to that conclusion. And Prince Charming only has Cinderella's best interests at heart. Cut Sloan some slack, whaddaya say?"

Mitch looked around, leaned over, and kissed Kevin. A light, playful kiss.

A smile broke out on Kevin's face. "I guess I could try."

Mitch couldn't read Kevin's next expression. He thought it just might mean Kevin was only going along to get along. If that was the case, he would have to keep working on him about the Sloan thing. After all, Sloan couldn't be anywhere near as bad as Spencer Fellows.

Kevin

"Good day. Welcome to J. Corden's. Myron Johnson. How may I help you, sir?"

The guy was everything he expected. Total faux charm. The kind of fake smile that would make his normal customers cream. *J. Corden's— Fine Menswear*, where all the pretenders like Step go shopping.

Kevin had cut out school early so he'd have plenty of time to set his plan in motion. This had been a long time coming. Weeks of planning, plotting, scheming. Everything had to be just right. When all this was over and done, Step would be furious. And that's exactly what Kevin wanted.

He fixed a smile on his face, thrust his hand out for this Myron to shake, and did his best imitation of someone who gives a shit.

"Myron, I'm interviewing for a summer internship at Peterson, Flores in NYC. I definitely need to dress to impress, particularly something that will add a few years to me. I may be second-year law, but I still look like I'm fourteen. Don't you think?"

The best way to cozy up and make this guy do his bidding was to act a bit vulnerable.

"Well, sir, if I may be so bold, you are quite youthful. Perhaps a hair trim would be in order, as well, sir."

Kevin liked how this schlong kept calling him *sir*. He had him in the palm of his hand.

"Never fear, Myron. I have a salon appointment in three quarters of an hour. So we must work quickly, if you please."

"Certainly, sir. What did you have in mind?"

"Suit. Something dark. Only the best. Nothing fussy. I want to look as if I dress that way all the time."

"I have just the thing. Zegna. Italian. Impeccably tailored."

"Just the thing, sounds like." Kevin knew repeating this Myron's own words was a good way to kiss up. "Show me what you have in mind." The salesman led Kevin toward the wall of suits. *I'm well aware of Zegna. That's what Step wears.*

Kevin bet Myron's johnson was almost as stiff as rebar as he presented the suit he pulled from the rack, holding it as if it were the crown jewels. But Kevin kept his eyes on the product, not Myron's well-clothed crotch.

"This is the Zegna Centroventamila. Night blue. Not as severe as black, but it does make a statement. And it would go well with your coloring, sir."

Could this guy lick my ass any harder?

Kevin fingered the fabric.

"Lovely texture, don't you think, sir. Would you like to slip it on?"

Even Kevin was impressed Myron could tell his size just by looking.

"If you please." And Myron helped him into the jacket.

"Fits you well. And, if you don't mind my saying, you look very nice. Very nice, indeed. Quite impressive. Shall we try on the trousers?"

Will we both fit into them?

"Yes, I believe we will."

Myron slipped the pants off the hanger like he was handling treasure and escorted Kevin to a dressing room. For a moment, Kevin thought Myron was joining him in the tiny cubicle, but the salesman simply opened the door, said "Oops" as he removed two suits from a hook inside, and then left.

Kevin had no sooner unzipped his jeans than a voice called out over the three-quarter door. "I thought you'd like to get the full effect, sir. Here is a dress shirt and tie I think will go well with the ensemble." And sure enough, a hand held a shirt and tie above Kevin's head. He took it and continued undressing.

The shirt was an amazing fit. He had to hand it to Myron. He knew his business. The tie, also a Zegna, was a muted cranberry and light grey stripe. He tied it carefully, and he pulled on the suit pants, buttoned and zipped, and completed the look with the jacket. He returned to the sales floor and stood in front of a mirror, Myron gazing over his shoulder.

"Don't you look stunning."

Stunning? Did Myron's johnson find its way into pussy more decidedly male than female?

"It does look good. Great choice, Myron, my man. But these pants. A bit baggy. And they're much too long, don't you think?"

"Not a problem. We have in-house alterations. We can get these done for you by Tuesday afternoon."

"No can do, Myron. Redeye flight tonight to the Big Apple. Surely you can persuade your tailor to get them done? If I can't have it later today, then I'll have to go elsewhere."

Kevin could see Myron imagining the dollar signs with tiny wings flying out the door.

"I'm sure we can accommodate you." Myron looked at his watch. "It's three now. Could you come back at six?"

"Sure thing, Myron, sure thing."

Myron marked and pinned, took the suit to the back, came out in a flash, and said, "And how will we be paying?"

Kevin whipped out Step's platinum card, and a sales slip with a balance just shy of $6000 was soon ready for his signature. Ah, the platinum card. The card company knew Kevin had charging rights bestowed upon him by Step himself, and the retailers never questioned him, no doubt because they loved the massive amounts he brought to their coffers.

"Six o'clock, on the dot. Thank you, Myron."

Myron gave him a bag containing the shirt and tie, and Kevin whistled as he left the store.

He stowed the bag away in the Spyder and then walked to Adrian's.

"Kevin! Good to see you," Adrian said as Kevin walked in the door. "Finished the last client earlier than expected, so I've been waiting for you." He motioned toward his chair.

Kevin sat at the stylist's station and looked in the mirror as Adrian, behind him, spoke. "Same as usual?"

"Time for a change, Adrian. Shorter. Not so wild. Want to look older, wiser."

Adrian had been styling Kevin's hair for a year or more. It was he who came up with that signature flyaway look Kevin sported.

"No prob, Kevin. But why the change?" Adrian fastened the cloth around Kevin's neck.

"Got me a new man, Adrian."

"If we're doing this so you can keep a man, then I want it to be a surprise. Let me turn the chair around so you can't peek in the mirror." He did that, and after spritzing Kevin's hair with his water bottle, he said. "Okay...give me the dish,"

"I'm ready to move up to the big leagues. He's older."

Adrian's eyes popped out. "How old, Kevin? You don't want to get yourself in a mess."

"Calm yourself, wise man." *Why did hairstylists always think they were shrinks too?* "He's only a year older than me, but he's in college, and he seems older. And before you decide he's some sort of predator pedophile, he hasn't made a move—not one little thing except a few kisses. It's frustrating, you know."

Adrian began snipping hair from Kevin's head. Even worldly-wise Kevin was always amazed at Adrian. He was a scissors wizard. "I know, Kevin. My José and me? We did nothing for almost a year after we met. Lots of cuddling, lots of hugs, lots of kissing, but José didn't want anything else. I thought I would go mad. I was getting *cojones azules*, you know—blue balls, like crazy, know what I mean?" He smiled as Kevin nodded. "But you know what? It was worth it. Just when I thought José was playing me and wasn't even gay at all, he blossomed. That night was a miracle. *Un milagro,* I say, Kevin. So you just wait it out, okay? Listen to Adrian."

Kevin pondered as Adrian finished cutting his hair, ran the electric clippers on his neck, pulled away the drop cloth, and said, "Now, time for shampoo." He led Kevin to the shampoo station.

Adrian always shampooed after the cut. All the stray, itchy hairs were washed away. Kevin loved Adrian's shampoo job. His fingers kneaded the minty shampoo into Kevin's scalp. After a warm rinse, Adrian applied conditioner. He even smeared the mint conditioner on Kevin's face, and then he applied a steaming towel. Adrian let that set for a few minutes, as he went to sweep up his station. When he returned, he rinsed the hot towel, used it to cleanse Kevin's face, washed the conditioner from Kevin's hair, and then he towel dried his head. And then Kevin was led back to Adrian's chair, with the stylist draping a dry towel over his head. Kevin knew what Adrian was doing. This was exactly the same thing he did when he created Kevin's previous style. Total secrecy until the big reveal.

"Okay, Kevin." Adrian had gently turned him around, away from the mirror. "Sit." Adrian began his magic with his hair dryer. When he cut the switch on the dryer, he applied some sort of concoction, used his fingers to smooth and tug the hair a bit, and then he swung Kevin around.

"Surprise! What do you think?"

Kevin stared at a new person in the mirror. He looked several years older. "Man oh man, Adrian, you're a miracle worker. This was exactly what I was goin' for."

"And keeping it this way will be easy. You just shampoo, apply a bit of this—" He handed Kevin a small, flat jar of something that said Hair Paste on the label, and then he continued. "And you just use your fingers to arrange it. If you want it to look even more businesslike, run a comb through it."

The platinum card covered Adrian's haircut fee—$75—the cost of the paste—$30—and a nice tip.

Then Kevin was off to Pace Opticians. He'd googled everything he needed to know about optometry. He knew if he got lenses in the lowest minus power, he could not only tolerate them but get used to them and be able to wear them all the time, if he so chose. Or at least as long as he needed them for his plan. He could have found some off-the-rack glasses with clear lenses, but he needed them to look expensive and authentic, like they'd been prescribed for him. In the course of his research, he'd managed to download a prescription slip, manipulate it to make it look real, fill in a prescription, and sign his fictitious doctor's name with henscratching that any self-respecting doctor would be proud of.

"Hello," a woman about his mother's age greeted him as he entered. "What can we do for you today?'

She was wearing a name tag, and Kevin looked at it and said, "Well, Elena, my doctor gave me this prescription, and I need to get it filled." He handed her his counterfeit prescription.

She glanced at it, and then asked, "Do you have something in mind, or do you want me to suggest some frames?"

"I don't mind telling you I was not really happy that I needed glasses, but the doctor said that this was a very mild prescription that would help me with my driving, especially at night. So I thumbed through GQ and some other magazines and decided I really like the Oliver Peoples frames." Oliver Peoples was what Step wore. He knew that because the last time Step got new reading glasses, he preened about in them, expounding on their virtues, until Kevin wanted to puke.

"Sure thing. Let me pull a few styles, and we'll start from there." She pulled out a chair at a small desk and motioned for Kevin to take a seat.

A few moments later, she returned with four pairs of eyeglass frames clutched in her hand. She placed them on the desk and sat down.

"These will all look great on you," she looked down at his prescription, which she'd also placed on the desk, "Kevin. It depends on the shape and color you like the best."

He picked up one of the frames, put it on, and looked into the mirror on the desk. No, those weren't right at all. He tried another pair. Not right, either.

Elena handed him a third pair. "Try these. My favorite: the Sheldrake. Comes in six colors. One's sort of a lighter color, the Semi-Matte Raintree. Then there's a black, a cobalt tortoise shell, two other shades that are currently on order, and these. Peoples dubbed these Cocobolo."

Kevin put those frames on, stared into the mirror and decided they were perfect for his plan. They added years to his face and complimented his new, more mature haircut.

"I'll take these."

"You want to try on the other colors?"

"No, I like these. You can make them up in thirty minutes or so, can't you?" He'd picked this place not only because they carried Oliver Peoples but also because they promised quick service.

"Sure can. Let me take a few measurements, and we can get them into production right now." She used a little ruler in front of his face and wrote down numbers. She then had him put on the frames. She felt them over his ears, mumbled something that sounded affirmative and then took the frames from him, picked up the prescription, and scurried away.

When she came back, she asked, "How would you like to pay for this?"

The magic silver plastic took care of everything to the tune of about $700. As he signed, Elena said, "Give us thirty minutes. See you back at 5:30, okay?"

"Sure thing."

He left the optical and headed to Nordstrom's. He needed shoes.

In the men's shoe department, a guy with a comb-over cemented in place accosted him immediately. "What can I do you for today?"

"I need something that will look good with a night blue Zegna. I'm thinking black. What do you have in a 9 medium?"

"Got just the thing." The guy disappeared into the back and reappeared with two shoe boxes in hand. "Have a seat," he said, and then he sat on one of those strange little shoe salesman stools. "I have other choices, but you look like a discriminating guy, so I present to you my two best—the Gucci Donnie Bit Loafer, and this one here's the Ferragamo Moccasin with Gancino ornament. I know you've heard of Gucci, but are you familiar with Ferragamo?" He lovingly took a shoe from its box and caressed it like it was his wife after he'd had half a bottle of champagne. "Feel the leather. Like butter."

Kevin decided to play along. "Oh, that is nice. How much will those set me back?"

"It's not the price, sir. It's the prestige. You walk into a room with these on, and every head will turn. And if you're sporting a Zegna suit, I know you're not truly interested in the cost. But to answer your question, these babies are $950. Care to try them on?"

Kevin slipped off his Nikes, and felt the softest leather he'd ever experienced as the guy slipped the shoe onto his foot. Then he repeated the move with the other foot, other shoe. Kevin stood. Walked around a bit. Looked in the mirror. Perfect.

"Whaddaya think?"

"I'll take 'em. Throw in a belt, size 32, and three pairs of socks, okay?"

"Sure." The guy gathered the purchases as he led Kevin to the register. Then he scanned each item and said, "That'll be $1052.28 with tax." Kevin handed over the platinum card, and soon a Nordstrom bag hung from his arm.

As he left the store, he looked at his watch. It had been thirty minutes, so he breezed back to Pace's. Elena was waiting for him. "I have your glasses ready."

He sat down. She pulled them from the case, placed them on his face, felt around his ears again, took them off, made some adjustments to the earpieces, and put them back on him. She pointed to the mirror. "Look great, don't you think?"

He did look good, he thought.

"Fit okay? Shake your head. Feel too loose, too tight?"

Kevin did as he was told, and they felt like they fit like a glove.

"Look out there in the distance." She pointed toward the door of the shop. "Things look clearer?"

They really didn't, but they didn't look any less clear, either. He played along, though. "Wow, I can't believe the difference."

"Sometimes a tiny bit of correction is all you need." She handed him the case and said, "Now, you come back if you need anything."

Kevin tucked the glasses case into the bag with his shoes, belt, and socks, and he stopped at the Spyder to deposit the bag in the car.

Then he headed back to J. Corden.

"My, don't you look nice," Myron said as he came through the door. "The haircut suits you, sir."

"Thank you, Myron." He was trying to act mature, old. That too was important to his plan.

Myron walked to a hook by the register. "I have your suit. All finished and pressed."

Kevin took the garment bag from him.

"And good luck on that interview. I'll be rooting for you, sir."

Kevin smiled at this supercilious prick and said, "Thank you, Myron. It's good to know someone is on my side."

When he left Corden's, he realized he needed to hustle if he was going to make his date with Mitch. Luckily, they were only going to a movie—and hook up big time afterward he hoped—so his jeans and T would be fine to wear. Mitch had said they'd get burgers before the show.

Friday afternoons were Markie's Boy Scout meetings, so he wouldn't be home until seven or so. That meant he wouldn't be questioned when he carted the suit, shoes and accoutrements into the house. God knows, neither Step nor Mom would be there. Mom would be at the office until her usual ten or eleven, and if Step got away from his desk, he'd be on the golf course. They were predictable if nothing else.

He pulled the car into the drive, gathered his purchases, and took the stairs two at a time to his room. He hung the suit bag in the closet and stashed everything else on the floor beneath it.

Stopping to pee because he hadn't taken time all afternoon, he thought of how he could win over Mitch. One thing he knew, he would have to cool it with the hardline he always took when he mentioned Step or the little monster. Mitch didn't like that at all. He would have to play nice if he was going to turn this thing into anything meaningful. And he did want it. From the minute he laid eyes on Mitch, Kevin knew he could be the one for him. Not just hot steamy bed play, but a rich, long-term forever coupling. Finally, someone who loved him and cared about him and wanted him and would take him away from Mom, Step and the chaos of his life.

Zipping his jeans, he ran his hands quickly under the faucet, and bounded down the stairs. If he didn't hurry, he'd be late. And if he was late, that would just be one more confirmation that he was a flake. He had to convince Mitch he was a standup guy, someone worth his trouble.

All the visitor spaces at Mitch's complex were empty, so he had no trouble parking. He cut his engine and ran past the pool to Mitch's. He kept looking at his watch as he ran. He was right on time, thank God. He rapped on the door.

The door swung open, and Mitch, beautiful Mitch, stood there, looking amazing in pressed slacks and a turquoise and green striped pullover with a Polo logo on the breast. *Uh-oh. I screwed up again.*

A strange look on Mitch's face shot back at Kevin. He looked like he couldn't believe his eyes. *He's all dressed up, and I'm standing here in my raggedy jeans and faded t-shirt. I'm such a fuckup.*

"Don't you look different," Mitch exclaimed. "With your new haircut and those scholarly glasses."

Kevin had a retort already planned to explain the haircut, but he'd forgotten he was still wearing the glasses. "Just needed a change, so I asked my hair guy to give me something different. And the glasses? My contacts have been giving me fits." *Good thinking, Kevin.*

"Let me get my jacket," Mitch said. He left Kevin standing in the doorway and returned in a moment. "Big Boy okay?"

"Sure. Love their burgers."

As they rode to the restaurant, they made small talk. "How was school today, Kev?" he asked.

"Okay. I actually left early." It suddenly struck him that was not the thing to say if he was trying to convince Mitch he was a responsible person. "Had to see the dentist," he adlibbed.

"Problems?"

"No. Twice yearly cleaning." One thing was good about having a mind like a steel trap. Kevin could talk his way out of anything.

"Oh. I hate the dentist. Even for cleanings." Mitch yawned. "'Scuse me. Today was a bitch. I had both a morning class and an afternoon class. Whatever possessed me to sign up for an afternoon class on Friday? Get thee behind me, Satan." He laughed. Kevin joined in. "I'll perk up when I get some food in me. I hear the movie's good."

They had decided on a new movie that had opened that morning. "Yeah, everybody at school was talkin' about it." *Why am I lying? I didn't talk to anybody in school today. Like most days.* "Got great reviews. Saoirse Ronan is Oscar bound, I hear." He glanced over at Mitch and smiled.

Mitch punched his shoulder. "Like you care. You're such a goof."

Kevin parked the car and a hostess led them to a table. They sat opposite each other. Kevin was scanning the menu from cover to cover. As if he didn't already know what he wanted.

His concentration was broken by Mitch's voice. "I just can't believe it."

Kevin looked up. "What?"

"You. You look thirty years old. But I like it."

"Thanks. I figured if I's goin' to date a college man, I needed to lose the teen pretty boy look." He primped the air around his head, like a model showing off her hair in one of those shampoo commercials.

Mitch laughed. "Well, you pulled it off. The hair's amazing. And those glasses. The color of the frames really brings out your eyes. I've never thought glasses were all that sexy, but you're bringin' it, man. Forget the contacts. You were made for glasses." He glanced over his shoulder, leaned over, and planted a kiss on Kevin's lips. "You turn me on, Kev."

The glasses were never part of his scheme to win over Mitch. They were a big element of the other plan. But wow. He was glad he'd forgotten he had them on.

They chowed down on burgers, fries, milkshakes, and hot fudge sundaes. Kevin loved the way Mitch never took his eyes off him the entire meal.

At the movie theater, Mitch took Kevin's hand in his and didn't let it go until the last credit rolled.

"You like it?" Mitch asked as they walked up the aisle.

"I loved it."

"Ronan was funny as hell, wasn't she?"

It dawned on Kevin that Mitch had asked about the movie. His answer to the *you like it* question was a response to the hand-holding. A simple thing, but he felt so in love because of it.

"Yeah. I loved the scene where she kept getting tongue tied."

Mitch laughed with Kevin. "So, so funny!"

In the car, Mitch grabbed him before Kevin could even start the engine and planted a warm, wet, tongue-probing kiss on him. Kevin felt his dick grow. *Please, please, please let this lead to something.* His crotch was aching as Mitch prolonged the kiss. Then he pulled away. "My place?" Mitch asked.

The Spyder, with all its horsepower, couldn't move them fast enough across town. The visitor spots were all filled, and Kevin freaked. "There's no place to park, there's no place to park," he shouted frantically.

"Try the side street. It's always empty."

Sure enough, Mitch was right. Kevin parked, and for his money, they didn't walk fast enough to the apartment.

As soon as they were through the door, Mitch was tearing at Kevin's shirt, pulling it from his jeans, his tongue once again halfway down Kevin's throat. He was backing Kevin across the room, and into the bedroom.

He pushed him onto the bed, pulled off Kevin's Nikes, unzipped his jeans, lifted him up by the pants legs, and ripped them off. Then he leaned over and pulled at the elastic of Kevin's briefs with his teeth. Kevin felt Mitch's fiery breath as the fabric snagged on his erection. Mitch gave Kevin's dick a sweet kiss. Then he stood.

He undressed slowly and seductively. He opened a drawer next to the bed and took something from it. Then he lay beside Kevin.

Kevin reached to remove his glasses. Mitch grabbed his arms. "No. Leave 'em on. Like I said, don't ever take 'em off again."

Mitch planted kisses of honey all over Kevin's face and neck. At this point, Kevin would have guided a lover's head to his crotch, but he let Mitch take the lead, totally.

With every inch of his upper body kissed and caressed, Mitch lay his hand on Kevin's penis. He was murmuring words of delight—nothing Kevin could make out, but it was obvious Mitch was enjoying himself.

Mitch reached over for the thing he'd taken from the drawer. He tore its aluminum foil covering with his teeth. Removed it from its packaging. Carefully and seductively rolled the condom onto Kevin's penis. He took Kevin into his mouth, his wet hot tongue exploring every millimeter of Kevin's member. Even the protection didn't lessen Kevin's ecstasy. Mitch sucked. Then he stopped. He sucked again. Then he stopped. This went on for what seemed like days until Kevin exploded, shuddering and quivering.

Then Mitch pulled his face back parallel with Kevin's. "That was amazing. You—you are amazing." He gently removed Kevin's glasses and kissed his eyelids. Then he placed the glasses back on Kevin's face.

Mitch laid his head on Kevin's chest. Contentment was like a warm blanket.

"I'm sorry," Kevin said.

"Sorry?" Mitch said, not looking at him. "What for?"

"Sorry I'm such an ass. You're right. Maybe I should cut my little brother and my stepfather some slack." The words were words he'd planned to use to win Mitch over, but right now, he thought maybe they made sense. Maybe he could try harder. At least with Mark. But Step?

That was another story entirely.

Mitch

Sun poured through the slats of the Venetian blinds, waking Mitch. He'd slept a bit later than he intended, spent from the night before. Dragging himself out of bed, he stretched and yawned. He scratched his privates as he headed to pee. A long, satisfying stream later, he turned on the shower, adjusting the faucet to hot. He had to wake up if he was ever going to get going and make it over to Brent's to begin their quest.

As he soaped up, his dick got hard again, remembering Kevin the night before. Did he let it go too far? It was certainly steamy and fun, but God, he'd let his lust take over, as he'd done so many times before. His plan was to treat Kevin differently than all those other faceless hookups. After his mom passed, he wasn't feeling anything. He knew all those meaningless beddings were a cry. He had to bring himself back to life. He fooled himself into believing they were all potential longtime partners, but he knew better, deep down. Love wasn't remotely a part with any of those guys, and so the empty void remained. Time heals all wounds, they say. He'd never get over losing such a big part of his life, but he tucked his mother away, hidden inside his heart most of the time, and he let his reason to live return. And as he revived himself, after he'd figured out sex wasn't going to do the trick, he'd decided to abstain. AA for sex addicts, sorta. No meetings, but still, he knew what he had to do. At least until someone special came along.

Mitch believed Kevin was that someone. He still wanted to take it slow, get to know Kev even more. Yeah, Kev's reckless. He talks about his stepfather and his little brother like they are subhumans. He barely mentions his mother, so she obviously is a big, big part of his problem.

Mitch convinced himself Kevin suffered from immaturity, and he'd grow out of it. It could be a very long process, but the day before, Kevin had shown he'd taken tentative steps. His words were kinder. His new look was much more mature. He was trying to discard his old self, bring on a new. Mitch appreciated that.

If only Mitch hadn't let his lust get the best of him. Baby steps were not a propellant to hot, steamy sex. Thank God he'd stopped short of coupling. At least, Mitch thought, *I reined myself in before the point of no return. But why oh why did I get so turned on over a new haircut and a pair of glasses?*

As he let the steam from the shower penetrate his lungs and the force of the water pound his body—and let his hard-on die naturally—Mitch realized he was hungry. Hungry for someone to hold him, to show him he was still a sexual being, still someone worthy of love. And that's what Kevin did.

But he couldn't let his own longing turn into something it wasn't. He may want it, but Mitch knew that getting it was a big misstep. Kevin *was* immature, no matter the strides he'd made so quickly. He owed it to both Kev *and* himself to get back on the slow track, let this thing develop. If it was meant to be, everything would fall into place. But pushing it into place via sex was not going to do anything but cause heartache. Yes, for himself. But most of all, for Kevin.

He would talk to Kevin that evening, he vowed. But, at the moment, he was going to be mucho late-o if he didn't dry himself off and get dressed. Brent was probably already antsy, waiting for him.

Fifteen minutes later, Mitch pulled in front of Brent's apartment. Cutting the engine, he looked up to see Brent standing on the balcony.

"Thought you'd never get here," Brent called as Mitch shut the car door and headed for the stairs.

Face to face, Brent asked, "You want coffee before we head out? We can talk strategy."

"Sure. I was dead to the world until half an hour ago. Make it strong. Feed me some battery acid to jumpstart me."

Brent led him into the apartment. "You take cream? Sugar? Or I have Stevia."

"Coal black. Perfect." Brent poured a mug full, and, steam rising off it, he handed it to Mitch. He motioned to the couch, where Mitch sat, blowing on the cloud of steam formed on the cup in his hand. After topping off his cup, Brent sat in the chair facing him.

Taking a baby sip of the hot brew, Mitch said, "Nice place."

"Thanks. My parents're only five minutes away, but I wanted m' own place after I graduated high school and started college. They indulged me."

"Sounds like you have some great folks."

"My mom and dad are crazy supportive. I'm an only child. They wanted more, but that never happened. So I guess I'm a little spoiled." He took a drink from his cup. He smirked. "More like rotten, some would say."

Mitch laughed. "I don't know you very well, but ya seem like a levelheaded standup guy to me. And from what you've told me about Callum, I somehow think he had high standards when it came to his men."

"Man."

"Come again?"

"Man. Callum never dated anyone but me, nor me, either. Dated anyone but him, I mean."

Mitch pondered that as he sipped his coffee. So these two fell in love in a flash. Maybe I should consider that's what's happened with Kev and me. Can it be that simple?

"So," Brent said, "first up, we'll go over to Callum's complex. Talk to his neighbors. See if they know anything or saw anybody."

It suddenly occurred to Mitch that Brent and Callum, as much as they loved each other, had lived separately.

"Sounds like a plan. But..." He paused. "Maybe it's not any of my business." He paused again. "If I can ask—why the separate cribs? I'd think you and Callum would have rushed from teenage home life to independent living together. From where I sit, you two were head over heels in love."

A sad look filled Brent's face.

Okay. I blew it. Mom always did say I was too nosy.

"I don't mind your asking. One of my greatest regrets. Not living together. If I'd had an inkling we had so little time left, I woulda made him move in together with me."

Mitch watched as the guy spoke. Brent's eyes wandered as if he were watching a film projected in the air before him. *The Contentment: Callum and Brent, the Happy Couple.* Mitch could see Brent imagining their life together. And probably how he could have protected Callum, saved him from his savage fate.

Brent gave his head a tiny shake. Like he was banishing his recent thoughts. He looked once again at Mitch, gulped some coffee, and continued. "Callum. Ultimate high standards. Devout Christian. Very involved in church. Got that from his parents. All that may be hard to believe because most people have this image of gay men rutting like rabbits." That hit a bit too close to home for Mitch. "But Callum, like a virgin penitent, was saving himself for marriage."

Surely this is a joke.

Brent must have seen that thought on Mitch's face because he said, "I know. I thought he was jokin' too when he told me that. That was early on. I figured he'd cave as we got to know each other because from the moment I saw that gorgeous god, my goal was to get in his pants. But Callum had steely resolve. He meant what he said. And before you ask, yes, we did kiss and hug and cuddle and sometimes I could talk him into a little mutual handplay, but it never went any farther."

Mitch was having a hard time swallowing this story, but Brent's earnestness told him the guy wasn't lying. This was the unvarnished truth.

"So Callum and I got separate apartments. I dunno. I respected his stance. He was firm in what he believed in, and I, never a real churchy person, began to understand my Callum. I even went to services with him most Sunday mornings. And he respected me enough not to insist on anything more than that. Maybe he thought he could bring me around, or—and I really believe this—he just accepted me the way I was, the way he accepted everyone. And so, every night, I went home to mine, he to his. His counseling and his Campus Pride duties kept him busy, so we didn't even see each other every day. But those dates we made were special, magical. I can attest to the fact that absence makes the heart grow fonder.

"And Callum could be mysterious. I dunno if he *meant* to keep secrets from me, or if he felt he had some sort of 'seal of the confessional' when he counseled, or if he was privy to so much sordidness that he wanted to shield me. I just know that many a night I sat right here, watchin' crap on TV, wonderin' where Callum was and what he was doin'. It wudn't that I didn't trust him, it was I ached to be with 'im. And then we'd meet for a date, and all that went away. We were together, and I was fulfilled. Sounds like soap opera, huh?"

"No," Mitch said, "it sounds like a man in love with a god."

"Callum was that. Yes, he was." He stood. "Ready to get some questions answered? We can take my car. It's a clunker, but it'll get us there."

Mitch rose. "I've seen your car. It's a Bentley limo compared to my Civic with its two different colored front fenders."

They laughed, and it felt good. This is fun, despite the shit we're goin' in search of.

An eight-minute drive brought them to a smallish, nondescript row of apartments straight out of the 1970s, sallow-looking grey brick with turquoise-painted trim.

Brent parked and they got out. He pulled out his wallet and removed a picture from it. "Knowing Callum, just the mention of his name will be enough, but I've got his picture just in case."

He knocked on the first door as Mitch stood behind him.

A girl, about five-seven, skinny as a rail, stringy, greasy-looking hair hanging halfway down her back, opened the door. She looked stoned out of her mind. Here's a dropout waiting to happen, Mitch thought.

"Yeah?" One tiny word and it was slurred.

"Hi," Brent said, all smiles. "I wonder if I could ask you some questions about one of your neighbors? Callum Slater?"

"Th' murdered guy?"

Mitch was amazed she could put three words that made sense together—and that she knew who Brent was talking about, as out of it as she was.

"Didn't know him," she said and shut the door. Brent looked over his shoulder to Mitch and shrugged.

"Thirteen more to go." He sighed.

Going door to door, they met with a lot of resistance and a lot of apathy. Number two knew Callum but had seen nothing the night he died. Three never opened the door, even though they could hear the TV blaring from inside. Four and five said they'd seen Callum earlier that day he—both of them stopped, like they couldn't say *died*— then they added he was alone. Six was a trip. He was one of those guys who talk to hear their heads rattle.

"Callum? Sure, I knew him. We was good friends. Smoked dope together all the time. Sorry to hear he died. What happened? Did he ram his hog into a wall? The guy never wore a helmet when he rode that Harley. Nice bike. Did it get totaled?"

Brent kept trying to stop his bullshit, but he couldn't get a word in edgewise until the guy stopped to take a drag off his smoke, which gave off an odor that was decidedly not Marlboro.

"Thanks for your time, guy," Brent said, and they walked to the next door as the guy called, "If ya need any weed, man, I can hook ya up."

The girl in seven was beautiful and articulate—a breath of fresh air. "I know you. You're Callum's boyfriend, aren't you? I'm so, so sorry for you."

"Thank you," Brent said. "I'm Brent, and yes, Callum and I were partners. I wonder if we could ask a few questions? This is my friend Mitch."

"Good to meet you, Mitch." She smiled at me. "I'm Sarah," she said to both of us. "Why don't you two come in? Can I get you anything? Coffee? Juice? Water?" As she spoke, she motioned us in and pointed to a sofa.

"Nothing for me, thanks," Brent said. He looked at Mitch.

"I'm fine," Mitch replied.

"Okay," she said as she sat, her longish skirt swirling a swath of lavender paisley around her legs. She adjusted the purple blouse she had on, and then she gathered her long auburn hair and sort of fluffed it out. Finally, she said, "Fire away."

"The night Callum was—" Brent faltered.

Mitch finished for Brent. "The night Callum died—"

Brent apparently had gained new resolved. "The correct term is murdered. The night Callum was murdered, did you see him?"

"Let me think." And she paused as she sorted her thoughts, it seemed. "I saw him the day before. We have—had—American Lit together. We talked about *The Scarlet Letter* as we walked home. We both loved the novel, and Callum had made some great points in the class discussion that day."

"That's my Callum," Brent murmured.

"So the next day was Tuesday. I don't have classes on Tuesday/Thursday. I wait tables at Hooters those days."

Mitch involuntarily took a loud breath at that.

She laughed at him. "Don't judge. It's good money and my student loans will kill me if I don't get a head start on saving up to pay them."

She looked back at Brent. "I work lunch—great tips from the businessmen—and my shift is over at four-thirty. I stopped at Needler's to pick up bread and milk and some veggies for dinner and got home about six. I remember seeing Callum heading out. We spoke."

"What did you talk about?"

"The usual. How ya doing? Nice day. You know."

"Did he say where he was going?"

"I just assumed he was going to counseling. He had his Bible. He always took it with him to the center. We'd talked about that. He said he never brought up religion when he talked to the kids, but if one of them brought it up, he wanted to be ready with scripture. He was that way. He didn't push anything on anybody. Just a nice, levelheaded, great guy."

"Yes, he was." And for all Brent's bravado about how he could talk about Callum's murder and funeral and everything else, Mitch caught him wiping a tear. "So, did you see him later?"

"No. I had a date. Got home about midnight. Went straight to bed."

"Now, I know this may sound strange. I, since Callum was the love of my life—as squirrely as that may sound—should know these things. But Callum didn't tell me everything, for whatever reason. So maybe this came up in one of your conversations. Did he ever mention counseling anywhere other than the center?"

She shook her head as if pondering the question. "No, I don't remember anything." Then her face lit up. "One night, he mentioned going to a gay club. I thought that odd because he was such a Christian, and gay bars just don't seem to fit with that image. I asked him why he'd gone there, and he said he'd gone with a guy he was trying to help. That made sense to me. Callum seemed like the kind of guy who would do anything, go anywhere to bring someone to his way of thinking."

"Did he mention the name of the club?" The tone of Brent's voice rose as if he were getting excited.

"If he did, I don't remember. I'm sure he did, but since I don't go to those places, the name didn't stick."

"You sure?"

"I wish I could help you with that, but I'm very sure." She paused to think again. "Oh!"

"You remember?"

"No, but I do remember something else. I don't know if it will help or not. One day Callum and I were shooting the breeze, and I mentioned Spencer Fellows. I'd just seen that asshole on TV, and I guess he was on my mind. Callum smiled at the name. I asked him why he was smiling. He said, 'nothing.' Well, I wasn't about to let him get away with that kind of answer. I kept begging, pleading, prodding until he told me the strangest story. If anyone else had come up with that tale, I woulda called 'bullshit.' But this was Callum, the standup guy who wouldn't make stuff up just to make himself look good. You know what I'm talking about?"

"Yes, I do," Brent said. "And yes, Callum would never invent things. And yes, Callum did indeed have that encounter with Fellows. But I never knew him to tell anybody about it after it happened."

"Sooooo—" She gazed at Brent. "Do you think his telling me can help you at all with your quest?"

"I don't know, but I certainly appreciate your sharing. Anything else?"

"I don't think so. I wish I could be more help. Callum was a great, great guy."

Brent stood. Mitch followed his lead. "Thanks, Sarah. You've been a big help."

"You think?" she said.

"If nothing else, it was great hearin' that someone else appreciated Callum as much as I did. And as for what you told me, I'll mull it over, talk about it with Mitch here, and maybe we can fit it with other puzzle pieces we hope to discover. Again, thanks. Have a great Saturday. Such a gorgeous morning."

Her faint perfume caressed the air as she walked them to the door. She offered a parting thought. "Talk to his next-door neighbor. If anyone saw or heard anything, it would be Tom. The walls here are thin as paper. Jen in eight works Saturdays, Ben in eleven will be nursing a hangover and probably not be any help. I don't know the others, really."

After she shut her door, Mitch asked, "Ya think we can use anything she told us?"

"I dunno. Hit me like a sledge to hear he'd gone to a club. Definitely not Callum's thing."

"But if he was tryin' to get through to some twink, it makes sense."

"Yeah. Callum would walk on coals to save someone on the other side of them. Let's see if Callum's next-door neighbor is in, huh?"

They bypassed the other doors and knocked on fourteen. A good-looking but almost Dracula-pale, slender guy opened it, a zip-up hoodie hanging open, showing his six-pack abs. A welcome smile suddenly shone bright as day, radiating from his light-brown eyes.

"Sarah told us you might be able to tell us about Callum."

"I recognized ya the minute I opened the door. Yer Brent, aren't ya?" the guy said. "I know ya from the thousand or so photos Callum had all over his place. Never stopped talking about ya. Total mo…tor…mouth. When it came to his Brent, that is." Mitch smiled at how the guy said the word, punching each syllable. Said a lot about Callum. And how he felt about Brent.

"That's my Callum," Brent said.

"Really, really sorry, bruh."

"Thanks. Did you see Callum the night he was murdered?" It seemed he gained strength and resolve from both Sarah's and this guy's attitudes about his partner.

"Yeah."

Brent turned to Mitch with a look that spoke a million words of hope.

The guy continued. "It wuz after the bars closed. I hooked up and had just got home with Sam? No. Pete? DaVon? Hell. Don't 'member. But I do 'member seein' Callum comin' outta his place as we wuz goin' into mine. He wuz pulling on a hoodie—it turned cool that night. A guy wid him."

"Can you describe the guy?"

"Nah, man. He had his own hoodie pulled up tight 'round his head, it wuz a dark night, and see that light?" He pointed to a light between his and Callum's apartments. "Been burnt out since September. I tol' the super a zillion times—"

"Did the guy with him say anything? Did you notice anything strange? Did Callum look like he was doing something against his will?"

"Callum never did nothin' 'gainst his will. You know that. I just figgered he'd picked up some guy in a bar, and unlike me, who wuz plannin' a little night of delight, he wuz takin' him somewheres to counsel 'im. Man, Callum wuz fearless. He told me once he liked quiet, deserted places to talk to these guys. Places like the hiking trail up at that park. The Arboretum, they call it? Also, the benches in Halloran Park. He said he could get into a person's soul bein' close to God in a place like that. Anybody else said that, and I woulda laughed m' ass off. But Callum wuz different, you know?"

Brent said nothing, so Mitch stepped in. "So did he just leave with this guy?"

"I guess. After I said, 'hi,' I pushed my trick inside and had me some."

Brent still was silent.

"Thanks," Mitch said, and he pulled Brent away as the guy shut his door. "You wanna talk to anyone else?"

"No. I've had enough. For now. Gay bars. Deserted parks. Fellows. I'm on overload. Let's head out."

Poor guy. Sounds like he's found out far more than he bargained for. And none of it seems to lead to anything concrete.

"Ya up for some chow? I'm starvin'."

Brent looked at Mitch and said, "I'm not hungry, but I'll go with you. I don't wanna be alone just yet."

Brent drove them to Chili's. He had a Coke while Mitch consumed a rack of ribs. "Sure you don't want anything?"

"I'm sure." Brent was mostly silent as Mitch ate.

Once they were back at Brent's place, Mitch promised to call him the next day.

Mitch didn't like the way Brent was acting. He worried that the blow Brent had been dealt earlier, all that stuff he didn't know about coming out, might do something to him.

"Ya need me to stay with ya, guy?"

"Nah. You can go."

"I'm concerned. Ya sure ya couldn't use a friend right now?"

"Mitch, thanks for offerin', but I really, really need alone time. I wanna process what Sarah and Tom said about Callum and try to make sense of it all." He looked into Mitch's eyes. "I see that look. Stop your worryin'. Yes, I learned a lot about Callum I didn't know, but no, I'm not thinkin' of offin' myself over it. Callum was caring, almost recklessly brave, and more secretive than I ever dreamed, but he loved me, and I know that whatever he kept from me, he had his reasons. So, I'm fine. I just want time to think. And I do that best when I'm alone. I'll give you a call if anything develops. In the meantime, come Monday, I'm gonna talk to his Campus Pride friends. Maybe they can shed light that will connect what we found out today."

"You need me to go with?"

Brent shook his head. "I can go it alone. I know or have at least met most of them—I went to most of the meetings they've had so far—and I doubt I can get myself into any trouble in daylight, on campus."

"Okay, man. But remember I'm here for you."

Kevin

Ah! God's golden heavenly rays of sunlight, Kevin thought as he woke on this Saturday morning he'd planned for so carefully. His first thought this fine day was what he imagined his target for the day would say. He stretched, yawned, and sat in bed, the covers bunched around his naked body. He laughed at the way his mind immediately described the same sun that woke him every day. Today, that description was infinitely appropriate times two.

Thinking about the night before, he reached over to the bed stand and retrieved the magical glasses. He'd never planned to wear them on his date. They were for his other scheme, this morning's outing. But oh, how glad he was he'd forgotten he had them on. Who knew a haircut and glasses could be such a turn-on? Mitch was an animal last night. And Kevin loved it.

He put the glasses on, and then he reached down, under the covers. *My hand in Mitch's at the movies.* He rubbed gently, getting harder. *The kiss in the car.* Kevin gripped himself, ran his fist up and down faster. *The way he undressed me. His teeth on my jocks.* He pulled harder, faster. *That beautiful body he unveiled with his seductive dance.* He tensed, waiting for it. *His tongue, his mouth.* He shot, over and over, convulsing. *Oh, god, oh god, oh god.*

Spent, he lay there, enraptured by the memories and the moment. A fleeting thought crossed his mind. What would Mitch think of me if he learned of what I'm about to do? But he dismissed it. Mitch will never know. Why would he? Besides, this is too important. I've planned for it for too long to turn back now. Step, the pretender, the lover of all things gay, the man who claims he loves me. How will he feel when he sees this and what he's now associated with? After a while, he grabbed the top sheet, wiped his crotch, and then pulled the wet part away, leaving a dry spot covering himself. He'd deal with the sheet later. The maid wouldn't be in until Monday, anyway.

Feeling almost as good as he'd felt with the real thing the night before, he reached over, pulled the drawer open from the bed stand, took out the Altoids tin he kept his stash in, opened it, and took out a big fatty. He reached for his lighter, put the joint in his mouth, and lit it. He took a long drag off it and held the smoke in his lungs.

"Kevin, what's that smell?" Mark. Outside his door. *Why isn't the little turd at the Scout Jamboree?*

"Nothing," Kevin called. "I'm just burning some incense. Aren't you going to your scout thingy?"

"Yeah. Can I come in? I don't like talking through the door."

Kevin thrust his ashtray, the lit joint in it, into his drawer and closed it as his room door opened.

The kid, in all his Boy Scout glory, merit badges galore on his sash, bounded into Kevin's room.

"Are you wearing Dad's glasses?"

"No. They're mine." He'd once again forgotten he had them on. But if Mitch liked him in them, he was going to be wearing them all the time, so he might as well establish his reason. "Went to the eye doctor yesterday. He said I need 'em."

"Well, they look just like Dad's. But you look better in 'em."

"Thanks, kid. Now, aren't you supposed to be at the jamboree?"

"I'm waiting for Mr. Blane. He's our troop leader. He's pickin' us all up in his van."

"Well, shouldn't you be waitin' outside for 'im?"

"You got your hair cut, too. I knew there was something else different about you."

Kevin was cool with trying to be nicer to the kid, but at this moment, he wanted him out of his room. "Mr. Blane may not wanna wait for you, you know."

"Oh, he said he'd honk—" A loud toot-toot sounded outside the house, cutting the kid off. "Gotta go." He ran towards the hallway. In the doorway, he turned around. "Wanna play catch in the park tomorrow?"

The last thing Kevin wanted to do was play catch, with his brother or anyone else, but remembering his vow to be nicer, he said, "Sure."

"Awesome," Mark said as he scurried away, leaving the door wide open.

With his brother safely gone, Kevin opened the drawer and tamped out the joint. He got out of bed. He listened for other intruders. Who, he didn't know, for the maid had the weekend off, his mother was never home, and if Step were home, he'd probably already have been in his room, trying to plan his day for him. No matter. He closed his door, then slipped on underwear, shorts, and a t-shirt.

Then he headed down to the kitchen for coffee. As suspected, the house was deserted. He loaded a pod into the Keurig, put a mug under the spout, and waited. He switched on Saturday Weekend to catch the headlines.

As he eyed the coffee dripping into his cup, he heard that familiar voice. Marlon Gordon.

"No new developments in the gay-bashing murders. District Attorney Miriam Welch's office spokesperson did confirm that they have decided that these are indeed the work of one person, and thus the word serial is now attached. They are still not being deemed hate crimes. The alt-right constituency applaud this, we hear, for they feel that LGBTQ+ citizens should not be a protected class. The serial killer designation, however, was a long time coming, but with this term now being used, we say the perpetrator, if caught and convicted, should be worried. Indiana has not often carried out the sentences of those on death row. But the threat of lethal injection looms over the head of this serial killer. Strangely silent on the whole issue is Dr. Spencer Fellows. We reached out for a comment, but his office declined. Strange indeed from a man who has been so vocal. Marlon Gordon, Force Four News."

Kevin tapped the remote, and the TV went black. He grabbed his now-brewed coffee and took it upstairs.

So no comment, huh? What's up with that? Well, I'd bet I find out.

As he sipped the hot coffee, Kevin laid out his purchases. The suit. The shirt. The tie. The belt. The socks. The shoes. Admiring them all.

You did good, Kev. Perfect. Very believable. And all on Step's dime. What a trip.

After once again stripping, he went into the bathroom. Stared into the mirror. *Looking good, Mister.* Methodically, he wet his face, applied shaving cream, and carefully scraped the overnight growth off his face. Then he took the Sonicare from its cradle, applied a swipe of Colgate, and brushed his teeth. He reached into the shower to turn on the water.

Taking off his glasses and laying them on the counter, he slowly edged into the shower, fearing the water would still be cold but finding it deliciously invigorating, the steamy rain from the showerhead penetrating and reviving his muscles.

Clean and ready for merriment, he opened the shower door, pulled the towel off the rack, and dried himself. He stepped in front of the mirror, gazed at his tousled, wet hair, grabbed his hair dryer, already plugged in, switched it on and went to work. It took no time at all to dry the new shorter look. He opened the hair paste and dug a glob out with his index finger. Replacing the container on the counter, he rubbed the paste between his hands and massaged it into his hair. Finishing up after running a comb through it, he looked just like a successful businessman. Replacing his glasses on his face completed the look.

He pulled on a pair of jocks retrieved from his dresser, then donned the shirt and the suit pants. They fit perfectly, he thought, as he buttoned and zipped. Then he took the belt, threaded it through the loops, and buckled it. Sitting down, he put on one sock, then the other. Tossing the shoes onto the floor, he slipped his feet into them. Then he rose and went to the bathroom mirror again, carrying the tie. Carefully, he knotted it, a perfect knot that looked like it had been done by someone who cared about every aspect of his image. Finally, he jacketed himself. He looked in his full-length mirror and admired his handiwork. From the hair to the glasses to the suit, shirt, tie, belt, socks, and shoes, he looked like a corporate wonder—a young exec who probably had amassed a fortune in his few short years in the business world. Not wanting to wrinkle the jacket, he carefully removed it and placed it back on its hanger. Swinging the hanger over his shoulder, he headed out to the Spyder.

The place was about twenty minutes away. A midrise tucked away, surprisingly, near a cluster of some of the most popular gay bars in the city. He chuckled to himself, remembering Michael Corleone in

Godfather II. "Keep your friends close, your enemies closer," he'd said, or something like that.

As he drove, Kevin let himself think of Mitch. This plan had nothing to do with him. Even so, he felt a twinge of guilt as Mitch's beautiful face floated into his consciousness. He would disapprove, but this was something Kevin had to do.

Arriving at his destination, as the sexy male voice of his GPS informed him, Kevin parked. Out of the car, he took the suitcoat he'd placed on the driver's side seat, removed it from the hangar, and put it on. He took his hands and smoothed it out, looking for anything out of place. Then he entered the building with Family Now painted on its door.

He'd done his research. He knew that every Saturday morning at ten Spencer Fellows held an open prayer meeting. Anyone in the community could attend.

"Welcome, welcome," a brightly smiling young woman at the reception desk greeted him. "Are you here for the meeting, sir?"

Kevin nodded and said, "Yes, I am. Would you be so kind as to show me the way?"

She flashed that smile again and pointed. "Right down this hall. You can't miss it. Straight ahead. Double doors of the auditorium are open."

"Thank you so much," Kevin said.

He walked in the direction she'd pointed, and he saw what she'd described. He walked through the doors and an usher accosted him. "Welcome, welcome. Don't believe we've seen you before, sir. Glad you've joined us. You're going to find Dr. Fellows very inspiring, I can guarantee." He handed him a pamphlet. "Sit anywhere you like."

Kevin surveyed the room and found it was filled with a variety of types, most of them, though, middle-aged white men. He saw a seat towards the back, a bit isolated from the rest, and took it.

As he waited, he perused the pamphlet he'd been given: "Family Now was created to celebrate marriage and children, God's greatest gifts to us. Dr. Spencer Fellows, our founder, is dedicated to the idea that marriage is between one man and one woman. Furthermore, our organization, through its outreach, fights to erase the scourge of homosexuality. But this fight cannot be won without the dedicated volunteers who steer the organization onto God's true course. Family Now has hundreds of volunteers who work tirelessly to spread our message. We have a dedicated TV outreach through our Sunday morning broadcasts, and Dr. Fellows frequently appears on news programs to explain the issues plaguing society. None of this is without cost. We invite you to search your heart and give generously to our cause. Ushers at Family Now gatherings are always happy to accept your donations." This message, Kevin noted, was spread out surrounding several glossy four-color shots of Spencer Fellows at his rallies, his cuddling a baby, his holding a Bible as he preached, and a particularly telling shot of him being interviewed by none other than Marlon Gordon.

Kevin looked at his watch. One minute. He looked around. He saw no cameras, but he knew they had to be there. Spencer Fellows never did anything that wasn't filmed for posterity. And for his own gain. About the only footage he'd never seen was of Fellows' private office. And if all went well today, he would get a firsthand look at that sanctuary.

"Ladies and gentlemen—" Ironic, since there were more gentlemen than ladies present, Kevin thought. *Maybe the announcer should have reversed himself.* "Please welcome Dr. Spencer Fellows."

The audience broke into thundering applause. Kevin was in awe that such a small crowd could make such a big noise.

The tall, lean, weaselly robot man entered from the wings and took the lectern.

With false humility, he waved his hands to quell the adoring ones. "Welcome, welcome." Kevin flashed on the receptionist and the usher having given the same greeting. Must be a cult thing. Something they are required to say, or that they picked up from their leader. "Shall we pray?" Like programmed androids, everyone in the room bowed their heads. "Lord, we thank you for this glorious turnout this morning. These are your warriors. They—each and every one of them—are here to fight for you, to propel your wrath and spread it to wipe out the evils in this imperfect world."

Kevin, head bowed, thought, "Each and every one? That's rather presumptuous. Is he so sure of himself that he knows every person in this room will fight to the death for him?" Then he glanced around. Saw how fervently they all seemed to be praying. "Maybe he is."

"May we all be your weapons, Lord. Weapons that will wipe homosexuality off the face of your beautiful, perfect earth. Amen."

Like automatons, the crowd echoed, "Amen."

As Kevin listened to Fellows preach—and that's what he was doing, despite the fact that he had no church, had no pulpit of his own, other than this lectern from which he bobbed and parried—Kevin marveled at how compelling the guy truly was. He was full of crap, but it was eloquently stated shit. It was no wonder that he had his minions, ready to do his bidding. The man was a doctor, after all—a doctor of psychology. Fellows had studied them, his sheep. He knew them. He used his training to wrap them all around his little finger. Maybe he did hate gay men, maybe he didn't. Maybe this was just a way to get money. Looking at him there, in a suit probably even more expensive than the one Kevin himself sported, it was clear that Fellows liked the perks of his chosen profession—the cult leadership, not the psychology practice, which he had abandoned long ago. Yes, this was a man who lived for attention. Craved the adoration. Adored fame and all its trappings. It was no surprise that he was always front and center when Marlon Gordon came calling for a comment. So why didn't he rear his head on Marlon's update this morning?

"And make no mistake," Fellows thundered on. "There is a warrior among us who will attain the Lord's greatest affirmation, sit at his side in Glory. But it is a sinful misnomer to call this soldier a serial killer and his righteous deeds hate crimes. He wields the mighty sword of God, and he does his acts in His name, smiting those who themselves are committing hate crimes against our children with their evil, filthy ways. We hope that he, one of God's angels, continues to right the wrongs of this world until authorities take notice and wipe out these so-called rights they have granted because of the homosexual agenda. Can I get an amen?"

Again, the crowd roared.

"Our ushers will now pass the offering plate. Please look into your hearts and give generously to support our cause," Fellows said, as if he were the gentle, loving servant of a gentle, loving God, not the angry God he'd just described in his message.

Piped-in organ music played as ushers passed the plates. As Kevin took the plate and passed it on to the person nearest him without putting any money in it, he felt a hot, disapproving "hmmph" from the usher hovering over him.

With the offering completed, Fellows spoke once again. "Thank you, thank you." Kevin rolled his eyes. *He sure likes to repeat himself, now, doesn't he?* "Each and every penny," Fellows said, "will be put to the Lord's use." *I'll bet. How much did that suit set the Lord back?*

"Remember now, be ever vigilant warriors for Christ. Go with God." He gestured—an almost *Heil, Hitler* salute—and left the stage. Folks rose and started leaving.

Kevin stopped to speak with the usher who'd greeted him when he arrived.

"I wonder if I might meet with Dr. Fellows?"

"Oh, no, sir. Dr. Fellows is always exhausted after his messages. He retreats to his office and secludes himself in prayer."

"Oh, I see. Well, you know," Kevin said ingratiatingly. "I wanted to make a contribution. You accept cards, don't you?"

"Surely, surely." *The repetition again.* "Just stop at the reception desk on your way out. Our receptionist will be happy to process your donation for you."

"Well, you see, I was thinking of a quite generous amount, and I wonder if I might give it to Dr. Fellows personally. It would mean so much to me." Kevin knew he had him at 'quite generous amount.' He saw the dollar signs in the guy's eyes.

"Perhaps I could arrange a meeting, sir. Wait right here. I'll return shortly."

Two minutes later, the guy ushered him into the inner sanctum.

"Welcome, welcome," Fellows said, walking over to him.

Kevin was certain he caught a whiff of whiskey on the good doctor's breath. *I guess a sermon like that takes it out of you. Need a little after-condemnation fortification.* Kevin held out his hand for Fellows to shake. "Sloan Howell, Dr. Fellows. Good to meet you."

Kevin's eyes were drawn to the man's lapel pin. A crown of thorns, below which was a W and a C superimposed upon it. Warriors of Christ. Kevin got it.

Like his sermon, his greeting was as fake as they come. An act. "And it's good to make your acquaintance, Sloan. I understand you want to give to our cause." *Cut to the chase, Doctor.* "Please, please. Have a seat." And he gestured toward one of two leather chairs that fronted his enormous desk. *Those chairs alone must have cost the Lord a pretty penny.*

As Fellows eased himself into his desk chair, he steepled his hands, as if in prayer, and leaned toward Kevin. "Now, Sloan, just how much do you feel you can offer our little group?" His smile alone lit the room, lamplight not needed. *Obviously, some very expensive teeth whitening there, Doc.*

"Well," Kevin began his prepared story, "I've been very lucky to have been quite successful in my profession. I joined my firm two years ago, and in that time I've attained a senior partnership, largely on my ability to bring in wealthy clients. I'm appreciated by my superiors, and as a result, I enjoy a salary that is, shall we say, much more commensurate than most my age are paid." Kevin gave him the humble smile he'd rehearsed in front of the mirror.

"Good for you, good for you."

"My younger brother, doctor, has not been so lucky. He struggled for many years. I'm afraid he wandered down the path that you so strongly warn against."

"I see, I see." *Yes, and I see that you have some highly practiced skills gleaned from your psychology training. You don't see shit, but you could convince the trained monkeys who follow you of anything.*

"My brother—whom I love dearly—love the sinner, not the sin, you know—" Fellows nodded, obviously chomping at the bit for Kevin to get to the bottom line. "My brother has turned his life around, thanks to you, Dr. Fellows. He has a girlfriend, they are planning their wedding, and he has renounced his old ways entirely. You were a godsend, doctor."

"Wonderful, wonderful," the supercilious buffoon exclaimed.

All you want to know is how much, am I right?

Kevin pulled the platinum card out of the pocket inside his suit coat. "I want to thank you for all you did for my brother. You never met him, but he listened to you, God's Messenger, and your words transformed him. He is a changed man. I want to aid you in continuing your wonderful ministry."

"Well, Sloan, we don't call it a ministry. I'm not ordained. I don't have a church. I'm just a humble man who helps to spread the Word."

What a crock.

Kevin handed over Step's platinum card. "I'd like to contribute five thousand dollars to your cause, Dr. Fellows. I can assure you I have an unlimited line of credit, and perhaps there will be more along the way, but for now, will you accept my little gift?"

Fellows grabbed the card like he was an addict craving smack.

"But, Dr. Fellows, I must ask that you keep this anonymous. My firm stays out of the limelight when it comes to charitable causes. One of my favorite verses is found in Matthew 6: 'But when you give to the needy, do not let your left hand know what your right hand is doing, so that your giving may be in secret. And your Father, who sees what is done in secret, will reward you.'" *Love that steel-trap mind of mine.*

"Of course, of course. Give me a moment." The clown left the room, was gone about five minutes, and then returned. "I have the receipt, Sloan. I assume you'll want that for your taxes. I assure you, I had the receptionist step away while I ran the transaction personally. Our accountant maintains the utmost discretion, so your secret is safe with us."

Sitting back down, he slid the receipt across his desk. Kevin took a pen that lay on Fellows' desk mat and signed the slip, perfectly, as Sloan Howell. He wanted to add Esquire after the name, but he didn't even know why people did that, so he restrained himself.

"And here's your copy, Sloan." Kevin took the slip of paper from Fellows and stood.

"So good meeting you, Dr. Fellows," he said, offering his hand again.

"And good to meet you, Sloan, good to meet you." *I know it was, you pig. And don't think I don't have your number. You know using my name over and over is Salesman 101. What you don't know is that Sloan isn't my name, now is it?*

"Wait, Sloan." Fellows opened a drawer of his desk. "A little token of our appreciation. It doesn't equal your generosity, but we like to give these to all our followers." He walked around the desk to face Kevin. He leaned in a bit and placed a lapel pin, identical to the one the pompous ass wore, in Kevin's lapel. *So you think you can push a hole into a five-*

thousand-buck Zegna without asking? You really think you're something, don't you? Kevin smiled graciously—as graciously as he could muster.

As he was escorted to the door, Fellows told Kevin, "Now don't be a stranger now, you hear?"

A bit too folksy, but he wants to appear sincere. As anyone who'd just pocketed 5K would. And, too, he craves the promise of more. *Wanna bleed me dry, huh, Doc?*

Sliding into the driver's seat of the Spyder, Kevin chuckled at the shitstorm he may have just created. He could picture Step seeing where his money had gone and trying to get that money back without implicating his stepson in a crime. No way would he turn Kevin in. That would not reflect well on his reputation as such a good father.

Yeah, right.

Mitch

At Brent's complex, walking to his car, Mitch thought the morning had been fairly productive. At least, he hoped so. What Sarah and Tom had told them might lead to nothing, but then again, every little thing they learned could add up to something big.

He worried about leaving Brent, but Brent was strong. Mitch understood Brent when he said he just needed time alone to process it all.

I hope whatever he hears from Campus Pride is helpful. Or at least doesn't throw him into a tailspin.

Starting his car, thoughts of Kevin flooded his mind. *I have to talk to him.* He grabbed his phone and texted: "Where u at?"

"The Cup."

"Join u?"

"Sure. Just Les and me."

"See you in a few."

On the way to the Cup, two things came to him. I'm glad Kevin has such a good friend like Les. I hope Les leaves before I get there so I can talk to Kevin in private.

Les and Kevin sat, appearing firmly entrenched, outside on the patio. *So much for Les vacating. Oh, well.*

Mitch threw up his hands, then pointed to the door. After getting a tall coffee, he joined them, all the time wishing Les would suddenly need to depart.

"Whatcha been doin', dude? My boy Kevin here's been cravin' you."

Mitch ignored him. What he wanted to do was tell Les to leave. Instead, he concentrated on Kevin.

Mitch looked at his *maybe* boyfriend, still beautiful in his new haircut, as Kevin shook his head slightly and rolled his gorgeous eyes behind his glasses.

"He told me he got glasses the better to see you with, Mitch, bro." Les was laying it on thick.

"Maybe he needed to see you clearer, playboy. You may not be what ya seem. Isn't there a hot cheerleader you need to nail somewhere?"

Les took that as a joke, laughing. But Mitch was hoping he'd get the vibe he wasn't wanted.

"Whoa. Got me." Les howled. "What's on tap for you two?"

Mitch wondered if Kevin had told his friend about their night.

Time to be more direct.

"Don't know. Guess we'll discuss the possibilities after you leave."

"Dude!" Les said. "That was a low blow. I could take the hint, but I don't think so." He crossed his arms, like he was planting himself for a long growing season.

Just then, Les's phone pinged. He looked at it. "M' girl. Summoning me. Guess I *will* be leaving you two lovers after all." He got up to take his leave. Mitch scanned his face, hoping to figure out if he'd said lovers because Kevin had spilled the beans or because Les was just a blowhard.

An almost-likable blowhard, but a blowhard nevertheless.

As his eyes followed Les to his car, Mitch said, "Regular comedian, that guy."

"Keeps me in stitches," Kevin said. Then he put his hand on Mitch's arm. "Missed ya, babe. Where ya been?"

"Had somethin' to take care of." He didn't want to fill Kevin in on his thing with Brent just yet. He was still hoping they could have the kind of thing that Callum and Brent had, and he didn't want to worry Kevin, telling him how he was pursuing a serial killer and all.

"You messin' 'round on me already?" Kevin smiled. A mixture of that goofy smile and love and concern, all wrapped in this new package—the years the new hair had added, the more mature clothes he was sporting, and the eyes shining through the lenses in the perfect mottled brown that framed them.

Mitch melted.

Mitch knew he could make this work. Be cautious. Take it nice and slow. You can build this thing without hurting Kevin's feelings. Kev may want to rush things, but that's not the way real love works. What was it Brent said about him and Callum? Lots of kisses, lots of hugs, some mutual hand play.

He could do that.

He just needed the courage to lay out his plan in the most gentle way he could. Maybe small talk would bolster him. "What ya been doin' all day?"

An undefined look came across Kevin's face. It was quick, but it was there. Then a big smile replaced it.

"Nothin', babe. Absolutely nothin'. Let's see...woke up with a raging hard-on. Took care of that. Mark came in before he left for his scout jamboree. Told him I'd take him to the park tomorrow to play some catch."

Mitch smiled hearing that. Yesterday, Kev's brother had been the little monster, and today he was not only *Mark*, but Kevin had made a play date with him. Progress.

"My bro left. I shaved, showered, and primped. Then I met Les for lunch. After chowin' down, we came over here for some after dinner drinks, so t' speak."

"Great."

"So what was this something you had to do this mornin', babe?"

Maybe it would go a long way to grease the wheels of this very difficult speech he needed to make if he told him about Brent. Not everything, but some.

"You remember Brent? The murdered guy's partner?"

"Yeah. Don't tell me you're hangin' with him too? I thought we had a good thing going."

Oh, great. I was hoping to make things better, and it looks like I tapped into some unexpected jealousy.

"No, no, no...nothing like that. He's hurting, you know. He just needs a friend." He didn't add *a friend who will investigate the crime with him.* The last thing he wanted to do was worry Kevin. "I thought if we hung out together, it might take his mind off what happened. So we had coffee this morning."

"Oh, okay." Kevin's response was so noncommittal it threw Mitch into a tailspin. *How to proceed?* He answered his question almost before he'd asked it. *Jump right in. Take the plunge. Dive right into the deep end.* But first, clarification.

"Know this: Brent and I are only friends." Mitch smiled at Kevin. He pulled Kevin to him. Touched his forehead with his own. "I think I'm in love with you." *Was that too bold? It could mean so much. Kevin might take it the wrong way.* Out of fear, he ratcheted himself down a bit. Lightened up. "Yes, indeed, I could be head over heels if we give it time." He paused for that to sink in. "For your sake, Kev, I wanna give it time. Time to grow, time to nurture." He squeezed Kevin's hand. "You're a wonderful guy. God knows, you're hot as hell, and you turn me on big time." Kevin grinned at that. "Can we turn down the burner just a little? Let this simmer 'til it's ready?" Before Kevin could answer, Mitch kissed him. And again. And again. He didn't care if people were looking. He didn't care if the gay-bashing serial killer was sitting right next to him, getting his fill of this, his blatant public display of affection, as his high school principal would call it. He simply wanted Kevin to understand he was committed to making this something good, something that could last forever. He kissed him again. And again. And a final time.

When he pulled away, it appeared that Kevin would do anything he asked, even if it meant staying out of bed. For now.

Why didn't I tell him 'bout all the others? How I'd treated them like shit? I guess I didn't want to scare him away. Maybe I don't want him to know the real me. Am I still that guy, though?

Oh, well, true confessions can be for another time, another place. For now, Kevin and I are back on track.

Brent

With a boring Intro to Econ winding down, Brent was antsy to get out of there and to the Campus Pride meeting. He'd skipped it the last two weeks, his wound far too exposed to see Callum's friends. But today, he was a man on a quest. He could do this.

Leaving Meachum Hall, he set his mental GPS to arrive at Room 479, Union Building, in ten minutes. Lately, he'd let his mind wander far too much. He had to stay focused. A trick of telling himself he had a self-programmed GPS in his brain was his way of coping. Coping. A word he never thought he'd apply to himself.

His life, those nineteen years that had gone before, was almost perfect. He was loved—yeah, almost worshipped—by his parents. His early school years were pretty much a blur. But that first day of kindergarten, that day he was terrified, was crystal clear. The day he expected to drop dead from dread, wandering into a big school building among hundreds of kids, leaving his tiny world at home where he was the center of it all. The day he made friends instantly, with not just one kid, but at least half his class. The day he knew he'd be okay. After that, he did well in school. Made good grades without trying too much. Joined about half the clubs on his high school campus and managed to juggle 'em quite nicely. Served on committees and never neglected the needs of one over another. Heads above everything was drama club. His beloved Amards. People would look at him like he was crazy when he said that name. He never tired of explaining it was drama spelled backward, a weird joke of the founding members. He loved that club like it was his personal savior. And turns out, it was. He wasn't one of those *hey, the spotlight's not centered on me here* types. He loved quietly working backstage, doing his part to make the magic happen.

But long before high school was when he knew. It was probably sixth grade when he began to feel he was different from most of the others. He looked at the other boys different than they looked at each other. He had no idea what that was all about, but he knew no other boy in his class acted like he wanted to hold hands with the baseball pitcher. Or looked adoringly at the leader of his history project group. Or rushed to sit next to the best-looking guy in class, and then spent lunch barely eating because he was staring at Billy, wishing he could go home with him. It was tough to figure all that out and still not know why it was happening.

Middle school. His first crush. Well, other than the totally unrequited secret love he felt for Billy. No, this was different. His math teacher was the seventh-grade football coach. Looking back, Brent should have seen the coach was using him. That coach asked Brent to be a team manager, but not one of those guys who handled equipment and stayed on the field during practice to do the players' bidding. No, Coach wanted Brent to do his paperwork for him. Pure and simple. A secretary, but with the manly title of *team manager*.

Brent didn't see Coach's motives. And wouldn't have minded if he had. His new position and new title made him feel like one of the guys. He'd proudly display the school letter he would be awarded for sports participation, even if, because he was in seventh grade, not eighth, it would be just a piece of paper and not a real cloth letter. And, it turns out, it would be a piece of paper that he, himself, had to fill in in his capacity as team manager extraordinaire. Brent smiled at what a dolt he'd been. Coach played him just as much as he played the star running back on his team.

And oh, that star running back—Tim Robinson. In all his seventh-grade-awkward boy glory, Brent thought he was the most gorgeous thing that ever held a football. Brent knew now Tim was nothing special then, but he saw Tom Brady's aquiline face, Victor Cruz's disarming smile, Matt Leinart's sexy flyaway hair, and Alex Smith's hard body, all rolled into one gorgeous—at least to Brent—amazing football player.

Brent laughed as he walked. How did I even know all those pro ballers? I wasn't even into football. But I was into Tim Robinson. And it didn't take me long to figure it all out.

Brent's longing for Tim didn't pan out. It's rare when a teenage crush does. Especially one in seventh grade. With a gay boy. On an unsuspecting, soon-to-be-aging heterosexual.

Brent bided his time. Sooner or later *the one* would present himself to him. He knew it. Someone, somewhere, someday would suddenly appear, and Brent'd know. Sure as he knew he hated broccoli, he'd know when his guy, *the one*, came along.

Callum. Callum came along. Brent had to work at it. Nothing ever comes easy. Your prince appears, then he disappears. But once they finally met, it was something Brent knew'd never be torn asunder, as they say in the marriage vows. 'Till death do us part.

He never got to speak those words, and thinking them made his heart ache. Death did, indeed, part them. Brent shook his head, shaking the tear forming in his right eye back before it fell. He'd arrived at his destination, his inner GPS informed him.

He went up the steps of the Union Building and rode the elevator to the fourth floor. He said a little prayer. Help me, Lord, to face these folks. Give me the strength to endure their condolences, to push toward answers to questions I don't want to ask, never thought I'd have to ask. Fortified by his prayer, he opened the door to Room 479.

About twenty people were gathered. Brent knew them as cis gay men, cis Lesbians, bi's, transpeople in various stages of transitioning, and a couple of heteros supportive of the cause. Most of all, he knew them as his and Callum's friends.

Standing in the doorway, he saw Melinda look up and rush over to him.

"Brent, you came," she said. After she'd spoken at Callum's memorial and again at the funeral, she told him they were all hoping to see him back at Campus Pride as soon as he felt able. She hugged him.

"Thanks, Mel," Brent said. "It's been hard, but I'm here now, and I'm ready to continue Callum's work. Has a new president been chosen yet?"

"Zina's taking over. She's been in the group since she was a frosh, and the board thought of all of us, she'd be the closest to Callum's philosophy. Her journey's a long, difficult one, and Callum supported her, she's told me, the last few months as she had her final surgery to transition from Harry to Hazina officially."

"Hazina? Where'd that come from?" Brent must have never heard her called anything but Zina.

"Means treasure in Swahili. Her mother, God love her, suggested it. So supportive."

Brent knew Zina was trans, but he knew little of her story. Hearing Melinda relate just this little bit made him feel a pain in his chest. Not a physical pain but an emotional ache. Callum really didn't share much with him, it seemed. Brent loved that Callum kept his work to himself, but these were their friends. You'd think Callum would have shared something as big as Zina's surgery.

But then Brent had a different thought. Quit beating up on Callum. You're Zina's friend, too. You coulda taken a bigger interest in her journey. You knew she was almost transitioned. You coulda inquired. But you didn't care as much as Callum did. That was why he was president, and you're just a member.

A few of the others noticed Brent standing with Melinda, and they, too, rushed over. "Brent, great to see ya," "Brent, my heart's broken for you," "Brent, good to see ya among the living,"—the guy who said the latter got a stricken look on his face and immediately waved across the room like he'd just seen his best friend, and then he retreated—and "Brent, if there's anything you need." They all meant well, even the poor guy who'd stuck his foot in his mouth. Brent asked himself, though, "Would they be so concerned with me and my loss if that loss hadn't been Callum? Would they even have made the connection between me and the victim of a serial killer?"

Zina went to the lectern. She was a beautiful girl. Eyes that lit the room. Flawless skin so black it gleamed in the light. Curly black hair that fell to her shoulders in abandon. She was dressed in African colors, red, green, yellow, black. "Okay, everybody, listen up," she said. "First of all, if you haven't already, welcome Brent back to the group. I know we all share his pain, and Brent, we're glad you're back." She gave him a genuinely sincere smile. Then she turned to the group once again. ""Now, people, I'm concerned, as I know you all are, about all this anti-trans crap coming out of the state legislature. We hoped we were safe, but this stuff is just kickin' up the dust again. It's scary."

Her declaration was greeted with shouts of "We're not gonna take it," and "Right on, Z," and a "I hadn't heard about that."

Zina continued. "So, we need you to get people talking. Stir up some noise, people. Get your friends, your relatives, people on the street to call their state rep's offices. Voice their displeasure. Let them know we're goin' to trash their hopes of being re-elected if they don't do something."

"My uncle's a state senator. He backs us all the way. I'll get on the phone to him as soon as we adjourn." Brent heard the voice of Lena Kapoor behind him. He'd admired her since the first day they'd met. Lena didn't take shit from anybody. And being an out and proud lesbian in her culture was not an easy path to walk.

Brent wondered if he'd had the courage to be as out as he was if he hadn't been a white gay man. It's tough being out, but being white makes a difference. Then he had a fleeting thought. *In this world, being a white man makes a difference in anything, whether it's bein' gay, gettin' a job, findin' housing, or a million other tasks.*

After that revelation he should have had long ago, he realized something else. His being out and proud was made easier because he knew—and loved—Callum. Callum gave everyone courage.

As Zina conducted the rest of the meeting, Brent lost himself in his thoughts, thinking of Callum.

He heard, "So let's fight the good fight, folks. Ready for some partyin'? Don baked some of his famous Cowboy Cookies, Tiny's got the punchbowl filled, and I got a great buy on mixed nuts at CVS. So get your party on, people."

The meeting officially broke up, and a few rushed to the refreshment table. Devon yelled out, "Get outta my way. I need me a Cowboy Cookie fix!"

Zina walked up to Brent, laughing. "Some people think we're different, but when it comes to cookies, we're no different from the rest of the free world. How ya doin', Brent?"

"I'm okay. Great job ya did up there today, Gil."

"Got big shoes to fill, but I'm trying. Callum left me a full agenda." Brent saw a look of regret on her.

"It's okay, you c'n say his name. And yes, I know he always had a mile long list of wrongs to right, so you've bitten off a big chunk to chew."

"Callum was a great guy. But you know that. He certainly helped me in the short time I knew him. I could be so down that I didn't want to talk to anybody, and Callum always pried open my clamshell. You never knew what he was doing, but in his gentle way, he dug, probed, and prodded until he got you to see things his way. I haven't shared this with most of the other members, but Callum was the reason I had my final surgery. He took me aside one day and asked, point blank, 'what's stopping you?' Deep down, I think I was holding back because I knew if I took that final step, I'd be giving up the me I'd been born with, the me my family still clung to the hope that I'd stay. It's hard enough to be gay in the Black community. Throw in trans, and it can be a shitstorm. I told him that, and you know what Callum said? He said, 'Z, you can cut off your dick but you'll still be the person you've always been.'" She laughed. "Callum was blunt. That he was. But he made sense. I could keep my penis and be unhappy or I could lose it and become me, the me that I had to be, not the me that my third cousin once removed thought I should be. Oh, I know there's a lot of us out there perfectly happy without having the surgery. And maybe it was the indecision that was killing me, not the actual act. But Callum certainly pushed me in the direction I know I was headed. Callum changed my life, Brent. Just like I know he changed yours in so many ways. He loved you. No, he was obsessed with you. Whatever point he made, it was punctuated with a *Brent and I* story."

Brent gazed at her, dumbstruck and awestruck. He'd begun to doubt Callum. He'd begun to think all the secrets Callum kept from him were because he didn't trust him. He'd begun to think Callum was pulling away from him because Callum wouldn't spend 24/7 with him. Zina, with her story and her statement, reinforced what Brent had known since the day he laid eyes on Callum Slater. They were soulmates, and nothing could or would ever change that.

"Z, you're a lifesaver. I needed to hear that. Callum didn't always tell me how much I meant to him. I never doubted it, but the words are good to hear sometimes, ya know? Callum could be a very private person. Especially about his work. It's funny to think about what he did as 'work.'

Counseling is something that people do after gettin' degrees, after settin' up shop, after advertisin' their services. But Callum was counselin' folks long before I met him. He once said he talked a friend off a ledge—not a physical one, but an emotional one—when he was nine years old, and he never looked back. He *knew* his purpose in life was to help people."

"Well, he helped me," Zina said.

"Z, speakin' of, do you know who Callum was workin' with during the last weeks of his life?"

"No, Brent, you know as well as I do that Callum didn't talk about his work."

"Is there anything, maybe someone you saw with him, maybe somethin' he let slip out, somethin' that struck ya as unusual? I really need to know so I can process."

The woman looked him in the eyes, and Brent could see her racking her brain as he looked back. It was that evident. She wanted to help him and searched for any little detail.

"Funny," she said eventually. "We were talking, a few days before his—you know—" Brent thought it spoke to her humanity that she still had a hard time saying the word *murder*. "I don't remember what I said, but Callum sighed. I asked him 'why the big sigh?' He said, 'I know a guy who has all the money he could ever need or want, and he's so unhappy. Proves that money doesn't buy happiness.' Then he added, 'Oops! I've said too much.' Then he clammed up, and I knew—well, I didn't *know*, but I got the feeling—he was talking about someone he was counseling. What that has to do with anything, Brent, I can't say. Couldn't even begin to tell you. But if it helps you, then I'm glad I told you." She put her hand on his arm. "You want some punch? Looks like the punchbowl is draining rapidly."

There was enough punch left for two paper cupsful, and a lone cookie remained on the platter. "You take the cookie, Brent. I'm watching my figure." Zina giggled.

That cookie was the best cookie Brent had ever put in his mouth. Why? Because he had one more puzzle piece, and it was time for him to party. It was only a tiny piece of a very complex puzzle, but sooner or later the jigsaw would be complete, and the face of Callum's killer would be staring out at him.

He couldn't wait to tell Mitch this new tidbit. They could brainstorm, tossing around ideas. He had a teacher who once told him that two people couldn't brainstorm, that it took a group to stir up a hurricane of ideas. But Mitch was his ally, and together they'd figure this out.

He headed home, armed with his newfound knowledge. It was just after five when he put his key in the lock. He hadn't eaten all day, except for the one cookie, and he was ravenous. Solving crimes can do that to you.

He opened the freezer door and surveyed his choices. Pizza. Marie Callender's Pot Pie. Half a pint of Chunky Monkey. A Hungry Man Dinner, Mexican-style. Well, he was hungry, he was a man. He took out the dinner and popped it into the microwave.

As it heated, he punched in Mitch's speed dial digit. One ring, two rings, three rings. Four. *Sorry. Leave a message. Get back to you.*

"Damn!" He told Mitch to call him as soon as he picked up the message.

The microwave dinged, and he took the dinner from the oven. He held it by the extreme edges so as not to burn his fingers. He plopped it on the counter and removed the remaining plastic film. He opened the refrigerator, saw a beer. That beer had been in there since almost the first day he'd moved in. Callum was a teetotaler, and he himself didn't drink much. One of his old high school drama buddies had shown up with a six-pack. Said it was a housewarming gift. Before the guy left, he'd drunk five of the six brews. This lone straggler Brent was staring at called out to him. Drink me, drink me. Fulfill my purpose in life. *What the hell. Might taste like piss, but it's supposed to go good with Mexican food.* And he popped the top on the can.

He grabbed a fork from the dish drainer and took the steaming dinner and his beer to the sofa. Balancing the dinner on his stomach, he reached for the remote and brought the TV to life. Five O'clock News. Force Four. *God, please no Marlon Gordon. I can't take it.* The weather guy was on, assuring us that there was plenty of sunshine coming our way. *Well, zip-a-dee-doo-dah!* Poking his fork into the steamy enchiladas, Brent thought of that old song he heard on the Disney Channel when he was little.

Blowing on his first bite of food, he put it in his mouth and chewed. Trinidad Garza, Force Four Sports, came on the screen. Brent mixed the beans and rice together and took a bite of his new concoction. This dinner was actually not bad, he thought. A flurry of scores and a tale of woe for some tight end he'd never heard of, and the familiar face of Chet Charles, the lovable Force Four anchorman appeared, flanked by the equally lovable Joy Jenson, his co-anchor. If you didn't believe they're lovable, just ask any of their trillion followers. "That about wraps up this edition, folks." Jenson said. "Join me again right here at six. And you can see Chet at ten this evening." The camera did a close-up of Charles, revealing every speck of makeup and powder covering his rather imperfect facelift. "Thank you for joining us. This has been Force Four News, your home for all the news that impacts the city of Greatwood, the state of Indiana, our magnificent nation, and your lives."

As Brent took a swig of beer, the screen cut to a screaming lawyer standing atop an eighteen-wheeler, proclaiming he would hammer until you got your dough. Brent switched the channel, and there was someone trying to get him to get his medical training and be working in a doctor's office in only a year. Another channel change yielded a shot of Sheldon, Leonard, Raj, Howard, and Penny. No Bernadette or Amy Farrah Fowler in sight, so this had to be a very old rerun of *Big Bang Theory*. He let it play out.

As he finished up his dinner, not really registering what antics the *BB Theory* gang were up to, his phone chimed.

He saw Mitch's name and number on the screen.

"Hey," he answered. The beer had made him a bit foggy in the head.

"Whazzup?" Mitch asked.

"Nothin'. Sitting here havin' Tex-Mex and watching *Big Bang*."

"Sounds productive," Mitch said.

"What you been doin'?" Brent said, as he tipped the can up and drank the last drop of the beer.

"Hung with Kevin and Les. After I saw you Saturday. That Les guy is a trip. I've always been good with a comeback, but I can't top him. He laid me low at the Cup on Saturday. I was tryin' to hint that he should leave so I could talk to Kev—it's a long story, don't ask—and Les picked up on it and acted like he was glued to the chair. But then his girl summoned, and he was outta there faster than a NASCAR driver at the starting line.

"Anyway, he always seems to be at the Cup with Kev when I get there. So yesterday, Sunday, I went to the park with Kevin and Mark. Here was a guy who had been badmouthin' his little brother, calling him the little monster, and there he was playing catch with him like he'd never had a bad thought about Mark. So fuckin' proud of him, ya know? I just sat and marveled at it all. Kev's made so much progress."

"I know you told me he was immature. Sounds like the love of a good man is changin' 'im."

Mitch laughed. "From your mouth to God's ears, Brent."

"Anyway, today I grabbed Kev at his house and made him ride in my clunker—he always drives—to Spaghetti Nation for happy hour. That place must be hurting, man, because between three and four-thirty, spaghetti and meatballs is buy one, get one. Can't pass up a deal like that. 'Sides, I needed to show Kev how the other half lives. Apparently, his stepfather is even filthier rich than I could imagine, and Kevin wants for nothin'."

Hearing that broke through Brent's beer fog and made him remember why he'd called Mitch in the first place.

"You're sayin' that brought me back to reality. I'm not much of a drinker and this beer I just finished gave me old-timer's disease. I forgot to remember, like my grandmother says. She names every cousin I have, all fifteen of 'em, before she says my name eventually, even when she's starin' straight at me. She's not senile or anything, but she's definitely forgetf—"

"Sounds like that beer revved your motor mouth too, Brent, m' man. Get to the point. You told me to call, and I'm callin'. You had to have a reason. I know we're becomin' friends, but we haven't made it to the *shoot the breeze* stage yet. What gives?"

"Sorry. So, I went to the Campus Pride meeting. It was hard because everyone seemed glad to see me, and they wanted to offer their condolences, and lookin' back, I wonder if they were glad to see me because it was me there or if it was a chance for them to remember Callum."

"Okay, okay, I get it. Brent, get to the point, I reiterate. A very good word, I might add."

"Anyway, the new prez is Zina, short for Hazina, née Harry. Get the picture?"

"I get it. I get it. What's that have to do with anything?"

"Well, Z just recently had her surgery. You know the snip-snip one?"

"That beer make you a standup comedian? I don't think this Z would appreciate your calling her surgery that."

"I know, I know. Z and I started to talk. Seems Callum convinced her to have the surgery. She was wafflin', and he counseled her. That was the perfect lead to ask her if she knew anyone else he was counselin'."

"And did she?"

"At first, she told me she didn't know anything, and we both agreed that Callum believed in total confidentiality. But as we talked more, she 'membered somethin'. She said she was reasonably sure, because of somethin' Callum let slip, that his last client was a rich kid."

"Hence why my comment about Kev jogged your drunken memory."

"Exactly. Now, I don't know who he was or if he really was rich or what it has to do with what Sarah and Tom told us. But I do know this, if we keep askin' around, sooner or later, we'll come up with somethin'. A criminal always slips up. I've seen enough *Law and Order* to know serial killers get sloppy. And if we uncover enough slipups, we can piece them all together."

"You may be right. So—next step?"

"So, I know we have Costner's class tomorrow morning, but that's not until ten. I was thinkin' we could go to the jogging trail and see if we can find anyone who saw anything. Even the least little detail might put the final chip in the broken china we're tryin' to glue together."

"Okay, I can do that. What time? Seven? Seven-thirty?"

"I'm thinkin' five."

"Ooooh, you're a tough taskmaster, detective."

"Well, think about it. You can't commit a brutal murder in a public place in broad daylight. Tom said he saw Callum with a guy—maybe *the* guy—at two in the mornin'. Said Callum was at his place to pick up a jacket. Given the time of night, he coulda found this guy at one of the bars and decided he needed his help. We know that Callum liked to be in a quiet place, preferably under the stars, when he did his best work. The Arboretum, where he died, fits that description. So he and the guy, most likely in the guy's car because Callum's ride was still parked at his apartment after he was found, woulda driven over there. Takes at least forty minutes, even in the dead of night, to get to the park from Callum's place.

"So, they get there, park in the joggin' trail lot, head into the trees to find a spot to sit. Callum woulda been very picky. He woulda wanted a spot that somehow fit his very specific requirements, formulated to fit this guy's particular problem and personality. So, they find their spot. The guy, say, brought some coffees for 'em—or maybe they stopped at an all-night Starbucks drive-through. There's no way he coulda overtaken Callum and beat him to a bloody pulp as soon as they sat down on the dew-wet grass—or a bench—or a rock—or wherever they 'lighted.

"No, he woulda had to drug Callum. No autopsy's been released, and there wudn't much left t' autopsy. So say the guy slips something into Callum's drink. Callum gets groggy, passes out. The guy hightails it back to his car to retrieve his weapon of choice. What that is—was—we don't know yet. He kills Callum, and then leaves. By then, five a.m. is approaching. Maybe, just maybe, there was a jogger..."

"Who saw something." Mitch finished his sentence. "So five it is. Meet you at your apartment, say at four-fifteen?"

"Sounds great. Early. But great."

"And Brent. I'm proud of ya."

"Why's that?"

"Only a few days ago, you wouldna let yourself be so detached about this. All that stuff you just said weren't the words of a victim's partner. It was Sherlock Holmes determined to solve a terrible crime. Yeah, I know you're still hurtin', and I know Callum's never far from your thoughts. The hurt's still there. But the only way we'll get to the bottom of this, find the killer and turn him in, is to be analytical, cold and uncompromisin'."

"Truer words were never spoken, Mitch."

"Now, get some sleep. I'm hittin' the sack. Five o'clock comes early."

As Mitch got off the line, Brent saw his phone said it was 6:45 p.m. He chuckled. Callum would have said the same thing Mitch said. When he was on a mission, no bedtime was too early if he had to get up and kick ass the next morning. Except, his beautiful, wise Callum never kicked ass.

More like a gentle nudge to understanding.

Mitch

The rumble and pounding of the hot shower not even waking him up fully, Mitch wondered why he'd let himself get pulled into Brent's scheme. They were two college kids, not battle-battered detectives on the city force. Detectives, who at a decent waking hour, would most likely be preparing to get to their desks and once again review their evidence—evidence that, hopefully, is more complete and more revealing than the tiny bits he and Brent have gleaned, tiny bits that may or may not be connected and/or valuable. The real police, not the rank amateurs he and Brent were, had training, access to crime scene photos and collected evidence, medical examiner's reports, and CSI findings. All that, coupled with experience, not to mention those guys were looking at four connected murders, would add up to the answer Brent sought. Mitch knew that. But here he was before the sun even thought about rising, getting ready to go fight Brent's good fight. And why? Why oh why oh why?

Because Brent's a man in pain. Because Brent's a man who lost the dearest person in his life. Because you'd want Brent to help you if, God forbid, Kevin, who you at this point aren't even sure if you're in love with, was brutally bludgeoned to a pulp. Brent needs closure, and this is helping him to get there. And that's why you are up at this god-awful hour. So deal with it.

The little talking-to Mitch gave himself helped enormously. He dried his body, slipped on jeans and a pullover hoodie, smoothed his wet hair, looked in the mirror to make sure he was presentable. Interviewing joggers at dawn didn't require any special dress, but he had no intentions of coming home before class, so he didn't want to shame himself by looking raggedy. He smiled. His mom used that term all the time. "You're not going to school looking all raggedy like that," she'd say.

He missed her.

The drive to Brent's was only five minutes, and he had an extra five, so he pulled into the drive-through of a twenty-four-hour McDonald's. He ordered two cups of their molten-steel hot coffee, figuring Brent would need fortification too.

He carried both cups to Brent's door, and not having a hand empty, he used his foot to knock on the door. "Coming," he heard from the other side.

Brent was pulling on a jacket as he opened up. Seeing the coffee, he said, "You, m' friend, are a lifesaver. I just barely woke up in time to get dressed. You think the sun will be risin' anytime soon?" He smirked.

"Your idea, not mine. I don't remember the last time I saw the sunrise, so who knows if we'll see daylight on this adventure."

They strolled toward their cars. "Separate cars, okay? I'll need mine later to get back home, and we might not be able to come back here before class," Mitch said.

"No prob."

They caravanned to the park. The sun was just beginning to peek over the horizon as they arrived. And joggers were already rounding the track. The parking lot contained three cars, plus surely there were those who lived nearby and had walked over. These were the diehards. The ones they really might get some info from because they were there every day at this time.

As they got out of their respective vehicles, Brent called over the top of Mitch's Civic, "I'm feeling somethin'. A tingle. Tells me we're gonna find somethin' we can use."

"Got your pic of Callum with you?" Slipping his keys into his pocket, Mitch walked over to face Brent.

"Yeah," and he pulled the tattered photo from his wallet.

"Ya know, ya could put that thing on your phone and not have to carry the copy around."

Brent seemed to have a moment of intense sorrow. "You're right." He held the pic in one hand as he snapped a photo of it with his other. Then he kissed the picture and returned it to his wallet. "This was the last photo Callum and I took together. A photo booth at the arcade on

Silvertown. Callum, serious as he was, had his moments. He *loved* pinball. I think it was 'cause it was the only arcade game he could beat me at. Anyway, after a particularly brutal beatdown, he screamed, 'We need to immortalize this moment.' He dragged me, almost kickin' and screamin' into the photo booth. I didn't wanna capture his triumph over my loss. But he tickled me, and I was fine. We did three crazy-faced shots. During the third one, he took my hand in his. That simple thing sobered us up, and the last shot was this one—serious, loving."

He put his wallet away, slipping it into his back pocket.

He stared at the newly captured shot on his phone. "We waited for the pics to come out of the slot, and Callum, back to gloatin' over his victory, grabbed 'em out of my hand. He tore off the three goofy ones and shoved 'em into his pocket. 'These are my trophy shots,' he proclaimed.

"Then he showed the fourth to me. We stared at this pic for a long time, and then he pulled me to him, 'And this is the kiss,' he said, 'that goes with this shot of two men in love.' And he kissed me, right there in the middle of the arcade, little kids runnin' around and screamin'.

"That—that was my Callum.

"So I'll never stop carryin' this picture. In my wallet, on my phone, in my heart. He'll always be with me."

Brent, who had come to be so stoic when he spoke of Callum, started to sob. Mitch had no Kleenex, no handkerchief. He felt helpless. Should he hold Brent or just stand there like a statue? Finally, Mitch grabbed the arm of his hoodie, extended it to Brent and said, "Here." One simple word.

Brent smiled and stopped crying. "Ya don't want my snot on ya, dude." He stood tall, wiped his eyes on his own sleeve and said, "Now—onward and upward."

It quickly became evident that you didn't stop a committed jogger in mid-run for any reason, not even if their shoes were on fire. They found a stretching station and waited.

The first runner sped right past them. It was like they were in a *Roadrunner* cartoon.

They were luckier with the second. He stopped to stretch. But when Brent thrust the phone in his face, the guy briskly said, "Never seen him," and resumed his run.

That, with different wording, was the response they got from several others who either stopped to stretch or slowed when they saw Mitch and Brent waiting on the path.

Brent, it seemed to Mitch, was getting frustrated and disappointed when an overweight guy, huffing and puffing and red as a beet, came around the bend.

"'Scuse me, but I wondered if we could ask you a question?"

His eyes had been pointed downward, and at the sound of Brent's voice, he looked up. He looked around and saw the bench at the stretching station. He sat and took great gulps of air, waving his arm at Brent, clutching his chest and laboring a gasp. "Gimme a minute."

Brent looked at Mitch, hope in his eyes. Mitch's thought, on the other hand was, 'this guy is gonna have a heart attack right in front of our eyes.

At last, the guy was ready to talk. "Whaddaya want?"

"I wonder if you've ever seen this guy before."

"I'm lookin' at him," the jogger quipped, a breath between each word.

Mitch saw Brent's disgust.

"No, not me. The other guy."

With his breath returned, the guy said, with a smile, "I know, I know. Just funnin' ya."

"Woulda been three weeks ago. Wednesday morning."

"I 'member."

Mitch saw Brent seem to get taller, his elation filling his body like a growth spurt.

"That was m' birthday. I wudn't gonna run on my birthday, but m' doctor's a real bastard. I could hear him tearin' me a new one if he found out I didn't come out here. See this thing?" He pointed to a wristband. "Records every step. Doc has it reportin' to his office. He knows every f-in' step I take. If it shows much of a difference in the total steps from the last time I saw him, he bitches me out. Only tryin' to keep me alive, he says. Sometimes I wonder if it's worth it."

Completing this diatribe, the guy took a water bottle from his waistband and drank. And drank. And drank some more.

Mitch wanted to knock the guy off the bench, so he knew Brent was frustrated.

Amazingly, Brent's voice was even and under control when he spoke again. "So, you remember the day. Did you see this guy?"

"Nah," the jogger said.

"Anything else out of the ordinary? Somethin' different. Somethin' that didn't seem right to you."

There was a long pause as the man thought.

"Ya know? There wuz somethin' that struck me as weird." He pointed in the direction of the parking lot. "The same cars're there every morning. Ya can count on your ten fingers the reg'lars on this track, and only 'bout three of 'em drive here. But that mornin', m' birthday mornin', there wuz a car I never seen before. One of them fancy-dancy sports cars."

Mitch heard the eagerness in Brent's voice as he asked, "What kind of sports car? Make? Model?"

The guy huffed. "Didn' I just say I never seen the damn car before? I don't know one car from 'nother. It coulda been some Eyetalian million dollar crap or it mighta been a Toyota knockoff. All look the same to me."

"Fine. Can you tell me what color it was?"

"The sun wuz barely up. It wudn't in the light. So no, I don't know what color the hell it wuz. Gray? White? Cream? Light blue? Who knows? I'm kinda colorblind in dim light, anyway. Doc sez my eyes're goin', 'counta the diabetes."

"Well, thanks," Brent said. "I guess that's everything."

Mitch thought a moment. The guy had seen the car. Had he seen the driver? "One more thing. Did you see who was driving this car?"

"Nope."

"Well, thanks anyway. We appreciate your help," Mitch said as he and Brent turned to go. They'd talked to or at least approached all the people who were out that morning, so this was the most info they would gather.

"Wait!" they heard the big guy call. "I do 'member somethin' else."

Mitch and Brent were back facing the guy before either could even take a long breath.

"I recollec' the guy. The one in that car. A guy in a hoodie whizzed past me. He wuz carrying a stick or something. He went by so fast I couldn't tell what was in his hand. Got in that car and burned rubber."

"Ya get a good look at him?" Brent almost shouted his question. Mitch heard hope and joy in Brent's voice.

"Now, didn' I just tell you I didn' see him?" The man's voice dripped with disgust. But Mitch figured he was disgusted with the fact he was out here doing this at all, and Brent had nothing to do with that. "He got past me before I could get a good look. He did stop, of course, at his car door, but like I said, it wuz dark, he had the hood pulled up, and my eyes ain't so good."

Brent's voice fell as he asked what Mitch figured was his final question. "Did ya tell the police any of this?"

"Didn' ask. Never talked to no police." A light bulb seemed to go off above the guy's head. "This 'bout the murder? Man, when I read about that and realized it happened on my birthday, I 'bout shit my pants. It coulda been me. Doc or no doc, I vowed I wouldn't be out here again—not at this hour. No way. But then I thought, 'It'd take a pretty hefty weapon, not to mention a strongman, to do much damage to my blubber.' And I figured whoever that murderer wuz wouldn't come back here. Each of those four wuz found in sep'rate places 'round the city. So here I am, living to run another lap." The guy chuckled at his joke.

Brent sighed. "Well, thanks again."

Back in the parking lot, Mitch was aching for Brent. He'd come so close to finding out something definite about the murderer. *Hoodie? They already knew that. Weapon? This guy hadn't seen what it was. The best clue was the car, and even then, there must be hundreds, if not thousands, of sports cars in a city this big. In River Glen alone, the swank neighborhood where Kevin lived, he'd seen five or six Ferraris, at least one Lamborghini, and ten or more Stingrays. Even Kevin drove a Boxter Spyder—that set his stepdad back thousands, Mitch was sure. And then there were all the knockoffs, the cars for Ferrari-owner wannabes. Toyota made a sports car that looked an awful lot like what Kev drives. So,* knowing Brent's not stupid and would have already run all this through his head, Mitch knew Brent was feeling mighty low.

"Hey, guy, we've got a few hours to kill before class. I do want to get to the library to work an hour, give or take, on a paper I have due next week. But what say we grab some breakfast?"

"Sure thing." Brent's voice was incredibly upbeat for someone who had just found out so little that helped him solve his partner's murder. "Molly's Table? It's near campus and open early. Know where it is?"

"Yep. Meet you there."

Just short of six a.m., the tables were already filling up. The door said Molly's hours were five-thirty a.m. to eight-thirty p.m. As he and Brent took seats at a two-top in the corner—his mom used to wait tables some, so he knew the lingo—they looked around, awaiting menus.

"I know that guy," Brent said.

Mitch looked in the direction Brent eyed. "Which one?"

"Red shirt. He's in Campus Pride. Name's Devon."

"Nice. If I weren't concentrating on Kevin, I'd jump that Devon guy's bones."

Brent laughed.

"But my casual sex days are over. I'm lookin' for a partner, someone to share with. Something like you and Callum." The minute he said that, he regretted it. But Brent didn't seem to react negatively. In fact, his response was upbeat.

"I wish ya well, m' man, I wish ya well. Ever'body deserves to find their one great love." He paused. "Was that too flowery? Did it sound lame?"

"Not at all, Brent. I feel like I know Callum now, and he was definitely your one great love." He started to add another in a string of condolences he knew Brent kept getting, but he decided it was best to just let it lay. Besides, it was too early, and he was too tired to think up any more flowery words.

"This place is jumpin', idn't it? Who knew people were up and at 'em this early in the morning?"

Mitch looked around again. "Well, ya gotta lotta people here that keep the world on its axis. The ones who get up early and stay up late, to make sure we got everything we need. See the postal carrier?" He pointed to a short black woman two tables away. "Within the hour, she'll be sortin' mail for today's delivery. And the guys at the table against the wall? Looks like they'll be pourin' concrete, nailin' up studs, or installin' Sheetrock in another twenty minutes. And—"

"I get your drift. We scholars who party all night and sleep all morning, strivin' to get a nine-to-five that pays us royally for very little labor, have no idea how the blue collar can chafe."

Mitch laughed, marveling at Brent's very intelligent sense of humor. His laughter was broken by a tall drink of water waitress. Her hair was concealed under a hijab. She had a smile pasted on, and she looked weary already.

"Welcome to Molly's Table," she recited rotely. "Coffee?"

Mitch wondered how many pots of coffee this place made every morning. "Yes, please, ma'am." He looked at Brent, who nodded. "Make that two if you would."

She went away to get their coffee while Mitch and Brent perused the menu.

"Turkey bacon? Turkey sausage? What's up with that?"

"You saw the waitress. This place is on the edge of a Muslim community. No pork. Absolutely forbidden."

"I see, said the blind man," Mitch remarked. "Well, I think I'll have the chicken fried steak and eggs. What you havin'?"

"The short stack and a Western omelet, no peppers—turkey ham, for sure."

"You must be starvin'."

"Ravenous. That Mexican dinner I pulled out of the freezer wudn't much food last night. And the beer I had...I don't drink much...musta made me wake up with the munchies."

"Brent, Brent, Brent. Alcohol doesn't give you the munchies. Are you sure that dinner wasn't laced with the ganja weed? You a pothead?" Mitch joked.

"Never touched the stuff. Callum woulda dropped my ass instantly. He was very, very anti-drug."

"I coulda predicted that."

Their server brought their coffee, took their order, and delivered it soon after.

"Best breakfast I ever had," Brent said. "So, let's recap. The fat jogger—" Mitch gave him the look. "I know. The *plus-sized* jogger confirmed that Callum's guy wore a hoodie, just like Tom said. And he told us there was a sports car in the parking lot. I'm thinking that hoodie, weapon-like object in hand, and leaving in said sports car add up to this bein' the guy who murdered Callum."

"I think you're right, but it's still not much to go on."

"Add to that what Sarah said about Callum going to gay bars. This all happened right after the bars let out. So, it's possible Callum picked the guy up in one of the bars."

"At last count, there were three gay bars, plus two gay-friendly clubs in this city. So how does knowin' that help us?"

Brent said, "Look. I'm just tryin' to fit the pieces into one puzzle. Any one of those might be from kitten playin' with a ball of string rather than sunset at Yellowstone."

Mitch looked at him like he was crazy.

"Jigsaw puzzles?" Brent said.

"Oooh! I thought you were losin' it man. Now I get your point."

"Get enough pieces in place, and the picture comes clear. So we just have to keep diggin'."

"And what, pray tell, is next?"

"I dunno." That should have thrown Brent into a tailspin, but Mitch saw he was still upbeat and confident.

They finished their breakfast. Mitch headed to the library.

Dr. Costner was his new gentler, kinder, more caring self again during class. Brent came to Mitch after class and said, "Still don't know. We'll talk."

Free for the rest of the day, Mitch texted Kevin. He would still be at school and probably wouldn't respond, but maybe he'd see the text during class change.

The rest of the day vanished as Mitch tried to concentrate, once again in the library, on his assignment he was almost ready to begin drafting. His mind wandered because it was long after public schools were out for the day, and he still hadn't heard from Kevin. Getting nowhere fast on his paper, Mitch closed up shop and went home.

He was pulling into a parking spot when he saw it—the Spyder.

"Thought you'd never get home, babe. Where ya been?" Kevin was all smiles.

"You couldn't call, you couldn't text?" Mitch asked.

"Wanted to surprise you. Come on, get in the car."

"Where we goin'?"

"You'll see."

He slid into the passenger seat, and Kevin sped—he always sped—away. Ten minutes later, he parked the car on a street in River Glen.

"Ever been here?" Kevin said, wickedly looking as if he knew what Mitch's answer would be.

"Where is here?" Mitch saw nothing but a tall hedge with a narrow opening.

"The fountains. The most romantic spot in the city."

"Can't say as I have," Mitch said.

"Well, you're in for a treat, babe." They got out of the car. "Let me just get my hoodie. The mist can get a little cold this time of year." As Kevin opened the trunk of the car, Mitch felt an overwhelming urge to kiss him. This whole idea, this surprise, was too, too sweet. He went to the back of the car to deliver that kiss.

As Kevin pulled a hoodie from the trunk, Mitch saw a metal baseball bat.

"I didn't know you were a slugger." He didn't know why he'd let the bat distract him from his objective, to plant a kiss on Kevin's luscious lips.

"I'm not. Ste—er, Sloan, my d-dad gave that bat to me when I was a kid." Mitch noticed he had checked himself.

He actually caught himself calling his stepdad Step and corrected it to the man's name. That's a very positive step. He also had a hard time with Dad, but that's to be expected. Kevin's still evolving on that front.

Kevin continued his explanation of the bat. "Anyway, Sloan hoped I would be a star little leaguer, but that didn't happen. No, I only have the bat there because I took it Sunday when we went to play catch with

Mark. I figured the kid might want to practice his swing. But that didn't happen. I just never took the thing out of the car."

"Ah. Sunday. You seemed to be havin' a ball. Pardon the pun. It was fun just watchin' you two."

As Kevin pulled the hoodie over his head, his muffled answer came. "Yeah." Fully clothed, his voice was unfettered. "And thanks for encouragin' me. Turns out Mark's a great kid. I guess I just let the age difference get the best of me. And I admit some jealousy. Mom doesn't take much time with either of us, but Mark seems to get more moments with her than I do. I guess that's understandable 'cause he's her baby."

Mitch loved the understanding he was hearing. "Well, before this conversation began, I was gonna do this." And he kissed Kevin.

"Hm-m-m, nice." Kevin pecked Mitch's lips in thank you. "Now, the fountains." He led Mitch through the narrow opening. Dancing sprays of water, set in a huge shallow, concreted pool, dazzled Mitch immediately. He'd never seen these before. He never even knew they existed.

"Whaddaya think? Fan-fucking-tastic, huh?"

"Wow! How ya know about these?"

"Actually, they're private. This is the backyard of one of Sloan's clients, hence the narrow opening. I think it's only there because one of the trees died and the gardener hasn't replaced it yet. Sit." He pointed to a bench under an arbor, facing the water ballet.

"And don't worry. The owner's a great guy. I called ahead to get his permission for us to be here."

"I was wonderin' 'bout that."

Under the arbor, nestled on the bench, a fragrance enveloped them. "What's that smell?" Mitch asked.

"That would be Sweet Autumn Clematis. See the tiny white flowers." He pointed above them. "They give off that fragrance. Some say it is the aphrodisiac of the gods."

"You made that up, didn't you?" Mitch smiled.

"Yeah. The clematis part is true. The god thing? Just my overactive imagination."

"You're amazing, Kev. I've never met anyone quite like you. I have t' say, when I first met ya, I thought you'd be too much for me to handle. But you're growin' on me, fast." He moved in, pulled Kevin into a cocooning embrace, and kissed him deeply, holding him in the kiss for as long as he could before he absolutely had to come up for air.

How long is too long to take time? I feel like the waiting period should be over.

They sat, content, holding hands, and watched the dancing waters. The day faded, and moonlight filled the garden. Soft, colored lights shone on the waters as they made their intricate, seductive moves.

Neither spoke. Mitch thought about how he's been happier than he'd been since his mother had passed. *I was lost, but now I'm found. Sacrilegious to quote* Amazing Grace *when I'm thinking of being in love? Maybe. But I don't care. I was attracted to Kevin the first moment I saw him, but I didn't want to let myself act on that attraction. I'd had enough of the physical, love 'em and leave 'em I'd been doin'. I wanted* this. *What we're havin' right here, right now. Kevin was young and impetuous, and I was right to hold back. He's come a long way in a very short time. Should I be cautious? Maybe. But this feels right. I want 'im. I want him so bad I can taste it.* And then Mitch thought of Callum. All this self-examination must have brought the ultimate counselor to mind. *Callum waited. Marriage was sacred to him. I want that. I want a sacred union, not just a lay in the hay. Kevin may not understand, but I have to wait. Maybe not until we stand at an altar, but until I'm very, very sure that I'm not still being led by my aching balls.*

"Nice, huh?" Kevin's voice was so quiet it almost didn't penetrate Mitch's thoughts.

"Yeah." He took Kevin's hand to his lips and kissed it.

"'S what I've always wanted. Someone to love. Someone to love me." Kevin's voice sounded so heartbreaking that Mitch wanted to take him to the nearest chapel so their journey together could start.

That's just the moonlight talking.

"Kev, I love ya. I'm here for ya when no one else is. But know this, you've found Mark now. He's your brother. He loves you. And even though your mom is dedicated to her career, I know she loves ya too. And Sloan. Your dad. He wouldn't drop several thou on that sweet ride of yours if he didn't care. I don't care how rich ya are, ya don't settle that much on a son unless you want 'im to be happy. So you have a lot of love in your life." He hoped Kevin had heard him, truly heard him.

He did flinch when I mentioned Sloan, though.

Kevin

"So how's it hangin', gay boy?" Les was being Les as they sat to have their coffee.

"It's been one week and one day since I took him to the fountains, but who's countin'?" He smiled at Les. "Best eight days of my life."

"So, bro, love this time?"

Les knew him well. As well as anyone knew him.

"Yeah, I think it is," Kevin answered. He swigged coffee. "I finally found someone to love me."

"Unlike Step and your mom who don't give a shit."

You really do know me, don't you, Les?

Kevin gave his best friend a look he was sure Les could read.

"I know ya like the back of my hand, dude. We been friends far too long to pull any punches. Your ultra-rich stepdad and your ultra-absent mother wouldn't care if you wuz beat to a bloody pulp by the city's infamous serial stalker. So I'm glad, bro, that ya found Mitch." Les could be understanding and caring and loving, all rolled into one. Then instantly, break it all apart. "He still won't fuck ya?"

"Well, aren't we being a potty mouth today," Kevin joked.

"Come on, bro, spill. You've had seven lonely nights since things heated up at those fountains. Surely, ya coulda made your move on 'im."

"Mitch's different Les. I don't want to move too quick, if ever. Maybe I just want to let him make the key plays."

"Well, if it'd been me, I would have—who am I kidding? My girl won't let me get in her pants, either. Guess we're both losers. By the way, I'm still laughin' at the fountain thing. How'd you even know those were back there? It's a wonder you didn't get caught. And Mitch bought the bullshit you told him."

"First of all, I saw 'em in *Architectural Digest*. I cased the joint and saw that break in the hedge. I went ahead of time to make sure there wasn't some sort of electric fence around the property—what's up with that? The owner is asking for it, I say. And what I told Mitch wasn't bullshit, it was just a little romantic fib. So there."

"Well, I just hope he's not *romantically fibbing* to you, m' friend."

"He's not. I believe him when he says he loves me." Kevin sounded too defensive. He toned it down. "We're a couple now, and it's largely because of the date I planned and executed. So you're not goin' to get me riled, Les."

"Okay, okay. You need a refill? I'm buying."

"Can't beat an offer like that. Yeah."

As Les went to get their new coffees, Kevin thought of the fountain date. *Everything was perfect. It went exactly as I planned, except for Mitch almost spoiling it bringing up Step. He insisted that Step loved me because he bought me the Spyder. Step just thought he could buy my love. Too bad, Step. It didn't work.*

Les came back with the fresh brews. "What ya thinkin' 'bout, bro?"

"Nothing."

"Yeah, sure. That brain of yours is always goin', always schemin', plottin', plannin'," Les said.

"That's the old Kevin, Les. This is the new improved Kevin."

"Kevin 2.0, huh? Seems like the original model to me, 'cept for the newer, more stylish look. But if you say you're a changed man, who am I to disagree?"

"Thanks, my friend. 'Til Mitch came along, you were the only person I could ever trust."

"That's good to hear. If I may be so bold, though, sometimes I thought there was a lot you weren't tellin' me."

"I would never hold out on you, Les." Kevin hoped that sounded sincere.

"What are you and lover boy doin' tonight?"

"Mitch has an important paper due Friday, so he made it clear he's incommunicado until he turns that thing in. He told me not to even try to call or text because he didn't want me t' get upset when he didn't answer."

"Kev, my man, surely you told 'im you could knock out a paper from inception to research to rough draft to typed copy in two hours, three tops? You saved my ass last year in American History."

"I offered to help, but Mitch is very principled. He said he had t' do it himself." Kevin smiled, thinking of the standup guy Mitch was. Refusing to cheat on a paper, even a little. Holding out until they could be together permanently. Helping that Brent guy with god knows what, just because Brent was in mourning.

Mourning—such a Victorian concept.

"Well, dude, I gotta hot date tonight. This might be the night she lets me. I gotta get home and make m'self pretty, know what I mean?"

"You're a trip, Les. You go ahead on, now, ya hear. Good luck. You'll need it with that Ice Queen you hang with. And don't forget your lock picks for that Iron Maiden she wears. You got your work cut out for ya."

"But she's mighty purty, ain't she?"

And Les was *outta there*, a phrase he'd used many times.

Kevin finished what was left of his coffee, daydreaming of Mitch. Daydreaming actually turned to evening-dreaming as the sun began to set.

He sneaked, once again, through the narrow passageway to the magic fountains. Sitting in the arbor, he relived it all. It was a magical date. He sat there, mesmerized by the fountains, until he was startled by a voice coming from far away. "Ringo! Come back here!"

Uh-oh, the owner must be out with his dog. I'd better get out of here before that dog comes sniffing around.

And Kevin rushed through the opening and jumped into the Spyder.

Adrenaline rushing and high on Mitch memories, he went home. Upstairs, he thought he might go for a run. Before he changed out of his recently purchased GQ-approved duds into running shorts, T, and Jordans, he switched on the TV just to hear the noise.

Damn! Mom! What's she doing on TV?

He turned the volume up. "This is a very important project," his mom said. "I'll be overseeing an international push to help children in a cluster of disadvantaged countries on the African continent. If I don't do it, no one will. Being a mother myself, I know how important it is to keep our children safe, see they are fed and clothed, and loved. That's the most important thing—that they feel they are getting the attention they need and are loved."

He pushed the off button and threw the remote across the room.

Tears welled in his eyes. *Let's see, Mommy Dearest, I'm safe. Check. I'm fed. Check. I'm clothed. Check. Loved? Not so much. Not by you, anyway. When was the last time you saw me? When was the last time we spoke, even on the telephone? No, you're always in your ivory tower office. And now I hear you're plannin' to mother all of Africa. Well, more power to ya, Doris, more power to ya.*

Kevin whipped out his phone. He was just about to push Mitch's digit when his door flew open.

"What's *this* crap?" Sloan was waving a piece of paper about. He was worked into a hell of a frenzy.

"I'm afraid I have no idea of what you are speaking." It always pissed him off when Kevin got all faux hoity-toity with him. "Pray tell, would you shed some light on the topic at hand?"

Kevin was pushing it. He didn't care. *First Mom's shit, and now Step's all hot and bothered.*

"This charge on my card."

So that's it. Kevin warmed inside. He hadn't expected a reaction so soon.

"I'm afraid, dear father, I don't know what charge of which you speak."

"Cut the bull, Kevin. I see the six thou worth of clothes you bought when you never have anything but t-shirts and ragged jeans on. But I'm not worried about that in the least. You know very well what I'm talking about."

Kevin stared at Step like he was totally clueless.

"This 5K donation to Family Now." He thrust the paper in front of Kevin's nose, jabbing at it like Kevin could read it with it flopping around.

"Oh, that. I just felt moved to help the good doctor with his cause."

Step was right up in his face. "That blowhard? That homophobic asshole?"

"But I thought your feelings were right in tune with his," Kevin said.

"Kevin, you know I'm not a homophobe. I supported you when you came out. Yes, I wanted you to make better choices when it came to who you went out with, but I've never been anti-gay. So your doing this hurts me even more, not to mention that I'm going to have to explain to my accountant what this charge is."

"You could contest it. Call AmEx and talk to somebody." Kevin was laughing in his gut, knowing that was the last thing Step would do.

"Or I could have your ass hauled into jail for credit card fraud."

That's a good one, Step. "And how would you explain all the other charges you approved of? And think of the publicity that would come raining shit down on you and my dear mother."

Step's tone softened. "Well, it's only because your mother and I love you that I won't press charges."

Kevin laughed out loud at that. He seemed to be making Step madder and madder. And he loved it.

"Stop that laughing. Stop it, I say!"

"Oooh, daddy. I'm sahwy." His baby talk inflamed Step more. "Did I hurt my wuving daddy's feewings?"

Step suddenly stood still, looked at the ceiling, took a deep, deep breath, and waited a moment. Then he stared at Kevin.

"Kevin, I'm not going to let you bait me. I know how kids your age can be, and I'm going to stand here, right here, right now, and say, 'I forgive you.' I've loved you since the first moment I met you, toy fire truck in hand, mumbling your little varoom, varoom. And your mother loves you more than life itself."

What a crock of overly microwaved bull dung. Kevin was having a hard time not breaking into an ironic chorus of *M-O-T-H-E-R*, that song they used to sing in kindergarten.

Step continued his hearts and flowers speech. "Kevin, I've tried to be a father to you, a real father. I know you hurt when your dad left you and your mom. I wanted to step in and make you see that I was there for you, will always be there for you." He sighed. "I don't know. Maybe I failed. Maybe I didn't have a good role model. My own father thought if he provided well for his children then he was showing his love. So I set out to make a name for myself, not because I wanted glory, but because I wanted to give you and Mark everything, everything the world has to offer. I don't ever want you to think that doors won't open for you. Money greases the hinges, and I wanted to have plenty of grease."

Like this lard you're slinging right now?

"Look, it's all over the news, this new project your mom is taking on, so I'm going to make an educated guess that you know all about it. I don't fully approve, but your mom is your mom. I told her she needed to tell you and Mark about this before it hit the press, but she gets so focused that she never got around to it. I'm sorry if that's what's bothering you. If I could talk her out of it, I would. Believe me, I tried."

Yeah, sure. When did you leave your office long enough to have a heart-to-heart with a woman who may not even know how to push the down button on her building elevator? She lives in that penthouse suite she calls her office. We both know it's her home.

"What your mom will be doing is going to make a huge difference in the lives of children who don't have much at all. You know what she told me? She said, 'Sloan, I want to help kids who don't have what our kids have. In effect, I'm honoring Mark and Kevin by doing this.' I swear to God that's what she said."

Don't take the Lord's name in vain, Step. He'll smite you with fire. But I have to hand it to you, that was quick thinking. I didn't know you had it in you.

"Look, Kevin. I'm a royal shit. I thought money could cure anything. But I know now I was wrong. I want us to turn over a new leaf. I know at this point you're busy leading your own life. But maybe we could have dinner together once a week or so. Catch up. I know this thing you did was a cry for help. I know you think I don't approve of your being gay and that's why you did what you did. But you can't mess with a megalomaniac like Fellows. He'll chew you up and spit you out."

So eloquent, Step. So eloquent. Did you think of that yourself, or did you consult Bartlett's Quotations before you stormed in here?

"I'm not contesting the charge. I'm not cutting you off. I gave you the card so you could buy anything you wanted. God knows, I've got the cash. I like that you feel free to use my credit however you see fit. By the way, I'm impressed by your new look. The shaggy hair, the ripped jeans, the faded concert T's were getting old and tired. You look your age now, like a man who will soon be going off to college and finding his place in the world. Good for you for seeing the need for change."

You don't get it, do you? If you spent more time around here, or kept your eyes open when you were here, you would have seen Mitch coming about, and you'd know why the change. It's all for him, Step, all for him. Then Kevin's brain backed up. *Okay, the haircut was for you—well, to impersonate you, at least.*

"And the glasses. Didn't even know you were going blind on us. See? That's what I mean about taking charge of your life. You saw you had a problem, and you solved it. You look good by the way. Like the frames."

I bet you do since they are exactly the same ones you wear, you butthole.

"Kevin, I was out-of-line when I came in here. You've shown responsibility and maturity in a lot of ways recently. I could have spoken in a civil tone and worked it all out with you. I hope that's how this has turned out. I love you, son."

And whatever good he might have thought he'd done with that last heartfelt oration, he'd ruined it with one three-letter word.

"Dinner, just you and me, next Tuesday, about this time?"

It was all Kevin could do to make himself respond. *Had Step not realized Kevin had said absolutely nothing for the last several minutes, throughout Step's canned 'I'm the greatest dad' speech?* "Sure." And then, just to mess with him, he added, "Dad."

Step rushed toward him, grabbed his shoulders, and hugged him like Kevin had just presented him with a Best Dad in the World coffee mug.

"Looking forward to Tuesday, son."

And between the spiders that crawled up and down his back as Step hugged him and the one-two punch of that word *son*, Kevin was plunged into a deep dark world after Step left his room, closing the door behind him.

He's such a fake. He doesn't love me. Nobody loves me. Mom certainly doesn't. She'd rather traipse all the way to Africa to practice her chronically lacking mothering skills than see she has a son right here that needs her. Well, to hell with her. She can feed, clothe, and rock little black babies all she wants. I don't care. Maybe her very private jet will go down over the Atlantic. She'd like that. To be martyred for her cause. I can see the public spectacle Step would make. He'd be distraught. Probably wing his way to the Big Apple, Rockefeller Center, do all the morning talk shows to publicly mourn his lovely wife who gave her life. Start a foundation in her name to aid the poor children on the Dark Continent. But would his sorrow be genuine? He's incapable of love. Proved it time and again. Mega-proved it just now.

All that purple prose he spouted at me. Pleadin' with me to believe he loves me. Beggin' me to understand about my mother. Even tellin' me he didn't approve of her new scheme. Good one, Step. Bad cop, good cop. But all he cares about is continuing to amass his fortune so he can throw dollars at me instead of truly offering his love.

I've got your number, Sloan Howell. As long as I toe the line, don't besmirch your good name, a name you never even offered to me, even though the man whose name I bear deserted me—there's another parent who doesn't love me. Oh, well, maybe I just have to make my mark in other ways. It's clear I'll never be motivated by the love of good parents. That's off the table.

And that Tuesday dinner? Ten to one, you'll cancel. With an oh, so *sincere apology, of course. You prick.*

Kevin was so pissed he'd started crying. A psychology book he once devoured said tears could signal frustration, anger, or a host of any other things. He decided anger. That's what he was feeling.

Angry. Sounds so not-right, so milquetoast, so pansy. Mad. Pissed. *Nope, not good enough.* He racked his brain. Provoked, disturbed, annoyed, riled, irritated, upset, aggravated, rankled, ticked, enraged, seething, sore, livid, steamed, ballistic. Yeah, that's what he was— ballistic. He praised his almost photographic mind. Ballistic. B-A-L-L-I-S-T-I-C, ballistic. 1.Extreme and unusually sudden reaction to something, i.e. The boy went ballistic when his sister threw the apple at him. 2. Pertaining to a rapidly moving projectile, i.e., Ballistic tests were run on the bullet pulled from the victim.

Yes, indeed, he was going ballistic. At this very moment, if he had a gun, he might go after Step.

But that would be rather messy, don't you think, Kevin, son? The blood spatter would just destroy your mom's house.

Kevin smiled as he thought of this fictitious comment he'd invented from his ever-so-eloquent stepfather.

So, there were other ways to ruin the great god Stepfather Sloan Howell.

Kevin sat on his bed. In the dark room. Not moving. Just plotting. *Step would regret. Mom would regret. Regret. Regret. Regret.*

But I won't regret.

He saw the time on his phone. *Four more hours. They'll be packed by then. I'll find someone. Someone to hook up with and do it. Make a fucking big splash!*

He sat in the silence, waiting. He didn't nod off. He didn't let his mind wander. He didn't do anything but meditate on what he was about to do.

At eleven-thirty, he got up. Went to the bathroom. Looked in the mirror. Tousled his hair. Made it sexier looking. Took off his glasses. Surveyed what he saw. Yes, he thought, I look more enticing without them. Went to his closet. Looked for something from the old Kevin. Picked out a shirt, jeans—an outfit that said, 'hey, lonely guy, come with me.'

Love me? I think not.

He headed for the Spyder and the beginning of his seduction.

15
Mitch

"You hear?"

Dr. Costner had barely dismissed class. Mitch hadn't even had time to save the notes on his laptop. The old spiral notebook and pen thing had gotten tedious, not to mention that his desktop had melted. With this paper deadline looming, he'd gone out the day before and picked up a new Macbook Air. Well, a refurbished Macbook Air. He was figuring it out, making sure he didn't lose his notes when he heard Brent.

"Hear what?" He closed the device and stored it in his bag.

"Another one."

Being holed up completing a five-thousand-word load of bullcrap hadn't left him time to think of anything else. And sitting in class with very little sleep had fried his brain. So Brent's statement didn't compute.

"Another what?"

"Murder."

He was so out of it, he almost didn't connect. *Murder?*

"Ya sure?"

"All over the news. Marlon Gordon's shootin' his wad, creamin' about his escalating ratings points. And that's not the only thing he says is escalatin'. The murderer. The victim this time didn't fit the profile. The rest of the MO's still the same, but this latest victim has brown eyes. What's up with that? Real or copycat? Gordon claims it's real. But then he's just panderin' for the ratings."

Brent going ninety miles a minute with all this wad, creaming, pandering shit is too much for me to take right now. I need coffee. Big time. Lord, please let me deal with this without a big scene.

Mitch willed himself to respond. Low key. "I been busy. Guess I missed the news."

"Where ya been? Under a rock? It's on all the channels." Brent wasn't hearing him.

"This eco paper's been kickin' m' butt. My desktop quit on me. Thank God I saved everything to a thumb drive. I rushed out to get a suitable replacement. Wound up with a Macbook Air. Been figuring it out while trying to finish the warmed-over shit I've dished up for that dimwitted professor. Haven't even turned on my phone in two days, much less the TV. If I didn't need to keep up with Costner's class, I woulda ditched it to finish the other crap."

He saw Brent's body tension release somewhat.

God, what a relief that is. I want to help him, but I'm not in any shape to deal with his intensity right now.

"Sorry, guy," Brent said. "I forgot the deadline you were facin'. How's it goin'?"

"Finally—finally, I carefully composed the final paragraph before I headed over here. Now all I have to do is print it out when I get home. Sounds easy, but before I can do that, I have to figure out how to link the Mac with my printer. If that proves futile, I'll have to go get a new printer, and you know what a hassle that can be. The walls're closin' in on me, man."

"When was the last time ya ate, Mitch? Sounds to me like low blood sugar talkin' here."

"Nah," Mitch protested. "That's not it. I had some Cheetos. When was it? This morning? Bedtime, which was four this morning? Oh, I remember. My stomach growled about six last night, and Cheetos were all I had in the place." He thought he'd made his point. He didn't have the energy to add anything else anyway. After a long pause, he said, unconvincingly—to himself—"I just need coffee."

"Get up." Mitch sat, in a semi-fog. Brent repeated himself, "I said, get up."

Robotically, Mitch rose. He almost collapsed back into the chair. He was weak in the knees.

"You been runnin' on adrenaline. Now it's caught up with you, m' friend. We're gettin' ya some food into ya, guy." Brent took two steps away and then turned around. "Come on," he commanded.

Mitch pulled himself up and took a baby step. "Get your bag, Mitch." Mitch did as he was told, and Brent grabbed his arm, pulling him from the classroom.

"I hope ya didn't drive over here in this zombie state," Brent said. "If ya did, you're leavin' your car. Y' c'n Uber back to get it once you're back among the livin'. Ya need food. And ya need sleep."

Mitch searched his addled brain, replaying his morning and finally working himself out of his stupor, a bit at least. "I was fine this morning. I only slept three hours, but I got up, showered, worked on the paper some more, and then I drove to class. I even was awake, for the most part, during Costner's lecture. It was only after I knew he was finished that I started fadin'. And somehow your mention of food and my lack of it threw me into a tailspin."

He stumbled as they walked and talked.

"Whoa!" Brent shouted, clutching Mitch to keep him from falling. "I rest my case. You need sustenance, my man."

By then, they were at Brent's car. Brent opened the passenger-side door and pushed Mitch in. "Buckle up." Mitch sat, the fog returning. Brent pulled the seatbelt across Mitch and buckled it. Then he went around to the driver's seat.

"What you need is carbs. Energy. Spaghetti. Macaroni. Fettuccini. I'm takin' you to Spaghetti Nation, m' friend."

Mitch sighed as he got out of the car after Brent parked. He hadn't realized how out of it he was. He took cautious, tiny steps as he walked toward the restaurant entrance. When he came to the stairs leading up to the door, he held onto the handrail like some frail old man. Brent hovered over him.

The hostess seated them. A server immediately appeared with a water pitcher. He filled glasses as he started the usual waiter banter: "I'm Jian. I'll be your server today. Been here before?" Mitch tried to say 'yes,' but he couldn't get it out before this Jian guy was onto his next canned remark. "We specialize in pasta, pasta, pasta. You choose your own combo or you can pick one of our chef-inspired dishes. Your placemat is your menu. Just so you know, we've been running a special from three to four-thirty. You can get spaghetti and meatballs, buy one, get one. So next time guys, hold your cravings a few more hours and save some dough." He laughed like that was the funniest thing anyone had ever said. "Now, while you decide, can I get you something besides water to drink? Soft drinks—Pepsi, Orange, Root Beer, Seven Up, Iced Tea, Coffee—all come with free refills. We also have a full bar with wine and mixed drinks." At that, he winked, a sort of *you don't tell anyone, I won't* wink.

Brent looked at the guy and said, "I'm happy with just water." When nothing came from Mitch, he said, "I think my friend here will just have water too." Jian nodded. "No, bring him coffee. Black. Strong."

With the waiter off to bring back the coffee, Brent asked Mitch, "What looks good to you?"

Mitch looked at the menu, shook his head like his eyes weren't focusing too well, and said, "I don't care. Anything's fine. I just need something to pull me out of this funk. You order for both of us."

Brent said, "Okay, then it's Callum's and my favorite—Spaghetti alla Carbonara."

"Sounds good."

Jian returned with a mug almost brimming over and set it down. "What'll it be, guys?"

"We'll both have the Spaghetti alla Carbonara, please, Jian," Brent ordered.

Mitch was pretty out of it, but he did see that look on the waiter's face. A moment before, they were just two college guys having lunch. Now, he saw in that shit's face, they were two gay guys sharing a romantic meal. *Well, fuck you, Jian. I have my own boyfriend. I don't need you marryin' me to Brent here.* That thought jolted him.

Eyeing the waiter as he walked away, Mitch said, "Ya see that?"

"What?"

"You ordered for both of us, and that little prick immediately thought, 'oh, I get it, these two're on a date.'"

"And?"

"Well, maybe I'm not in any state to make judgments, and maybe I'm readin' him wrong, but I just don't think it's right for him to make assumptions about anyone. We could be two raging heteros, come to scope out the place for picking up pussy."

"Damn, son, you're not yourself today. Drink some coffee. The caffeine'll help." Mitch did as he was told. "And what difference does it make if this guy thinks we're a couple? Maybe he's gay himself, and he needs two good role models. That's what Callum would say."

Mitch softened, a combination of Brent's Callum-based reasoning and the caffeine kicking in. "You're right. I need food."

"It'll get here. Just keep swiggin' that caffeine, m' man."

Mitch took another gulp. The coffee was barely warm, which was good because he could consume it quicker. Let the caffeine invade his bloodstream. "You know, Brent, maybe I didn't like that implication because I'm missin' Kevin. I didn't think I was in love with him. I fought the idea. But just two and a half days without him, and I need a Kevin fix."

Brent shook his head and smiled. "Definitely in love, guy. You know how I told you I might go for days without seein' Callum? The only thing that kept me goin' was knowin' when we did get together, he was all mine. Callum compartmentalized, and our time was our time. But those days when his time was taken up elsewhere? I was crazy. Stark starin' mad. I had to make myself find projects, do things to take my mind off not seein' him."

"That's kinda the way I'm feelin' about Kevin. But you and Callum were together for years. Kevin and I have only known each other for a few weeks."

"Doesn't matter. When it's right, it's right."

And with that confirmation, Mitch rejoiced that Jian was approaching with their food. As he set the plates down, he said, "Now, you take the raw egg in the center—" There was indeed a raw egg in a half shell in the center of the pile of spaghetti. Mitch had never seen this before. "—and you dump it into the pasta, then stir it. The steam cooks the egg and makes the sauce much creamier. My favorite dish on the menu," he added as Brent and Mitch followed his instructions. Jian turned to the tray he'd left on a nearby table, and turned around with a block of cheese wrapped in a dish towel and a micro plane. "Fresh parm, guys?" Mitch declined, but Brent more than made up for his not having any of the Parmesan. Brent didn't give the all-clear signal until his pasta was covered with a half-inch of grated cheese. "Enjoy," Jian said as he left.

Almost inaudible through the mouthful he'd just stuffed into his mouth, Brent asked, "You don't like extra Parmigiana, paisano?"

Mitch laughed, having come much more alive now. "Been watchin' the Travel Channel a little too much lately?"

Brent flashed a smile. He knew what Callum saw in him. He'd noticed before, but Brent was glowing, enjoying the food, the banter, and especially, the aid he was offering. No wonder Callum loved Brent. They were two peas in a pod, two counselors in search of counselees, or whatever we lost souls in need are called.

"Never have liked parm a whole hell of a lot. I don't mind if it's part of the sauce, as long as it's not the dominant flavor, but extra? Not for me," Mitch said.

"So, whaddaya think? The Carbonara? Incredible, isn't it?"

"Pretty damn good. I'm glad you turned me on to it, Brent. I'll have to bring Kevin here when the buy one, get one isn't calling my name. He'd probably love this stuff."

They chatted about nothings—their high school years, Dr. Costner's change, what major Brent would be declaring—as they savored their lunch. At one point, Jian stopped by to ask how things were, and Mitch asked for some bread. Hot, crusty bread arrived, and both pulled off chunks to sop up the sauce pooling on their plates. With every noodle devoured, every drop wiped clean, they pushed their plates away and sighed.

The ever-lurking Jian appeared and picked up their plates. "How 'bout some dessert? Tiramisu? Gelato? Cannoli?"

Mitch looked at Brent. Brent looked at Mitch. There was no stopping them.

"Tiramisu, Jian. Brent?"

"Bring me the cannoli. How many on the plate?"

Mitch pointed at Brent and wagged his index finger. The classic naughty-naughty.

"One, but our cannoli are huge," said Jian.

Brent shook his head. "Make it two, Jian, m' man."

"Excellent. Coming right up." And Jian scurried away.

Two Carbonaras, a tiramisu, two cannoli, a cup of coffee—Jian was probably already computing his tip in his head. Mitch just hoped he had enough in his wallet to cough up a generous one. He felt guilty about thinking bad of the guy earlier.

Brent opened his iPad. He'd brought it in with him, and it had sat on the table the whole time they'd been eating.

"While we're waitin' for dessert, let me pull up the Force Four app."

Mitch drank the last dregs of the coffee Jian had refilled earlier. Then he waved his mug in Jian's direction, signaling for another refill. "You want coffee with your dessert?" he asked Brent as Jian made his way to the table.

"Nah. I'm good," Brent mumbled as he fiddled with his device.

As soon as Jian returned with the filled mug, set it down, and walked away, Brent thrust the device at Mitch. "Just push play."

Marlon Gordon. His head looked even bigger on this small screen. Mitch tapped the play button, and Gordon came to life.

"Just when hopes were high that the scourge of our city had taken a permanent vacation, the serial killer has struck again. A body was discovered in the city's gay enclave early this morning." Mitch saw a bar he recognized as Gordon stood in front of it. "Once again, police are in a quandary. The victim seems to fit the description of previous ones, except this latest one has brown eyes. The coroner's office tells us once again that identification will be difficult.

"An unnamed source, however, told Force Four News that this time the assailant's DNA may have been left at the scene. If this proves accurate, then the DNA can be run through a myriad of databases, and a match could be found.

"Interesting to note is the location of the body. It was found in an alley near the city's cluster of gay clubs. But that's not all. The alley is just around the corner from the building that houses Family Now.

"Here to comment on this development is Dr. Spencer Fellows, who, as you know, is the founder and leader of Family Now, an organization that strongly supports so-called traditional family values. Dr. Fellows, what is your take on this newest development? Do you think the perpetrator targeted a patron of one of the bars? Do you think his murder in such proximity to your offices is some sort of statement?"

The camera cut to Spencer Fellows. If Mitch hadn't already been revived by the food and caffeine, seeing his father would have certainly awakened him from his fog.

"Marlon, I think you're right in both cases. These sinners debauch in these dens of iniquity, drinking and doping, engaging in filthy, vile acts. And then, closing time comes, and they have nowhere else to continue their sin except to follow each other home. It stands to reason that this particular sinner could have followed God's warrior into the alleyway. If this alley was chosen on purpose, I say, 'Good for you, avenger. God will smile on you for bringing one more of these miscreants to justice while honoring family.'"

What did Mom ever see in you, you snake? She must have been in a very dark place indeed to hook up with the likes of you. But someday—someday, you'll get your comeuppance. I'll see to that. Mitch almost smiled at the thought, but he caught himself. He didn't want to have to explain to Brent.

Gordon's giant talking head came back. "Thank you, Dr. Fellows. In counterpoint, we have a comment from Hazina Graham, president of Campus Pride at the university. Zina?"

A beautiful young woman was presented, the background showing she was in the studio, rather than the on-the-street interview that Mitch's father had given.

"Marlon, I have to disagree with Dr. Fellows. He calls himself a Christian, and yet he condemns those of us who live good lives, try to follow Christ's teachings of 'love one another.' My predecessor at Campus Pride was a victim of this monster stalking our gay community, and Callum Slater was one of the finest human beings I've ever met. From when he was really young, he decided he would give counsel to our brothers and sisters. Well, truly to anybody in need, not just those in the LGBQT+ community. Our group, our university, our city, and the world lost a good, good man at the hands of this monster. We can only hope that our law enforcement officials can find him before he decimates our community—not just the gay community but the city's community, for each loss is a loss to this city—again. As for Dr. Fellows, I pray for him."

"Thank you, Ms. Graham," Gordon, back on screen, said. "This has been Marlon Gordon, Force Four News."

Mitch handed the iPad back to Brent. "Sad, sad. But that Graham woman sure told fa—" he caught himself "—Fellows, didn't she?" *That almost slip. What a shitstorm that would create with Brent.*

"Z's great. Beautiful and articulate. I told you she's trans. At least I think I did."

Mitch's eyes almost popped their sockets. "Really? You'd never know it by lookin'. She's gorgeous."

"Stunning, is how Callum always described her." Brent took a drink of water. "So, this is good news, huh?"

"I don't follow. Another murder is good news? How?"

"The DNA. The killer's never been that sloppy before."

"Yeah," Mitch nodded. "Could lead to somethin'. But don't get your hopes up, Brent. The guy's DNA might not even be in any data base. So we're not talking instant ID—maybe."

Brent's face fell. Then he smiled again, "I don't care. I'm gonna look at this positively. More and more, people're givin' up their DNA. Surely some database, somewhere, will show a match."

Mitch loved his optimism.

Jian brought the desserts. They ate them hungrily and joyfully. Then Jian brought the tab. Mitch reached for his wallet, but Brent held up his hand. "My treat. I just got my monthly stipend from my scholarship. I'm flush."

"Well, thank *you*, money bags. And leave a nice tip for m' boy Jian, if you would."

Brent laughed. "You got it."

Totally revived, Mitch insisted he could drive, so Brent took him back to his car.

He drove home and set about linking the new laptop to his printer. The process was easier than he'd expected, and a test run proved that everything was good to go. He was calling up his paper on the new laptop when there was a pounding on his door.

Startled and worried that a neighbor was in trouble, he rushed to the door and flung it open.

Kevin stood there. Disheveled. Frantic. Raggedy clothes. No glasses. Looked like he hadn't slept.

"I fucked up!" Kevin shouted, and burst into huge, heaving sobs.

Mitch pulled him into the room, walked him to the sofa, and eased him down.

"It's okay, Kev. Stop cryin'." But Kevin was far past comforting words. Mitch rushed to get a glass of water, like they always do on TV. He grabbed the box of Kleenex off the kitchen counter as he took the water to Kevin.

He sat beside him and held the glass to Kevin's lips. "Here, drink this." Kevin was so distraught that he acted like he didn't know what water was. Mitch tried and tried to push the glass to Kevin's lips. Kevin knocked the glass out of Mitch's hand, a violent move. The glass flew across the room, hit the wall, and shattered.

"Kev, talk to me." Mitch pulled him close to him. Kevin fought the embrace. He acted as if he were living on another plane of existence. Planet Chaos. Planet Despair.

"Kev. Baby. Whatever you did can't be all that bad. You're not capable. I know you. I love you."

Kevin's sobs lessened, but they didn't cease. *I'm worried about you, Kev. What'd you do to bring all this on?*

"Kevin, listen to me." Mitch put his forehead on Kevin's. Spoke quietly. Gently. "Nothin' you did can't be fixed." He held his lips to Kevin's forehead. Then he released them. An angel's kiss.

Kevin sucked air like he was a swimmer who'd almost drowned. Fifteen seconds or more of this rough inhaling. At last, his sobs stopped.

Mitch didn't push it. He gave Kevin time to process. He'd talk eventually. When he felt safe.

A small, still voice. "You weren't there for me. I called. It kept goin' to voicemail. I texted. You ignored me."

With the kindest, most caressing tone he could muster, Mitch said, "Kev, I told you my phone wouldn't be on. I was doin' my paper, remember?"

What a shit I am. I put my needs above his. If I'd only known he was somehow in trouble. I could have at least checked messages. And then Mitch switched from beating himself up to thinking of Kevin again. *Just what trouble did he get into?*

"Kev, you said you fucked up. Tell me how."

A long, long pause. Kevin stared into his hands. Then he looked into Mitch's eyes.

"I went to a bar last night. Met a guy. Hooked up."

Shit—he's bludgeoning himself because he had sex with another guy? That happens. Especially when your potential lover won't commit. Like me.

"'S okay, Kevin. I don't blame ya if you slept with another guy."

"That's just it. I didn't." Another pause. Another sigh. "I needed you. I was pissed at you for not pickin' up. I wanted to punish you. So I went to The Rotor and I saw this guy. We started talking, and come last call, he asked if I wanted to see his place. We both know what that's code for. So I left with him. But I didn't sleep with him."

Mitch continued with his calm, soothing tone. "That's good. You had a choice to make, and you chose wisely. Proves your growin' up, Kevin." Mitch took Kevin's face in his and kissed him. He felt new tears fall on Kevin's cheeks.

Mitch pulled a tissue from the box and dabbed at Kevin's cheeks. "Here, dry those tears. You showed great judgment last night. I'm proud of ya. I really, really am. But why do ya look like ya slept in your clothes? And where are your glasses?"

"Left 'em at home. I dressed like the old me because I thought I'd be more appealin' to the younger guys. Somehow I convinced myself it wasn't cheatin' if it was someone my age, but someone older was, like, betrayin' you. I know, I know—any cheatin' was a betrayal, but I wasn't thinkin' straight." He wiped the new tears that came with the back of his hand.

"Look, Kev, I'm sorry. Really, really sorry. I would never ever want to cause you this pain. But come on, is there somethin' you're not telling me? I promise I won't be mad. You knew I was holed up with my paper. You said you were cool with it. So did somethin' set this off besides that?"

"I don't wanna talk about it."

"Babe, you *have* to talk about it."

"Well, I went home after seein' Les at the Cup. I thought I'd go for a run—yes, I sometimes run to clear my head, but this time I wanted to run because I could think of you the whole time. Anyway, while I was gettin' ready, I turned on the TV. I hate the silence in our house. Well, who should be on the news but my loving mother."

So, the way you said that tells me that your mother is a big part of this meltdown.

"Doris, that's dear ol' mom, was layin' out her newest plan to stay away from me. She's startin' some shit about helping kids in Africa. She can't even come home long enough to share a cup of coffee with her own son, but she c'n raise money and fly halfway 'round the world to take on a buncha children who the day before never even knew she existed. She's *my* mother, not theirs. She's supposed to love me." And the sobbing started again.

Mitch let it play out. *There had to be more to this. Kevin's disappointed in his mother, but he's spent a lot of years gettin' used to her absences. He's told me all about her neglect.*

"I know it hurts, Kev, but that's the way she is. You made that abundantly clear. Tied to her job. If that job takes her to Africa, she'll charter a plane ASAP."

Kevin reached for another tissue. "Yeah, I know. I really didn't get all that worked up over her provin' once again she doesn't care about me. It was him."

Him? The guy in the bar? Some other him?

Mitch's answer came instantly.

"Sloan. I'd no sooner switched off the tube than he came into my room, yellin' and screamin'."

"What about?"

"Some charge on his precious platinum card. I can charge a zillion dollars a month without a word from him, but he sees this one item, and he goes ballistic."

"What'd ya charge? And for how much?"

Mitch was having a hard time believing Sloan Howell could get worked up over any amount.

"Doesn't matter. He didn't like it, and he burst into my room to ream me out about it. He's such a pretender. I gave him lip, which pissed him off. And then suddenly, he was Mr. Good-Father. He tried to reason with me. Spread unadulterated grade-A cow manure. 'I've loved you since the first time I saw you, little man.' Or something like that. 'I tried to tell your mother she shouldn't do this new project. I wanted her to spend more time with you and Mark.' Like hell he did. 'I'm proud of you. You've really matured in the last few weeks.' Okay, I'll give him that. But he wanted to take the credit for it, and I did it all for you. That asshole doesn't have a clue that I found you, Mitch. He doesn't know how happy I am with you. And he thinks when he says 'I love you' that I'll buy his lie. I admit he talks a good game. Anyone else would have bought his supercilious smile, his smarmy 'let's schedule a regular dinner, once a week, just you and me' shit. Fuckwad. You know what really set me off? The last thing he said ended with the most fraudulent, filthiest term he could have come up with. He called me 'son.' I'm not his son, and I never will be. Sons love their fathers. Fathers love their sons. And Sloan Howell? He's incapable of love."

And now it comes out. Poor Kevin. He's so torn apart. Beggin' for love and never getting it. Words are words. Things are things. Sloan doesn't understand you can't buy love. You can't pay homage to the concept. You've got to show it. And sometime, long ago, he and Kevin's mother quit showin' it. Or maybe they never even started. His own mother came into his thoughts, and Mitch felt warm all over. *Mom may have had her faults. Her youthful indiscretion may have saddled me with a father far worse than Sloan Howell, but oh, how Mother loved me.*

He cradled Kevin in his arms, the way his own mother had cradled him so many times.

"I love you, baby, I love you, baby, I love you, baby." Mitch spoke his mother's mantra over and over.

He sat there, Kevin in his arms, cooing over him. Afternoon turned into night. Night turned into morning light.

Mitch felt like Kevin's savior.

Kevin

"Wake up, sleepy head." Kevin heard Mitch's soft, sweet voice and felt the nudge at his shoulder. He opened his eyes a slit to see Mitch hovering over him with a coffee mug. Seeing the steam rising from the mug, Kevin pulled himself upright and took the coffee, craving the reviving brew.

Mitch sat on the sofa beside him, taking his own cup he'd put on the coffee table. "You were dead to the world, babe."

Yawning, Kevin asked, "What time is it?"

"Nine. I let you sleep in. I figured ya needed your rest. Like you got any rest on this resale relic of a couch. But I had the gift of holdin' you in my arms the entire night." Mitch closed in and kissed Kevin on the nose. Then he laughed as he set his cup down and massaged his shoulder. "How can you have joy and pain, all at the same time? You feel any better, babe?"

Kevin took a sip of coffee. "Yeah. Sorry t' be such a pain."

"Now, now, now," Mitch said. "Stop talkin' like that. A little stiff shoulder is a tiny price to pay if I brought you out of whatever funk you were in last night."

"A mess, wudn't I?"

"You sure were. I'm just happy you're better now. Makes me feel good."

"Did you really mean it? That you love me?" He looked achingly searching for his answer.

"Yeah."

A grin burst out on his face.

"Good." Then the grin left. "Because somebody needs to."

Mitch instantly reacted. "Now don't go into all that. Just know I'm here for ya." And he kissed Kevin again, this time on the lips.

They sat without speaking, drinking their coffee. Eventually, measured words came from Mitch. "So, babe, what'd you do between the time you left that bar and the time ya showed up here?"

Kevin stared at him. Not replying to his question.

"You don't have to tell me," Mitch told him. "It's okay if ya don't wanna talk about it."

"'S not that." Kevin put the mug to his lips again and sucked a tiny draft of the scalding drink. "I just don't want ya to think I'm psycho."

"I could never think that, Kev." He placed his arm on Kevin's. It gave Kevin courage.

"So," Kevin began. "I left the bar, trailing after that guy. I knew I didn't wanna fuck 'im, but I was kinda on autopilot, thoughts of my mother and of Sloan drownin' me. I wanted the voices t' stop, stop, stop. I tried callin' you. The guy saw me on the phone and was pissed. 'What? You lookin' for sumpin' better?' He scared me. I said I wasn't, and since we were right by my car, the key fob in my pocket unlocked it. I got in and quickly relocked the door. The guy pounded on the window, screaming, 'You shit, you shit, you shit' over and over.

"Believe you me I got outta there as fast as I could drive. My adrenaline was pumpin', having just almost gotten myself into a situation that coulda led to who knows what—"

"Babe! My heart's racin' just listenin' to ya. What if that guy was the serial killer? Oh my God, I don't know what I'd do if I lost ya, Kev."

Kevin flashed a smile that he hoped showed devotion and love.

"Well, you weren't pickin' up—and yes, I know why. Knew then, but I wudn't bein' rational—and I didn't wanna go home because at that hour, my mom might finally be getting home from the office for her nightly nap, or Sloan might be waitin' up for me. I didn't wanna deal with either of them. Running on empty emotionally, I just drove. I was way on the edge of town before I decided to stop at a flea-bag motel in my headlights. I figured I could sleep some—if my mind and heart stopped racin'—and shower. I had these clothes in the bag of shit I was plannin' to take to Goodwill. I knew they'd look like I'd slept in 'em after being wadded up for a week in the trunk of my car, but they were clean, and I could feel whole again, I hoped.

"I slipped under the covers about four, couldn't stop my thoughts, felt very, very sorry for myself because you weren't pickin' up my calls or answerin' my texts, so finally, I got up, showered, and dressed. I looked like shit warmed over to the fourth power. And I didn't care.

"So, there I was, six a.m., in the motel room from hell, wonderin' what I was gonna do with myself. I thought I could just keep drivin'. But I knew if I didn't show up for a couple of days, Sloan would cut me off, call AmEx and cancel his card. By then, I was reconciled to the fact you really were incommunicado, like you said you'd be—and I really, truly didn't wanna disturb you. So what could I do? I went to school, pretendin' like my life was normal as the proverbial blueberry pie.

"I was officially in-fucking-attendance. But I wudn't there. I couldn't tell you a word that was said in a single class or who was sayin' those words I wasn't hearin'. There coulda been a crazed shooter armed with an AR-15 stormin' the school, and I wouldna noticed. By the end of the school day, I knew I should just go home, get some rest, and live to face another day.

"But I wanted to see you. I *had* to see you. At that point, I didn't give a shit that my mother didn't love me or that Sloan was an asshole. I just kept thinkin' how I'd almost cheated on you, and that destroyed me. So, incommunicado or not, I came straight here when I left school."

Kevin inhaled, a long, deep, endless breath that spoke volumes, he hoped. He knew he was spent. He was through with it all. He didn't care about Sloan. He didn't care about his mother. He only knew he cared about Mitch.

"Quite a nightmare. I'm ecstatic you're okay, that you're processin' all that's happened with your folks, but most of all, that you came. Babe, I was jonesin' for a Kevin fix, and as much as you scared me last night, I felt so good just holdin' you all night and spillin' out my love to ya."

Kevin laughed, a tiny, loving laugh, not a big guffaw. "Tell me you didn't hold my heavy butt all night long."

"Well, not your butt, but I did have you in my arms. I told you I have the sore shoulder to prove it. There was no way I was gonna let you get away until I knew you were okay. I only pulled away a couple of hours ago because I had to print my paper. If I don't get that turned in this mornin', my ass is grass."

Kevin laughed at that. *You love me, Mitch. Nobody else. But you do. And that's all I need.*

Mitch pulled his phone from his jeans. "Half past nine. M' class starts at ten. I really do have to go. I feel like I'm desertin' ya once again, but babe, you know I wouldn't cut outta here if I didn't have to."

"I know. I know. You go."

"So, what ya gonna do? Ya c'n stay here and wait if ya want."

Kevin surveyed Mitch's apartment.

"Know what I think?" Mitch said. "I think ya need to go home. Your parents'll be at work. Mark'll be at school. You'll have the whole place to yourself. Ya can clean up. Peel those contacts off your eyes. They must be plastered to *tus ojos* by now. Not good to leave them in so long." *So he just assumed I was wearing contacts? That's good, I suppose.* "And, all bubblebathed and powdered, you can slip under those fancy sheets of yours and get a much needed rest. What say?"

"I think you're right." *Except about the contacts. Since I don't have any on.* "But I want to see you this evening."

"I'm yours, babe."

Mitch left. Kevin left.

Kevin's house was quiet as a tomb. Always at least one servant somewhere, but they never made a sound. Never reported anything about him to Step. Always kept an eye on Mark when Kevin wasn't there. Strange life he led in this mausoleum. The silence normally bothered him, but it was comforting then. He did, indeed, take a bubble bath, something he hadn't done since he was a kid. And after a long, soothing soak, he dried off and slid under the 1200 thread count Egyptian cotton sheets. He feared his mind would start its roller coaster again, but he slept the sleep of the dead.

When he awoke, it was approaching five. He thought about the amazing slumber he'd just experienced. *It's all about Mitch. He loves me. I will never have another problem with Mitch at my side. My life will be peaches and cream. Whatever that means.*

Kevin sat up in bed, reached to the drawer beside it. He smoked a leisurely joint. He luxuriated in the fragrant smoke. Then a twinge of guilt overtook him. *Why'm I doin' this? I just told myself that Mitch is enough. But I guess old habits die hard.*

Tamping out the burning fatty long before it became the roach he usually left, he reached for his phone. Two texts: 5:45, the cup. 6:30, the cup.

He quickly Febreezed his room. Then he pulled a brand new shirt and jeans from Abercrombie out of his closet. Slipped them on. Slid on new loafers. Stood in front of the bathroom mirror as he used his fingers to tousle his hair into that of a perfect GQ model. Then he put on his glasses. He was ready for the love of his life. Later. But first, Les.

In the Spyder, he got an answering text. It was Les. Got your text, bro. 5:45 on the dot.

Good. Les needs to know how much in love I am.

When he pulled the car into the Cup's parking lot, his phone pinged again. Mitch: Be there.

Two words. Seven letters. Seven's a holy number. It's a sign.

"Spill, bro. You cut today. Whazzup?" Les said as Kevin sat with his coffee. Les had seen him come in and waved, but this was the start of their conversation.

"I'm in love."

"You're fulla shit, guy. Like I didn't already know that. Tell me somethin'. Somethin' new, this time."

"Les, you can't really be in love unless you get it back. Mitch is in love with me."

"And you know that how?"

"He told me."

"When? When you were locked in an embrace doing the nasty in his bed all day today?" Les laughed like he'd made the best joke ever.

"Cut it out, Les. We don't have to have sex. That'll come. But right now, I know Mitch loves me." The warmth of Kevin's smile felt like it started in his toes and moved all the way to the top of his head.

"So, no change. Still no booty calls. Still no pokey, pokey. Doesn't sound like love to me, bro."

"You don't know what love is, obviously. You're stuck in a give and take relationship—you give, she takes. And you haven't realized there's something better in the world."

"You gettin' all phi-lo-soph-i-cal with me, man?"

Kevin didn't like the way Les drew that word out. Like he was mocking him. Kevin neither liked nor stood for being mocked. "Damn, Les. Are you listenin' to me, or is your skull so thick you can't hear what I'm sayin', let alone understand it?"

"I didn't come here to be yelled at, bro. I c'n get that at home. Hell, I get plenty of that from my woman."

Kevin looked at his best friend. *Maybe he's too immature to understand. That's okay. Les is my best friend, and I just need to accept he needs to mature a little bit more. He's not as smart as I am. How can I expect him to understand? Especially since he hasn't walked in my shoes the last two days.*

"Les, I love ya, man." He smiled. Les returned the look with a smirk. "Not in the same way I love Mitch or the same way Mitch loves me, but you're my bestie, as the girls at school say. I don't like us fightin'. Agree to disagree?" He stuck out his hand. Les shook it.

Then the inevitable ping on Les's phone rang out. "Gotta go, gotta go, gotta go." Les jumped up and exited stage left.

Kevin shook his head, and under his breath, so Les couldn't possibly hear, he said, "So pussy whipped."

He drank his coffee and thought of Mitch. That's all he thought of. *He loves me. My Mitch.*

Drinking the hot coffee and staring out to the parking lot, willing Mitch to get there earlier than the appointed time, Kevin's own phone pinged.

He lifted the phone from where he'd put it face down on the table. "Crap! A text from Sloan." He read the text. Missed seeing you the last couple of days. Booked us a table at the club for Tuesday. 7 ok? I can change it if not. Looking forward to it.

Kevin plunged into the depths. *Did he really mean it? Did he truly think we can make it through a whole dinner without one of us bludgeoning the other? In a public place?*

While he stared at the words, trying to absorb what they truly meant for him, he felt lips graze the top of his hair. Then Mitch sat next to him. "Sorry I'm late. Brent called, and when I saw his name on my caller ID, I sat in the car to talk a moment."

Brent? What's that all about? "Mitch, if you're holdin' out on me, I swear to God—"

Mitch stopped him with a kiss. A kiss that thrust him back into his earlier great mood.

"I promise, Kev, Brent and I are friends, just friends. He has a project I'm helpin' him with. That's all."

"What kind of project?"

"It has to do with Callum. Remember? Callum was a great, great guy, and Brent is plannin' something that will honor him."

"I could help."

"You've got enough on your plate right now. Did ya have a good rest? Did ya see your mom? Sloan?"

"Yes, no, and no. But I did get a text just now from Step—I mean, Sloan."

"And?"

"Everything we talked about last night is kinda hazy, but I think I told you his bull hockey about having dinner with me once a week? So—my dear stepdad wudn't kiddin'. He's made a reservation and everything. Damn him."

"Kev, this could be a good thing. I still believe that Sloan cares about you. Maybe you could give him a chance." Mitch said all this with his hand on Kevin's arm.

Feeling the warmth of Mitch's clutch, Kevin said, "Why don't you come with? I want Sloan to meet ya. If he saw that I'm in love with someone like you, he might finally accept me as a gay man. Please?"

"I can't come, Kev. You said Sloan made it clear he wanted alone time with you. And besides, a third person would just add to the check. I eat like Bigfoot, ya know." Mitch beat his chest. "Me hungry. Bigfoot no like berries. Need steak. Need chops. Need prime rib."

Kevin laughed at him. When he stopped, he said, "Mitch, this is Sloan Howell, ya know. A third dinner guest? It's not like he'll have to wash dishes afterward in the kitchen to cover the tab. Besides, that sense of humor you've got? Exactly one of the things I want Sloan to see."

With a wary voice, Mitch said, "Well, okay. But only if you clear it with Sloan ahead of time."

"He won't care. I guarantee it."

"And where *is* this reservation?" Mitch inquired.

Kevin replied with a British society matron's voice, "At the club. Where else would we dine?" Then he dropped the accent. "You don't expect Sloan Howell to eat ribs and potato salad at some beer joint, do you?"

"Kev, you got five days to change your evil ways."

Kevin started to protest.

Mitch added, his voice all smiles, "I mean it. If I'm gonna join you two, I refuse to slather my prime rib with animosity sauce. I prefer horseradish." And, for the third time in this very public place, Mitch kissed Kevin.

"You got it, boss."

Kevin started looking forward to the dinner date. After all, with Mitch there, Sloan would be on his best behavior.

Mitch had asked what he should wear. Kevin offered to take him out and buy him a new suit, but Mitch refused. He said his old one would be fine. He added, "Especially if the lighting is dim. The rich bitches won't notice the threadbare sleeves." And he cackled.

With Mitch refusing his offer, Kevin decided he would buy him a new dress shirt and tie. The man he loved would not refuse a nice gift.

Saturday morning, he drove to J. Corden. Myron greeted him at the door. "How was your interview, sir?"

Kevin didn't want to engage in fictitious banter, but he was impressed that Myron remembered him. He ignored the question.

"Need a shirt and tie. Present for a friend."

And Myron helped him select the shirt and tie he presented to Mitch that evening.

"Kevinnnnn," Mitch drew his name out. "I told you."

"It's a shirt, it's a tie. A fraction of the cost a suit would have set Sloan back. Take it in the spirit in which it's given, babe. I love spreadin' Sloan's largesse around."

"I bet you do." He sighed. "I guess I can't expect ya to change totally overnight. You've had too many years spendin' that largesse of which you speak. Next time, though, no gifts unless you yourself earned the money to buy 'em. Clear?"

Kevin nodded.

"That bein' said," Mitch continued as he took the items from the J. Corden bag, "thank you, thank you, thank you, babe. These'll look great with my tired ol' raggedy suit, plus the pale color of this shirt will bring the focus away from that mess I made when I dropped food the last time I wore it. It's barely noticeable—a tiny spot on the pants—but I know it's there."

"All the more reason we shoulda bought ya a new suit to go with the shirt and tie. There's still time," Kevin answered.

I want Sloan to like Mitch, and I know Sloan. He's impressed with things.

"No way. My suit'll be fine. But the shirt and tie? They're great. Thank you again, Kev. And thank Sloan for me."

"I will."

Tuesday evening arrived, and Kevin decked himself out in the Zegna. He hadn't worn it since his big confab with Fellows.

He parked the Spyder and went to Mitch's door.

I wish I could have brought him a boutonniere, just to prove this is an important, realer-than-real date, but I guess that would have been a bit much.

When Mitch opened the door, in unison they said, "Damn! You clean up good!"

Kevin laughed. "Great minds, huh?"

They hugged.

Then they headed to the car.

Kevin spent the drive to the club spouting inanities, hoping to put Mitch at ease. After all, Mitch might blow his stack if he figured out Sloan had no idea Mitch was joining them.

He pulled up to the gate. Lowered his car window.

A guard said, "Kevin. Haven't seen you in ages."

"Life gets in the way, Samir. You seen m' dad?"

"Yeah, he was on the golf course this afternoon. You meetin' him for chow?"

"You better believe it. It's been too long since I had that prime rib."

"Well, he's probably waitin' for ya."

"Thanks, Samir."

As Kevin drove through and left the car with the valet in front, Mitch tugged at his sleeve. "I'm proud of ya."

Kevin squinched his eyes.

"You called Sloan your dad when you were talkin with that Samir guy."

"Oh, that," Kevin said. "Sloan wants me to do that, and I figured I didn't need to start the evenin' off on a sour note, pissin' off the guard of all people. Samir's big on family. He needs t' be. His parents, his wife, and his six kids all live together. A cultural thing, I guess."

"Well, I'm proud of you even more. Thinkin' of some guy who works a gate and bein' s' nice to him." He pecked Kevin on the lips. "'No kissing in the front drive' is not in the club bylaws, is it?"

"Probably is. But I don't care." He took Mitch's hand, and together they entered the double doors of the huge colonial-style mansion.

They turned right, with club minions nodding at Kevin about every six feet, and they soon reached the maître' d.

"Good to see you, Kevin. Your father is already at the table with his pre-dinner libation. I didn't realize you were bringing a guest."

"Is that a problem, Mario?"

"Certainly not. We'll simply set another place at the table."

Mario walked Kevin and Mitch toward a table very near the center of the room.

Good. Out in the open. Sloan won't even think of making a scene here.

They were about halfway there when Sloan stood up.

I hope Mitch doesn't read something into that look on Sloan's face.

Mitch whispered in Kevin's ear. "You didn't tell 'im I was comin', and he dudn't look happy."

"I texted him." Then a pause. "Or maybe I forgot."

Mitch surreptitiously swatted Kevin on the bottom.

As Sloan walked toward them, a waiter quickly set another place setting.

Sloan immediately held out his hand for Mitch to shake, saying, "Sloan Howell. And you are?"

Well, he's pissed, but he's hiding it well. Not a trace of anger in the somewhat combative greeting.

Kevin plunged ahead before Mitch could speak. "This is my *friend* Mitch, Sloan." He punched the word friend, and the look on Sloan's face left no doubt what Kevin meant.

Mitch shook Sloan's hand and said, "Good to meet you, Mr. Howell."

Kevin saw a calm come over his stepfather.

I knew Mitch would win him over. I didn't expect it so soon, but I knew it would happen.

"Now Mitch, it's Sloan. And it's good to meet you too." He looked at Kevin. His eyes were filled with approval. "You guys hungry?"

"Better believe it, Sloan," Mitch said. And Kevin, expecting tension from both men, sat, feeling relieved.

"Sit, sit, Mitch. Drinks?"

"Sorry, Sloan. The government doesn't approve."

Sloan chuckled. "Well, you look older, my man. Wouldn't have guessed it."

"Thanks. I guess my mother called me little man so much when I was younger that I started believing her early on." Mitch laughed and Sloan joined in.

"So, Kevin, I like this man."

"Thanks, Sloan,"—*what the hell, throw him a bone—* "er, dad."

Mitch stared at Kevin like he'd just found the Holy Grail.

And the look on Sloan's face was priceless.

Bet you didn't expect that, huh, Step?

But Kevin's thoughts didn't bring him as much joy as he thought they would. Sloan was being very genuine with Mitch. He seemed to actually like him.

What's not to like? Could it be that Mitch is right about Sloan?

Soon a waiter came to the table. Decked out in a full tuxedo. "Drinks, gentleman?"

Sloan held up his glass. "Another Macallan, neat, of course, Petrov."

"Most certainly, Mr. Howell. And the gentlemen?"

Kevin said, "Coke. Rocks." He smirked at Mitch.

Mitch said, "I was wondering if they even served that here. Thanks for piping up, ba—er, Kevin."

"Two Coca Colas with ice." And Petrov, the penguin, waddled away.

"Okay, that confirms it." Sloan, too, had a smirk on his face, but it wasn't a hostile one. "I thought I caught Kevin's drift when he introduced you, Mitch, but your slip of the tongue just now was classically Freudian. You two are a couple? Am I right?"

Oh, shit. Is this question a good thing or a bad thing?

Kevin stared at Sloan, trying to decipher.

"You hit the nail on the head, Sloan," Mitch confidently answered.

"Well, if you're taking my son away from me, I'd better interview you. I made up a list of questions long ago that I keep in my breast pocket. Let me get those out." He reached inside his jacket. Then he looked at Kevin, holding up his empty hand. "Gotcha." He turned his attention back to Mitch. "I don't have no stinkin' questions, Meech." Sloan was affecting a very bad, stereotypical Netflix-style south-of-the-border drug lord characterization. Then he got serious in tone. "But I have to ask. What's your profession?"

What? An ordinary laborer is not good enough for your little Kevin?

"Sloan, be easy on Mitch. He's not used to you yet."

Maybe that will put him on his best behavior.

"I'm being easy. I do have a right to know something about this fine young man you've just thrust upon me without warning."

So now the real Sloan comes out.

Mitch turned to Kevin. "Kev, it's only right that your dad knows a little about the man who loves you."

That was bold. And I love you for it.

Mitch continued. "I grew up an only child. My father was out of the picture. My mother had what she called a 'youthful indiscretion' that produced me. She never treated me like I was anything but royalty, her little prince. She somehow managed to provide for us with meager means. She was very good with money. I found out later she amassed not a fortune, but enough to put me through college, pay my rent, and provide what I needed. I adored her to the day she died. No—I still adore her. Anyway, I'm a freshman at the university. I haven't declared a major, but I'm leaning toward counseling. I know I'll need at least a master's degree, but I plan to take it all the way through to Doctorate."

Kevin's eyes widened. He had no idea of Mitch's master plan he'd just laid out.

Sloan looked pleased. "Very honorable profession, Mitch. What drew you to it, if I may ask?"

"A friend's partner died recently. I never met the guy, and I only met his partner following a memorial service on campus. This guy Brent and I have become pretty good friends, and I've tried to help him through his grief. Well, it seems his slain lover had the understanding of a wise old man and a knack for counseling from a very early age. Brent tells me tidbits of the good things Callum did in his short life, of how many people he helped, and I've kind of thought that I like helping people, I enjoy listening, and I would like to honor Callum by following in his footsteps."

Sloan leaned forward in his chair. "Callum? Slain? Are we talking about one of the serial killer's victims?"

"That's right. Callum Slater."

"Horrible things, those murders. I don't mind telling you that I worried so much about Kevin here. Not more than a month ago, I feared he was going down the wrong path. My son has a mind that won't quit, but sometimes, he forgets to use it. I was so afraid he might get himself into a situation he couldn't talk himself out of. But you know what I've seen in recent weeks?"

"No, Sloan," Mitch said. "What?"

"Kevin has matured almost overnight. He changed. He's looking like he cares about his appearance. He's got a sensible haircut. And, except for one transgression we won't get into, he seems to be joining the adult world. His choice of partner tells me that."

"Thank you, Sloan." Mitch blushed.

"Mitch is the reason for all that, you know. He's been tellin' me I need t' grow up, and I been tryin'." Kevin thought he sounded like a seventh grader, but this was something he wanted Sloan to know.

"Well, thank you, Mitch. You're doing a great job on my kid here. Now, what shall we order?" Sloan pulled out his reading glasses and perched them on his nose.

Mitch looked at Kevin, looked back at Sloan, looked again at Kevin, then looked back at Sloan. One final look later, he made eyeglasses with his fingers curled together in front of his eyes. Sloan saw none of this. Kevin pointed at his own glasses and nodded. Mitch smiled.

"Oh, hell," Sloan said, putting the menu down and removing his glasses. "I don't know why I look at this menu. I always get the prime rib. Three King Cuts? Medium rare?" He looked at the boys.

Kevin nodded.

Mitch nodded vigorously and beat his chest. "Mitch want meat. Mitch hungry."

Kevin smiled, and hearing Sloan's laugh made him fall in love with Mitch even more.

Brent

"I wanna know everything. Start talkin', guy." Mitch had agreed to join him after Brent's morning class.

They were in the Union building cafeteria, having lunch. Wednesdays were pork chop days, and Mitch loved them. And they were cheap.

He cut into one of the two delicious chops the steam table lady had put on his plate, liberated a piece from the rest, popped it into his mouth, and chewed. Mitch's eyes rolled heavenward. "Food for the gods," he exclaimed.

Brent followed all this and wanted to slap him. He knew he was playing him. They'd got closer, and Brent figured out Mitch's weird sense of humor. He reached over and pulled Mitch's hands away from his plate. "I'm about to murder you, guy. Did Kevin's stepdad like you? Did he walk out? Did he deck you in the middle of the River Glen F-ing Country Club for even thinking you could date his son? Come on, guy, spill."

Mitch laughed at him. He made a grand gesture. "All of the above."

Brent was about to take a bite of his own pork chop, and that response stopped him cold, bite in midair.

"Eat your lunch, Brent. I'm just funnin' ya."

Relieved, Brent put the bite in his mouth and chewed.

"Brent, it was great. Kevin was pretty much on his best behavior. He hadn't told Sloan I was comin' with him, but Sloan took it well. Sloan—"

"Wait a minute. You were an interloper? A tag along? The dreaded uninvited guest?"

"Yep."

"What was Kevin thinkin'?"

"I think he was so rattled at the thought of havin' dinner with his stepfather—this is a screwed up family who never gathers in their largely unused, over decorated dining room for a sit down meal—that he had to have me there for courage or backup or whatever and, despite my makin' 'im promise to tell Sloan ahead of time, he couldn't bring himself to do it. I didn't mind. Really, I didn't."

"Gotta hand it to you, Mitch. You're a very understanding and considerate boyfriend."

"Callum."

"Huh?"

Mitch smiled wickedly. "Oh, doesn't work when I do it, huh?" Brent still didn't understand. "I don't know how many times I've said something to you or asked you a question, and trippin' from your tongue's that one word—Callum."

"So? You know how much he meant—means—to me."

"Well, you've talked so much about him that you've got me performin' your little trick. Callum had so much understanding, so much compassion. And all your tales of him are so vivid that he's rubbed off on me. So to answer your question, I seem to be seein' people, especially Kevin, in a different light. I did tell you I was declarin' a psychology major?"

Brent thought he hadn't heard right. "Run that by me again?"

Mitch laughed. "How far back do I need to go?"

"Just the declaring part."

"It's true. Dealin' with Kevin's angst, workin' together with you, hearin' 'bout Callum, I realized there aren't enough good counselors in the world, and I seem t' have a knack for it. So that's the course I'm a chartin', matey."

"Callum's smilin' in Heaven. Proud of you Mitch. And I'll be supportin' ya all along the way." Brent scooped some sweet potato onto his fork and gobbled it up. "But please, you're killin' me. Tell me more about last night."

"So, Sloan Howell is an, how do I put it, *elegant* man. Kevin wore a suit that had to have cost at least a coupla thou, and Howell's duds left Kevin in the dust. Meanwhile, there I was in my high school graduation suit from J.C. Penney, a bit worse for wear. But I digress. Sloan was impeccably clothed, carried himself like he owned the world he inhabited, and was articulate and seemed to really care about, dare I use the word *love*, Kevin."

"The rich clothes part I expected. The love part doesn't jibe with what you've said Kevin has told you about him."

Mitch finished one pork chop and started on the other.

"That's just the thing. I told Kevin he was judgin' his stepdad too harshly. I went there last night fearin' Kevin had assessed Sloan correctly but hopin' *I* was right. I didn't expect Sloan, however, to be so forthcomin'. The man really does love Kevin. He proved it in his words and the looks he gave him. Speaking of, funny thing—Sloan pulled out his readin' glasses to look at the menu. The frames? The exact ones Kevin wears. Unless Sloan Howell stood over Kevin at the opticians, and that sorta thing dudn't seem to be in his DNA, then Kevin picked out those frames on his own. Despite all Kev's diatribes against Step, as he used to call Sloan, he had to feel somethin' good about the man if he wanted to look like 'im."

"Yeah, that says a lot."

"Certainly does, Brent. Back to the royal occasion. Sloan seemed t' warm up t' me as quickly as I warmed up t' him. And Kevin sat baskin' in it all. I was so happy for him. Sloan approves of my degree choice, and when I mentioned Callum and the way he died, Sloan expressed how worried he'd been for Kevin with a serial killer on the loose. Then he told of how happy he was that Kevin seemed to be maturin'. Kevin told Sloan I was the reason for it, and Sloan bestowed his greatest accolade. He was pleased, indeed, that I'd helped his son. All in all, it was a great night. And the prime rib. Oh my God, it melted in my mouth. We each had the sixteen-ounce cut, and if it wouldna made me look like a pig, I coulda rocked another order!"

"You never cease to amaze me," Brent said, laughing uproariously. "One minute you're sober as a judge, the next minute you're bringin' the house down. I'm happy we found each other. You're a good man to have around, Mitch. Especially right now."

"Now, now, now. Let's keep it light here. No need for—"

"Don't worry. I'm not goin' into an *I miss Callum* funk. I do miss 'im, but his death brought me you, and you make me laugh."

"Okay. Good. Cool. Glad I can help. Anytime. Just call out—" and Mitch began singing "You've Got a Friend." Brent knew the Carole King song, and he knew it was actually written by James Taylor. And that Carole King and Taylor were friends. For some twisted reason, Callum knew that bit of ancient history.

"Quit your caterwaulin'. I get it. I've got a friend." Brent almost had to shout because Mitch was singing at the top of his lungs, and others in the dining hall had joined in. Brent, at first, was embarrassed, but it didn't take long for him to join in on the fun.

The song finished, the cafeteria ladies applauded, and the diners returned to their meals. Mitch said, "I'm thinkin' it's time you met Kevin. I know you already met him at the funeral, but that was weeks ago, and you two really didn't talk. You certainly didn't get to know each other."

"You've told me s' much about his incredible and rapid transformation, I been wonderin' when you'd offer me a sit down with him."

"True confessions, Brent. I feel a little guilty. Kev knows I've been spendin' time with you. I keep puttin' him off when he asks why. I don't want 'im t' worry. If we, you and I, uncover who this monster is, things could get dicey. Kevin doesn't need to add worryin' 'bout me to his already full list of angst. He's finally comin' to some understandings about his family, and I want him focused on that, not all het up about how I could confront some maniac and get beat to a bloody pulp. I know that won't happen. You and I, so far, have been cautious. If—when—we solve the puzzle, we'll take our findings to the police, not go on some vigilante style hunt. We're safe. But Kevin may not think so. So I haven't told him anything about what we're doin', only that I'm helpin' you with a project. For all he knows, it might be a presentation for Dr. Costner's class."

"I think you're wise, Mitch. Very wise to keep him in the dark."

"But I do want 'im t' meet you, get to know ya. I think he and I may be together a very long time. Maybe a lifetime. I hope a lifetime. And I never want to lose you as a friend. So it's high time you two got to know each other. I'm not talkin' the three of us movin' in together and livin' happily ever after. No, I'm thinking more like coffee at the Cup. This afternoon? Say fourish?"

"Sounds like a plan."

"Great. I'll text Kev. He's there just about every day, so he'll be cool with the idea. You might even get to meet the infamous Les."

"Whoo-hoo. How you've described him made me think he was mythical."

"Oh, he's real, Brent, very real. Now, let's finish up because I got my eye on a piece of that cherry pie over there." Mitch tossed his head in the direction of the dessert section of the cafeteria line.

"I've been sittin' here in a deep dark dire depression, fearin' you would not mention pie."

"Listen to you with your oh so literary allusion. Did I hear alliteration fit for a king, there?"

They both laughed at Mitch's joke.

With lunch, topped off with luscious cherry pie with a marshmallow cream crown, completed, Brent said, "Well, unlike you, m' friend, I have another class to flit off to. *Ciao!*"

Brent rushed off as Mitch pulled out his phone, no doubt to text Kevin about their coffee date.

Class dragged, as it always does. Gathering his things right after the 3:45 p.m. bell, Brent decided he had just enough time to swing by his apartment, drop off his crap, and maybe put on a fresh shirt. The Cup was nothing fancy and would be mainly filled by high schoolers and university students at that hour, but if he was meeting Kevin—the first time they shook hands and exchanged greetings didn't count—he wanted to look good.

Mitch, Kevin, and a third guy, perhaps the infamous Les, sat as he entered. He walked to the table. Mitch stood.

"Am I late?" he asked Mitch.

"No, man. You're actually a minute early. Kev and Les have been here for over an hour, and I got here five, maybe six, minutes ago. He gestured to his tablemates. "Kevin, Les, this is Brent."

Kevin sprung up and shook his hand. "We've met, Brent. Not the best of circumstances, so you may not remember me."

"Kevin," Brent said, "you're pretty unforgettable." Brent smiled. "But you've changed. Like the new look. The haircut. The glasses. The snazzy clothes."

"Enough of this lovefest," Les interjected. He forced his hand at Brent. "I'm Les, the best friend. Beginnin' t' think you guys forgot I wuz here."

Brent shook Les's hand and said, "Great to meet ya." And then he added, "I'm gonna get a latte. You guys need anything."

Kevin and Les gave a *we're cool* sign. Mitch said, "I'll join you. I haven't ordered yet."

As they went to the counter, Brent got nearer Mitch. "You told me about the physical change, but I wasn't expectin' what I just saw. He looks five years older than the first time I saw him."

"Remarkable, isn't it? And most of the time, he acts five years older. Makes me feel like a middle-schooler," Mitch quipped.

Coffees handed to them, Mitch and Brent sat back down. Mitch sat next to Kevin while Brent took the seat on the other side of Les. Les had his head buried in his phone.

"Your girl ignorin' you?" Mitch said to Les.

"Fucking incommunicado. Cheerleading practice was over thirty minutes ago."

Mitch looked at Brent. "Les and his woman have a complicated relationship."

Kevin added, "Not complicated at all, really. She tells him to jump, and he asks how high."

Les narrowed his eyes at Kevin. "I'm this close." He held up his two fingers just barely spaced apart. "She wants me. I know she does."

"Ah, the trials and tribulations brought about by young, unrequited love," Kevin said. "I'm rootin' for ya, guy. One day, it'll happen."

Les gave Kevin a go-to-hell gaze that lasted a few seconds, and then he broke into raucous laughter. "The fun's in the anticipation, buddy." Then his phone dinged. Les jumped up. "Gotta go. Dreamgirl's callin'."

After winding up into a runner's stance, Les mimed hearing a starter pistol, and he slow-motioned a run out of the coffee shop.

After the laughter among the three of them died down, Brent said, "He's everything I thought he would be."

"Yeah, he's a trip," Kevin said.

"So, Kevin, Mitch told me all about your dinner last night."

Kevin smiled.

Obviously, he thought it was a good experience.

"I'm glad it turned out so well," Brent said. "Sloan sounds like a good guy."

Mitch quickly added, "Yes he is. I really enjoyed talkin' to 'im."

Kevin said tentatively, "He wanted to make a good impression, I'm sure."

"Not the Sloan you've described to me, Kev. He's a take-charge kinda guy. He proved that last night. But he doesn't put up with nonsense. In a nice way, he grilled me like I had just asked for your hand in marriage. And it was clear to me that he was not givin' his son away to just anyone."

"He did seem different somehow," Kevin said.

"No, babe, *you're* different. I'd venture to say that Sloan is the same man he always was. He loves ya, Kev."

Brent saw that Kevin looked uneasy and pleased, both.

"Maybe I shouldn't chime in here," Brent said, "but I think Mitch is right. From what I hear, Sloan had Mitch on the griddle like he was crispin' a grilled cheese sandwich, and the questions he asked were mostly about you. And if Mitch related it all correctly, your dad's been worryin' about you bein' in the midst of this shit in the city. I know we're gonna catch this guy, but we all have to be cautious. And that's what your dad was sayin'." Brent went quiet, fearing he'd said too much. He also worried that Kevin might pick up on his slip, the *we're gonna catch* part.

"Okay. I hear ya." Kevin's response wasn't long and profound, but Brent thought he meant it as an acceptance of what he'd just told him.

"Kev, babe, I'm proud of ya. You're growin', acceptin' what I felt all along and what was confirmed last night. Sloan cares for ya. He worries about ya. He wants the best for ya. I love ya so much for comin' to this realization."

"Mitch, you love me and that's what's changed my life around. And Sloan can stop worryin'. I'm not about to get into anything I can't handle. Not with that stalker, anyway."

Kevin leaned toward Mitch and placed a soft kiss on his lips.

Brent felt a tiny bit uncomfortable. This was more intense than he had expected. But seeing them reminded him of Callum, and the discomfort fled.

"Enougha this mush," Brent said, trying to lighten the mood. "Tell me, Kevin, whaddaya plan to do with yourself after ya graduate?"

Before Kevin could answer, Mitch said, "I did tell you he's valedictorian, didn't I? Colleges been beatin' down his door."

"Amazing. I suppose that means scholarship offers."

"Tons of 'em. Not that he needs 'em 'cause Sloan'd give him anything he desires."

"Let the man speak for himself, Mitch," Brent admonished. "I didn't come here to hear you rattle on."

"Yeah, Mitch." Kevin playfully swatted Mitch's hand. "I c'n speak for m'self." Then he looked at Brent. "You're both right. Sloan's always pushed Harvard, and bein' a legacy'd go a long way toward gettin' me in. And with my grades, my class standing, and my SAT scores, I could probably get a full ride. Sloan's insisted he'll pay for everything, but I'd love it if he didn't have to. Make me feel like more of a man. And truth be told, I'm leanin' t'wards Yale. We visited New Haven once, and I liked what I saw. Those scholarship offers Mitch referred to are his wishful thinkin'. They're yet to pour in, but I'm applyin' at all the Ivy Leagues, and who knows? And, of course, there's always the university here. I might not want to go too far from my Mitch."

"Mitch's lovable mug might be a reason to stay, but believe you me, if Harvard or Yale or Dartmouth came callin', I'd be out of here in a flash. 'Course, Mitch is just my *friend* friend. He and I don't share what the two of you do."

I hope that last reassures Kevin that Mitch and I have no romantic inclinations whatsoever. Life will go on, as I know it has to, but if I have my way, I'll never love another man but Callum.

"Yeah, Kev. Listen to Brent. Your mind's too good to waste on the university here. I'll be here, waitin' for every moment you c'n fit me in. Summers. Spring Breaks. Winter Breaks. We c'n squeeze the life outta those. And when you're away, you'll be s' busy becomin' a future CEO or President of the United States, you won't even think 'bout me," Mitch said.

"Don't even think of believin' that bullcrap," Kevin said. "You're never away from my mind, and you never will be. My plan's to have a long, long life, the two of us."

Abruptly, Brent said, "Anybody want more coffee?"

This is getting too, too heavy for me. I miss Callum.

"Sure," Kevin said, leaping up. "Same thing, all around?" Brent reached for his wallet. "Sloan'll get it," Kevin said, motioning for Brent to just sit still.

With Kevin away from the table, Brent said, "I like him, Mitch. Funny and charming. And you're right, he's growin' up. Ya told me ya worried 'bout datin' a younger guy, but Kev's intelligent and sensitive. Makes him seem much older. And the change in look dudn't hurt. The first time I saw 'im with ya, I thought, 'what's this guy doing with a twink?' But now he looks and acts like somethin' much older than I woulda guessed then. That's your influence, Mitch."

"Thanks, Brent."

Kevin returned, three cups in hand. Sitting down, he asked Brent, "What's this project you two are working on?"

Uh-oh. Tread lightly. For Mitch's sake. "It's sort of a tribute to my partner. You know, don't you, that he was one of the serial's victims?" He paused for a nod because he knew Kevin knew about Callum. *That inane question was just me stalling to put together an answer for Kevin.* "So, Brent and I're working on somethin' that'll honor Callum's memory in a big, big way. Hush, hush. Under wraps. I know you'll respect that. I swore Mitch t' secrecy, and even though not tellin' you all about it's eatin' away at this standup guy, he's so far kept his promise."

Mitch added, "And I will. This is your project, Brent, and I'm not gonna tell a soul until you gimme the all clear."

"Okay. I get it. You two're in cahoots, and you're afraid the high school kid will blow your cover." Kevin's words could have been taken as petulant, but his tone said otherwise. "I promise I won't blow the sand out of your sandbox. You two build your sandcastles, and I'll be at the unveiling, as curious as the rest of the world."

I can see why Mitch likes this guy. He thinks like a wise old scholar, not like someone who is frettin' over which cheerleader he'll be screwin' after prom.

Brent tried to initiate small talk as they sat and drank, but Kevin's intelligence got in the way of that. And then, too, he, himself, had just lived several years of his life in the presence of a very serious man. Callum had his fun moments, but he mostly was very earnest and didn't have much use for small talk. So Brent wasn't very good at it.

Thank God Mitch saved the day. "Whaddaya think about them Knicks?"

Both Kevin and Brent looked at him like he was crazy.

"What. Youse guys don't follow no hoops?" Mitch said.

"More like you don't have a clue what you're talkin' 'bout, guy," Brent said, knocking Mitch's arm.

"Yeah, babe," Kevin added. "I haven't known ya very long, but I can testify on the Bible that I ain't never heard ya talk 'bout no hoops or no innings or no first downs or no anything else remotely connected to the wide, wide world of sports." Kevin stuck his tongue out and made a face.

"Well, I was just tryin' to get a little light conversation going. The air was getting' a little too thick in here. I'm tired of talkin' 'bout Ivy Leaguers, scholarships, and such, much less bringin' up the killer trash. I only wanted to lighten the mood." He looked at Brent. "Don't you wanna know where Kevin gets his hair done?"

Kevin did his faux primping motion. "Adrian's on the Plaza. You like?"

And the three finished their coffee laughing and talking. Brent and Kevin got in some good ribs at Mitch.

"Well, guys," Mitch said, wadding up his paper cup. "If you're just gonna beat up on me, I'm gonna bounce."

"Don't go, Mitch," Kevin said. "Let's get some dinner. Your choice, Sloan's dime. Wanna join us, Brent?"

"No, I'll let you lovebirds carry on without a third wheel." He stood. "Gimme a call later, Mitch, unless you're too busy." He put every salacious intonation he could muster into that.

"Oh, I'll be callin', guy. If only to rake you over the coals for suggestin' I would do such a thing and ruin my guy here's reputation." Mitch and Kevin stood together.

"Glad I got to know ya a bit, Kevin. Take care of m' friend here. And watch out. He c'n be a handful."

"Don't I know it," Kevin answered.

Brent was glad Mitch had suggested the coffee date. He reflected on it as he drove home. He liked Kevin. He hadn't known if he was going to meet the great guy that Mitch bragged about, or if Kevin had the wool pulled over Mitch's eyes, and Kevin was really the screwed up, petulant teenager that he could have very well been. *I'm glad Kevin's working his problems out, because he deserves a good life.*

The time at the Cup was exquisite distraction. Brent's mind was always racing, trying to fit those damned puzzle pieces together. His latest idea would probably lead to zilch, but he knew, as exhausting and mind-numbing as it would be, he had to do it.

As soon as he got home, he opened his laptop and began.

Three hours later, his eyes feeling like they'd been stuck with needles, his phone chimed.

"Mitch, so glad you called," he said snarkily, not even knowing why except that he'd just had three excruciating hours of abject disappointment. "You at CVS to pick up more rubbers?" *This is not like me. Not like me at all. Callum would be shocked.* "Sorry. What a shit I am. I'm glad you called."

"I was beginnin' t' think you weren't gonna let me get a word in edgewise. You sound tired and irritable."

"Very."

"Well, in answer to your question, I had to go to three drug stores. They were out of the supersize, and you know I just break the extra-large much too easily."

"I deserved that," Brent said. "How was dinner?"

"Good. Kevin's gettin' more and more open with me. I think he's findin' out sharin' can be a great way to figure out stuff."

"So said Callum."

"He spoke truth. So—Mark, remember Kevin's bro?—apparently he's having a harder time with the *mom goes to Africa thing* than Kevin is. She sat them both down and tried to explain. Kevin doesn't like it, but he wrote her off long ago. Sad, to detach from your own mom, but it's helped Kev deal with it all. Poor Mark, though, feels totally abandoned. Kev told me that since he's away from home a lot, he never knew his mom and Mark actually had some mother/son bonding moments. Kevin's voice broke when he told me that, and I think it was part feeling sorry for his brother losin' out on his mom moments and part feelin' sorry for himself, losin' out on that mom bondin' time. Anyway, Mark, like a kid—they're resilient as hell—had this fantasy that his mother actually was gonna increase their quality time. Her goin' off to Africa for an extended period's throwin' Mark into a tailspin. But Kev, God love him, is steppin' up to the plate and tryin' to help Mark deal."

"That's great. I know the kid's happy to finally have his brother on his side, at least."

"Yeah. And ya know what? That just makes me love Kev even more. So caring. He used to talk a big game, but I always knew he would never do anything to truly hurt his kid brother. Kevin wouldn't hurt anyone. It's just not in 'im."

"I don't really know him, Mitch, but if what I saw today's any indication, Kevin's a really good guy."

"Anyway, we finished dinner, and Kevin said he wanted to go home to spend some time with Mark. He invited me, but I figured they needed brother/brother time. Without me around."

"You're right." Brent yawned.

"What's up, guy? It's only nine-thirty, and you sound beat to hell."

"Started a new phase of our investigation. And don't worry, I'm doin' this part all on my lonesome. No risk involved whatsoever. Just me, my couch, and my laptop."

"Explain, please, Holmes."

"Certainly, Watson. The last murder occurred very near the Family Now building."

"Yes, and also near a bunch of gay clubs."

"You're right, but I think the two could be connected. That prick Fellows keeps praisin' this monster like he's some avengin' angel. So, what better place to lay a sacrifice than at the Spencer Fellows altar. It's like when your cat delivers the mouse he's just killed. The clubs are the mouse holes, a patron is the mouse, and our stalker is right outside the little hole, ready to club the mouse, scoop him up, and deliver 'im at the feet of the master, Dr. Spencer Fellows himself."

"Your metaphor's a bit overdrawn, but I see your point. But with all this elaborate plot you created, how are you gonna discover anything by sittin' on your couch with your laptop?"

"I was canoodlin' the other day, Mitch. Googling around, hoping to uncover the least tiny thing to cement our puzzle pieces together. I 'lighted on the Family Now website. Right on the homepage was a video, a film of the good doctor ranting and raving about the wrath of God and how the only thing, yes, the only thing, in this world that could make ol' angry Holy Trinity happy was the annihilation of the entire gay population. Wipe them off the face of the earth, and sit at His feet in Heaven."

"Okay. So?"

"The message wudn't new. But I saw something very unexpected. And why it surprised me, I dunno. The man's the ultimate narcissist, God knows. He's recorded every word, it seems, that he's ever spoken. That website archives hundreds of rallies, TV appearances, prayer meetings, and almost every time he's ever taken a crap, it seems. And what I saw on the first video I watched, and have seen over the last three hours of endless YouTubing, is that the Family Now videographer's fond of audience reaction shots."

"And?"

"You're not computin', Mitch, 'cause it's such a long shot. What if our killer's one of those followers, and his ugly mug's on one of those tapes?"

"Oh, Brent, are ya mad? It'll take ya weeks, maybe months, to go through all that. And what makes ya think you'll recognize our guy when ya see him?"

"I dunno. Okay, I'm bonkers. I'm loony. I'm delusional. I'll never see the killer on the screen, and if he's there, I won't know I'm lookin' at him. It's just something I need to do. I have to try it. Maybe some brain-addled psychopath will pop out of the crowd, I'll have a Eureka moment, and say aloud 'I know that guy!' and just feel in my gut that he's the one."

"Brent, I like your *just do it* spirit. But don't be surprised if it all comes to nothin'. And don't go blind."

"Look, luckily, they're catalogued by date. This guy's only been stalkin' the city for what? Three months or so? I only have to look at the tapes from the middle of the summer. That narrows it down."

"T' what? A coupla hundred. Spencer Fellows loves the camera."

"I think it's only a hundred or so if I counted right. And some of those are TV soundbites, so they'll go quickly and most likely don't show any onlookers. I might get through 'em in a couple of weeks or so. Or maybe, just maybe, the first one I watch'll have our killer in it with a sign saying, 'are you lookin' for me?'"

"But you already watched a bunch, haven't ya?"

"Yeah." He tried not to let his answer show disappointment. "But the next one. The next one."

"Good luck, guy. Stay in touch. I assume you won't be neglectin' your classes, so I'll see ya Tuesday. Or should I stop by with pizza regularly? Don't get so wrapped up in Fellows' mesmerizing personality that you forget to eat. I'd hate to see Marlon Gordon, Force Four News, intoning 'A university student's shriveled body was found in his apartment this morning. Neighbors said there was a peculiar odor, so they notified the super, who discovered the body. It appears to be suicide by starvation.'"

"You can laugh at me all you want, Mitch. You'll be laughin' out the other side of your mouth when I identify Callum's killer."

Mitch

"Awesome. That creature leaped right out at us. I dodged 'cause it felt like he was gonna stab his horn right into me." Mark was still wearing the 3D glasses as they came out of the theater.

"What about that sword fight? Jake's moves were dope!" Davy, Mark's friend, was equally hepped up on the movie.

Mitch was ecstatic. This stupid monster crap had been just the thing that Mark needed. He was glad Kevin suggested it.

"Ice cream, guys?" Kevin asked.

"Cool," Mark said.

"Duh," his friend said to him. "Ice cream *is* cool—really, truly cool. It has ice in the name, you doofus."

"Oh, yeah." And Mark laughed raucously.

They piled into Mitch's car, and he headed to Baskin Robbins.

This might be the only time in these two's young lives they ever rode in a beat-up, six-year-old Civic. But, what the hey. All four of us would not fit in that death car. No way.

Rich kids or not, Mark and Davy were just like every other kid at the ice cream counter. They couldn't make up their minds on the flavor or whether they should get a regular cone or a waffle cone. Mitch suggested hot fudge sundaes, and that settled the debate.

"I'm getting two scoops in mine—cherry vanilla and peanut butter. I love hot fudge with cherries, and I love hot fudge with peanut butter, so this is gonna be one awesome sundae." This was about the four hundredth time Mark had said the word awesome since they picked up his friend. Mitch loved how much fun Kev's brother was having.

"Well, you'll have to give me a taste if ya wanna convince me," Davy said. "I'm goin' with chocolate mint and butter pecan."

"Ewwww, that sounds gross," Mark said, scrunching up his face.

"Mark, everybody's different. You might *like* Davy's choices, and I bet he'll let you try 'em if you ask nicely." Kevin was in more than big brother mode. He was in father mode, Mitch thought.

Six weeks ago, Kev would have been talking trash at Mark. I'm so proud of this change in him.

Kevin got a waffle cone with a scoop of butter pecan of his own. Mitch had rocky road, one scoop, in a cup—it was his mother's favorite, and she never, ever had a cone because she thought melted ice cream running down your hand was icky. Mitch smiled, thinking of her expression when she said, 'icky.'

The two younger boys wanted to sit at a table outside. Kevin told them they could, and then he and Mitch sat at a table near the window inside, so Mitch figured Kevin could keep an eye on the boys.

Licking the creamy amber of the butter pecan, Kevin asked, "So how's Brent?"

"Kev, you've asked me that just about every day since you got to know him. And I'm not countin', but that's seventeen times, seventeen days, since. And like I've said, every time, 'he's fine.' He's stuck in a rut doing research, so I've only seen him in World Affairs class, but he looks like he's eatin' and poopin' regularly."

"Ease up, babe. I liked the guy and since he's your friend, I just wanna keep up."

"Sorry, Kev. I'm kinda pissed at Brent right now. He's goin' 'bout this research all wrong, and he won't listen t' me. Yeah, physically he's fine, but otherwise, he's kind of a wreck."

Kevin looked at Mitch, a huge smile on his face. "I'm a whiz at research. I could cut his time down to nothing, if he'd let me. Tell 'im I'd be glad to help."

If only you could, but I don't want you even near this thing.

"Brent's hell-bent on doin' it all 'imself. I offered t' help, and he politely declined my offer. What bothers me is this thing he's workin' toward is closely tied to his slain boyfriend. He's dredgin' up feelings he doesn't need to have."

"Well, he said he was puttin' together some sort of tribute. I know that's important to him, and he probably wants to do most of it himself to show how much of a loss he's suffered. So I guess we, you and I, just have to let him take the reins."

Kevin's so caring. So understanding. So loving.

Mitch decided to steer the conversation, move far away from Brent and the killer. "You do anything more about the college apps?"

"I'm just about ready to send them in. Early, I might add. I got the essay. It alone is gonna get me that Yale scholarship."

Mitch smiled, knowing that anything Kevin set his mind to, it would happen.

"Oh, really," Mitch said. "And what's this award-winning tome about?"

"You."

Mitch looked at Kevin incredulously.

"Well, me, actually, but it's the *after meeting Mitch* me. I read online that schools want an essay intensely personal and revealing. They wanna know about momentous events in your life, and how ya dealt with 'em. They wanna know about your growth."

Mitch nodded, eager to hear more. "Go on. I'm listenin'."

"So—I started with the old Kevin. The Kevin who didn't give a shit about school, content to let his intelligence get 'im through. That was kinda hard to compose without soundin' totally conceited. I described my look, which was a big part of my attitude. I looked at life sloppy, so I dressed sloppy. I also searched deep inside and decided to share how I used to feel about Sloan. I figured a college admissions officer would get excited about a petulant son, rich stepfather saga. And then came the hero character. Mitch. The savior. The man of my dreams. The greatest influence on my short life. The Svengali who transformed me, made me see my life in a new light. And to add a final flourish, I waxed eloquently about the value of maturity and the lessons I've so newly learned." Kevin finished with a flourish of his hands and a wide grin on his face.

"You make it sound like a big, big fiction, babe. FYI, I've never been on a horse, so cut the part about me riding in on a white stallion to save your ass." Mitch laughed. He didn't want to diss Kevin's essay, but it sounded like a load of crap.

I wanna believe he wrote his own personal truth. Maybe his delivery here was just for show, a bit of the old Kevin peekin' out.

Kevin quickly grabbed both of Mitch's hands in his. "No, no, no, no, no—I meant every word I wrote. You *are* my savior, babe. I just told it that way right now to be funny. And because, I have to say, I'm a little embarrassed to share out loud. I'd gladly let you read it if I had a copy with me, but somehow talkin' 'bout it seems self-serving. And by the way, there's no white horse. But there's definitely a white knight."

Mitch melted like the ice cream from Kevin's cone dripping on the hand Kevin was holding. He licked his hand. Then he said, "I bet the actual thing dudn't have a whiff of overkill in it. You're a very humble man, Kev. More and more, ya prove it. To me. To Sloan. To Mark." Mitch leaned in for a kiss, and his eyes caught Mark, outside. "Uh, Kev, I think your brother is about t' fling whipped cream at his friend Davy."

Kevin jumped up, pushed the entry door open and yelled, "Mark! Cease and desist!"

Through the window, Mitch saw Mark put his spoon down and heard him laugh.

"'S' okay," Mitch heard Davy say. "I threw my cherry at him first. I deserved it." And Davy joined Mark's laughter.

"Well, if you guys're through eatin', bring your cups in, put 'em in the garbage, and we'll head out."

Kevin came back to the table and picked up his cone, now melting onto the tabletop. "Guess we're goin', babe." Mitch quickly scooped the last of his rocky road into his spoon and put it in his mouth as he stood. The boys were back inside, tossing the remnants of their sundaes into the garbage bin. Mark went over to the water fountain and ran his fingers under the water. "Mark! Go to the restroom if you wanna wash your hands."

Mark looked over his shoulder, a guilty smile on his face, and then he went past the water fountain and pushed the men's room door open.

Soon Mark returned, and the four of them got into the Civic.

"I like your car, Mitch. Reminds me of the one our maid drives," Davy said.

Kids, Mitch thought, *never a filter.*

"Best I can afford, Davy, best I can afford."

"Oh, I didn't mean anything by that. I like it, really I do—"

Mark punched Davy's arm. "Just shut up, okay?"

There was silence in the car until they got near Davy's house, a grand mansion compared to the relatively smaller palace Kevin and Mark lived in. As they got closer to the house, even though Mitch had picked Davy up earlier there, the boy started directing him, showing the exact driveway to turn into.

A guard greeted them. He was the same guard who'd met Mitch, Kevin, and Mark when they arrived earlier. Mitch rolled down his window, wondering why the guard didn't just wave them through.

The guard leaned over and put his crossed elbows on the windowsill. "Hey, Davy," he said. "Have a good time?"

"Sure did, Frank."

"Good for you." Then Frank touched Mitch on the arm. "Thanks for taking m' boy Davy out today. He's a good kid."

Mitch said, "Happy to," and then he drove on up to the front door of the behemoth house.

Mark and Davy hopped out of the car. "Pick me up tomorrow, Kevin? It's a teacher conference day at my school, so we don't have to go. I can stay here all day. I'm thinkin' 'bout four or five, but I'll text you," Mark said.

"Sure thing, bro," Kevin answered. "Have fun. Love ya, kid."

Mark smiled. Then he joined Davy as they entered the house.

"I know you're thinkin' what the hell about that guy Frank," Kevin said to Mitch. "I couldn't say anything before without Davy maybe overhearin'. Davy's parents're never at home. I mean, never ever, unless there's some charity event they just absolutely have t' attend. Otherwise, they're in Dubai or Jakarta or Tokyo or Paris or London—you get my drift? Poor kid."

Mitch nodded.

"They make *our* mother look like Mother of the Year. I feel sorry for the kid. So that crack he made about your car? He didn't mean anything by it. If he ever gets outta the house, it's 'cause the maid takes him places, hence his knowin' all about her car. I'd venture to say, he loves that car. And Frank? He sometimes takes Davy to his own house to play with his son. Frank has a boy about Davy's age.

"It hurts my heart, Mitch. Always has, but even more now that I've made peace with Sloan. Hell, I even made peace with Mom. I hate she's not here, but she never was here much, anyway, now was she? At least she's helpin' kids who need her help. Davy's mom and dad're so filthy rich all they do's travel around in search of meaning in life, not even knowin' the real meaning's right here. They got a kid, bein' raised by a housekeeper, who needs their love. And who'd give it back tenfold."

"Wow," Mitch said. "I hope that last is a centerpiece of your essay. If it is, you'll definitely get into Yale. They'll be fallin' all over themselves to get you before some other school snaps you up."

To think, the Kevin I met and was attracted to's a far cry from the Kevin I love now. I was worried he'd screw up his life in a heartbeat, but now I know he's gonna live a very long, supremely happy life. And he'll do so while bringin' joy to others.

"Okay." Mitch looked at Kevin, a wicked smile on his face. "I'm assuming the rest of the day's ours to do with what we desire?" He punched the last word.

"Oh, yeah," Kevin nodded salaciously. "I asked Cook to come in today to prepare a scrumptious feast for us and leave it in the warming oven. I know it's Sunday, and she was working on her day off, so I gave her tomorrow off. Sloan's on a business trip. Won't be back until tomorrow. We just got rid of—er, left Mark to his own devices. And the stage is set for a night of infinite joy." The look on Kevin's face was priceless. "And that's just dinner—Lobster Thermidor with all the trimmings, Cook's famous Pavlova for dessert, and Sloan always has a bottle of Dom in the fridge. We're good to go. And afterward, if we're not too stuffed, maybe another little *sumpin, sumpin*." He raised his eyebrows up and down as he said the last two words.

"Why, Kevin, I cannot believe you would suggest that I would take advantage of you," Mitch said, faux indignation dripping in his proper Southern gentleman imitation.

Kevin stuck out his hands and used his index finger, left hand, to count off on his right hand. "Let's see, last Wednesday, your place. Friday, my bed. Saturday *and* Sunday, your place again. That little number you did on me in the secluded spot in the wilds of the park—when was that? Monday? Tuesday? And—"

"Enough. I surrender. You're just so cute, I can't resist. Now, is there a quicker way to get to your house than the way we came here?"

"I think I can guide the chariot swiftly, o god of food and debauchery."

Mitch didn't need directions. The *quicker way crack* was a joke, punctuating their talk of mutual lust.

They made it back to Kevin's house in five minutes, tops.

"Put on some music while I get the table set," Kevin said.

Mitch headed to the media room. The thing was filled with CDs, plus they had Spotify, iTunes, and God knows what else on the myriad of devices. He couldn't decide. Then he saw the white plastic goddess of commands. "Alexa," he said, "Play quiet romantic music." The velvet crooning of John Legend softly set the mood.

I'd really just like to cut to the chase, but lobster does sound amazing.

The dining room table was set with what were no doubt the finest linens money could buy. The utensils gleamed. The dishes were so delicate that you could almost see through them. Waterford champagne flutes stood at each place. Mitch had once upon a time not known they were Waterford—he didn't even know what that was—nor did he know the skinny tall glasses were exclusively for champagne. Kevin gave him that lesson when he brought two glasses and an ice bucket with a champagne bottle into his room one evening. The table had a beautiful arrangement of cut flowers—the identity of which Mitch could not name—and Kevin had lit a sparkling crystal candelabra, five slender candles flickering in the dimly lit room. He'd never seen *Downton Abbey*, but he imagined this was exactly what one of their dinner parties must look like.

Kevin came through the door that led to the kitchen. He had two plates filled with incredible-looking delicacies. "Sit." Mitch did as he was told. Kevin put one of the plates in front of Mitch. He set the other at his own place, and then he seated himself. He reached over, took the Dom Perignon from its ice bucket, and poured them each a glass.

Then Kevin raised his glass. "To Mitch. My life."

They clinked their glasses while Mitch said, "And to Kevin. The man I never want to live without."

I never thought I'd be feeling these feelings. Can people fall head over heels in such a short time? I hope so. Because that's what this feels like.

They sealed their toasts with sips of champagne. Then they began their meal.

Moving a forkful to his mouth, Mitch said, "You outdid yourself, Kev."

"Cook's doin', not mine."

"She mighta made the dinner, but this, all this—" he gestured over the table—"is all your doing. I know it is."

"So? Anyone can light candles, order flowers." He took another drink of wine.

"But you're not anyone. You're my Kevin. And I love you." Mitch leaned in and gave Kevin a kiss so full of love that Mitch didn't want it to end.

Lips still pressed together, Kevin made a mumbled sound. "Ooooooh. Hmmmm."

Moving their lips apart just enough to talk, Mitch said, "You taste good."

"As do you." Then Kevin pushed Mitch away. "And so does this lobster. I'm starvin', babe. If ya think you're gonna get some later, I needs me strength."

Mitch laughed at him. "Okay, okay, okay. I can control myself until we get through this here." He made the end of his statement sound like eating this was a chore.

"You're lovin' it. I know you, babe," Kevin said. "And just wait until you have Cook's Pavlova."

Mouth full, Mitch said, "Whuzzat?"

"Oh, man oh man. Prepare yourself for a treat. I refuse to describe it and spoil the surprise. You'll just have to wait."

They finished up, and Kevin began to clear. He poured the remainder of the Dom bottle into Mitch's glass. Then he put the bottle upside down into the ice bucket.

"Why'd you do that?"

"Dunno," Kevin said. "I've seen the sommelier at the club do that. Always wanted to do it."

Mitch shook his head. "You never cease to…"

"I know…to amaze you." He picked up their plates and carried them to the kitchen.

Mitch sipped the last of the wine.

I'm glad I made my decision. It's time.

Kevin returned with two full-sized dinner plates with enormous identical concoctions on them. Sitting Mitch's down, he said, adopting a French accent, "Je vous présente, monsieur, le Pavlova, a creation designed to lift you straight to Mount Olympus to play among ze gods."

Mitch was almost speechless. He waited for Kevin to sit before he said, "Damn, boy. This shit looks guuuuud. Map it out for me."

"Well, you've got your lightly browned meringue and whipped cream, dressed with an apricot sauce, a bit of French vanilla cream, topped with mixed berries. Dig in."

Nothing could have ended that meal more perfectly, Mitch thought.

This is indeed food for the gods, and it's the perfect way to start a journey I hope will take Kevin to Mt. Olympus.

Literally licking their plates, they sat back in total satiation.

I'd bet a zillion bucks no one at Downton Abbey ever pulled that *stunt with their dessert plates.*

Mitch rubbed his belly. "Oh my God, my God. I'm so full I don't think I can do anything but go to bed."

"Well, m' friend," Kevin said, "I hope you're not alludin' to sleep, because I'm hungry for the after-dessert course."

"Don't worry, my pretty, your time will come. You'll get your comeuppance." Mitch cackled like a wicked witch.

Kevin stood and pulled Mitch up by his lapels. "Plenty of time t' clean up later." He rattled off. "Fill up the whole night, and there's always tomorrow." He pulled Mitch toward the stairs.

They both took the stairs two at a time, and when they got to Kevin's room, Mitch pushed him down on the bed. He leaned over and plastered his mouth onto Kevin's. Mitch ran his tongue all over and around Kevin's while he undid the buttons of Kevin's shirt. Pulling away to tug at Kevin's zipper, Kevin wiggled out of his shirt. Mitch got the zipper down as Kevin undid the buttons on Mitch's fly. Mitch stood to remove his jeans and shirt. Kevin pulled his pants off and flung them across the room. Together, they peeled each other's briefs off, tripping over each other and landing back on the bed, Mitch on top of Kevin.

"Ohhh, I love the weight of your body on mine," Kevin moaned.

Mitch flicked his tongue all over Kevin's body. Flick, flick. Kiss. Flick, flick, Kiss. Over and over. Kevin screamed, "Hold on. You're makin' me come."

"It's okay. You'll come again."

He rushed to the bathroom, wet a towel, returned and bathed Kevin's penis. Then he took from his jeans one of the square aluminum foil packets he'd put in his pocket early that morning.

He tore open the packet and carefully rolled the condom onto Kevin's still-hard member.

With the protection in place, Mitch took the member into his mouth. He lovingly caressed it with his tongue. Kevin moaned as his penis grew even more. Mitch felt his entire body tingling, so he knew Kevin was feeling the same.

When Kevin screamed he could take no more—for a while, he was quick to add—Mitch jumped off the bed, grabbed his jeans, and thrust his fingers into the pocket again. He pulled out a second condom.

Holding it up, he said, "Not even for this?" Then he flipped Kevin over onto his stomach.

Kevin

They lay together, the soft sheets caressing their two bodies. Kevin felt like they'd both been high atop a mountain. *Mount Olympus. Food for the gods, only not for the mouth this time.*

A half hour or more had passed, and Kevin still was intoxicated with Mitch-nectar. "So that's what it's like?" he whispered.

"Yeah," Mitch said. He leaned over to press his lips to Kevin's forehead.

"How many times have you done this?" Kevin asked. *I feel the highest I've ever felt. I don't think I'd survive this high if I'd done this as many times as Mitch must have.*

"You don't wanna know."

"Oh, yes, I do. We're gonna be together forever, and I wanna know everything I can about you."

"Yeah, babe. Okay. I've done this very act many times, but ya know what? I always felt empty afterward. Just somethin' to do. Somethin' I wanted, needed, to make me feel whole. But it never did. Until tonight." He leaned over and kissed Kevin gently, with all the feeling he could put into one kiss.

"I love you, Mitch. I love you more than I ever thought I could love anybody. I love you for eternity times a hundred, infinity times a thousand, forever times a million. You're mine. I'll never, ever let you get away from me."

And all those other times with all those other guys mean nothing. Now I'm in love. And I can't let Mitch ever know that he wasn't my first.

"Aw, babe. You're just sayin' that. You're goin' off to Yale, make somethin' of yourself, find someone better 'n me."

"Nobody's better than you, Mitch."

Contented. Complete. Wrapped in each other's arms. They drifted off to sleep.

The sudden jangling of Mitch's phone shattered their peace.

"What's that?" Kevin asked, bringing himself from the depths of another world.

"My phone." Mitch ripped off the covers and climbed to the edge of the bed to reach for his phone in his jeans pocket.

He pulled it up and looked at it.

"What, babe? Somethin' wrong?"

"Brent. Accident. Needs me to come get 'im."

Starting to get out of bed, Kevin said, "I'll come with."

"No—you stay put. Just a fender bender. Not hurt. Rattled. I'll go calm him down." He placed an angel kiss on Kevin's forehead. "Get your beauty sleep, Kev. I'll call you in the mornin'.

Brent

Brent pushed send on the text: *Get here, now. Don't bring Kevin.* And then he waited.

The minutes ticked away, but time stood still. He could see the time changing on his phone, minute by minute, but Mitch wasn't there yet, and Brent was certain he'd had plenty of time, no matter where he'd been.

Maybe he didn't pick up the text. Oh, God, no. This will be hard enough to do without having to delay it. Please, Mitch. Get here.

He gazed at the frozen image, closing the laptop, immediately reopening it and pulling the image back up. Closing, opening, closing, opening. Brent didn't want to believe what was staring him in the face.

Twenty minutes after he sent the text. A millisecond after, he'd closed his laptop for the fortieth time. *Rap, rap, rap* on his door. He leaped up. Rushed to it. Flung the door open.

"'Sup?" Mitch said.

Brent pulled him into the room. He pointed to the couch. "Sit."

Mitch chuckled. "A bit melodramatic here, ya think?"

"I said sit." And again, Brent pointed.

Mitch held up his hands defensively. "Okay, okay. I'll sit." He plopped down. Brent sat too. He was careful to put space between them so he could make his case without Mitch thinking anything. The last thing he wanted was for Mitch to think he was coming on to him. Brent reached for his laptop. With it turned away from Mitch, he opened it. Brought the screenshot back up.

"Brent," Mitch said. "Stop the cloak and dagger. Why'd ya get me over here with that cryptic message? And why'd you say not to bring Kevin?"

Brent sat a moment, collecting his thoughts.

Finally, taking a breath as deep as the Grand Canyon, he spoke. "You know what I've been doin', right?"

"Yeah. Combin' through the Fellows tapes. Don't tell me ya found somethin' promisin'?"

"I think so."

Brent let that lie, not wanting to proceed but knowing he had to.

Oh, God, give me the strength I need to do this. I never thought I'd shatter Mitch in order to honor Callum. This is so hard.

Slowly, Brent opened the computer. Equally as slow, he turned the screen toward Mitch. Mitch looked at the screen.

Then he looked up at Brent.

Say something. React. Scream. Throw something. Just don't sit there and stare.

Again, Mitch looked at the screen. Seemingly not making any connection whatsoever, Mitch said, "Why's there a pic of Kevin on your laptop?"

"Mitch." Brent had to gather his thoughts. He had to work up the courage he needed to do this. He repeated himself. "Mitch." He faltered.

"I know m' name, Brent. You don't have to keep repeatin' it. Answer m' question. Why do ya have a pic of Kevin?"

With almost despair, Brent said, "I found it."

He let that sink in, but for whatever reason, Mitch was still not making the connection.

Is he in denial? Or am I not making any sense?

"This, this shot of Kevin, is a face in the crowd. The crowd? Family Now. A Spencer Fellows meeting."

"No. You're makin' that up. Why you doin' this, Brent? We're friends. You like Kevin. Why ya wanna turn me against him?"

Mitch's questions were frantic. Brent heard the cries of someone who was clutching onto life itself, not wanting to hear confirmation of Brent's allegations.

"I'm not makin' it up. I c'n show you the entire video. There's no way I'm computer savvy enough to insert Kevin into it. Mitch, I wouldn't even have a video of Kevin to insert. No, it's him all right. He was there, at that meeting."

"Okay. Say he was. Dudn't prove a thing. I told you when you began this it'd come to nothin'. That even if you recognized someone, it wouldn't prove anything." Mitch pulled out his phone. "I'm gonna call Kev right now. Get him over here to explain. Maybe he was doin' research of his own. Kev's a smart guy. He probably wanted to find somethin' out to expose that buffoon."

Brent reached over and pulled Mitch's hand away before he could make his call.

"Don't do it, Mitch. Hear me out. Then if you want to get Kevin over here, it's okay."

Mitch set his phone on the table. "I'll listen. That dudn't mean you can make me believe somethin' that bizarre. Kevin's not a killer. He might be many things, but he's not that."

"Okay. Let's start with this..." He pulled printouts from a folder. The neon of a yellow highlighter pen shouted out passages. "Read. Out loud."

Mitch took the first printout Brent handed him. "The victim is of slight build, with sandy colored hair and pale blue eyes." Brent gently pushed another sheet of paper into Mitch's hand. "My son was such a handsome man with his sandy hair, his piercing blue eyes." Another article. "Police say the victim was brutalized, but he does fit the killer's profile; sandy hair, blue eyes, slight build." A fourth. "Callum Slater was well known around campus, a striking young man who cut a wide swath. Despite his slight build, he carried himself like a god, a friend said. And like a god, he had sandy golden-brown curls with moonlight blue eyes." And finally, a fifth article. "A patron at the Rotor, a gay club, couldn't describe the assailant, but he remembered the victim. He said he was attracted to the man's sandy hair, slight build."

Brent wanted that to sink in before he connected the dots. Mitch finished reading and said, "So? We always knew the victims were similar. This dudn't prove anything. I don't see what you're gettin' at."

"Describe Sloan Howell."

"Light brown hair, medium build, not too bulked up, blue eyes."

"Uh-uh."

Doesn't he see it now?

"What ya getting' at? What does Sloan have to do with anything?"

"You didn't use the same words, but do you see any similarity between him and the victims?"

Mitch shook his head in disgust. "You're in the deep end treadin' water, Brent. A lot of people have the same physical characteristics. And besides, the last victim had brown eyes."

"An anomaly." Brent knew it was time to clench the deal. "Now, describe yourself."

"Brown hair, blue eyes. Five-eight. Shirt, medium. Thirty-two-inch waist." Mitch spat out the words.

"*Sandy* brown hair. *Pale* blue eyes. Height, shirt size, waist size—*slight build*."

Mitch's look was inscrutable. He was either putting it all together, or he was in terminal denial, or he was writing Brent out of his life for even thinking this.

I can only hope he'll see this. For his *sake.*

Brent continued, speaking rapidly, wanting to get it all out and make his point. "Here's what I think, based on what you've told me, Kevin had a love/hate relationship with his stepfather. You say he's changed his attitude about Sloan now, and maybe he has. But just a few short weeks ago, it was clear he was conflicted about Sloan Howell. He said he hated his guts, but he got a haircut like him, he got glasses just like Sloan wears, and he picked up a man—granted someone, I hope, that he fell in love with and you with him—who looks very much like the stepfather he professed to hate. And all, every last one of them, the victims? Virtually clones of Sloan Howell."

"Coincidence, Brent. A fuckin' coincidence. Kevin idn't capable of murder. You can't make me believe that. I love him. I know he's a good person."

Despite their outward meaning, Mitch's words had a tinge of doubt in them.

Brent knew if he pushed this too far, too fast, Mitch would shut down. So he searched for something, anything, to delay the inevitable. "You want some coffee?"

Mitch screamed at him. "No, I don't want no fuckin' coffee! You bring me over here to tear my lover apart, to accuse him of heinous, vicious, brutal crimes, and then, like Betty Fuckin' Crocker, you offer me coffee?"

It was now or never.

"What kinda car does Kevin drive?"

"A Spyder," Mitch spat.

"And what kind of car did that jogger see?"

"A sports car." This time Mitch's tone had changed, but only a bit.

"A sports car so exotic the guy had no idea what kind it was. Now, the time you and Kevin went to those fountains? What'd Kevin get from his trunk to wear?"

"A hoodie." Mitch's tone was weakening.

"And what'd the jogger say the guy who ran past him was wearing?"

"A hoodie." Mitch was almost inaudible. "But that dudn't—" He didn't finish what he started.

"And what'd ya tell me was in Kevin's trunk with the hoodie?"

"I don't remember," Mitch said unconvincingly.

"Yes, you do, Mitch. A bat. A metal alloy bat. You told me you saw it, and you asked him about it. He told you Sloan had given it to him." *He does remember. He just doesn't want to admit it. Not to me. Not to himself.* "The kind of bat that could do some serious damage to a human head. The kind of thing that guy in the hoodie might have been carrying when the jogger saw him."

Mitch began to sob. Quietly. Brent knew he had gotten through to him. *It was all circumstantial evidence, as the TV lawyers would say, but it was very compelling.* As Mitch cried, Brent, feeling like he was bludgeoning Mitch with his words, summed it all up, bringing it home, his closing argument.

"Kevin hated Sloan and everything Sloan stood for. He took the expensive car, he spent Sloan's money liberally because in Kevin's brilliant but flawed thinking, he was punishing his stepfather for not being his real dad, not giving him love in the way he wanted it. I can't even begin to fully analyze Kevin. No one probably really knows him and his motives. Not even you. I'd bet not even him. But he's opened up to you, Mitch, more than to anyone ever. I do think he loves you. And I know you love him. But we can't ignore all this. Maybe Kevin felt so sorry for himself and hated Sloan so much that he lashed out. Irrationally, he *had* to kill Sloan. But we humans often can't punish ourselves for doing what we know is wrong, and we can't punish those we love. Kevin, in a twisted, incomprehensible way, loved Sloan, the only father he's ever known. So if he couldn't punish Sloan, he found Sloan stand-ins. Maybe he was spurred on by Fellows's hate-filled messages that gays don't deserve to live. Maybe Kevin thought he was punishing himself by wipin' out gay guys like himself. Maybe he fell in love with you because you gave him the love and understanding that he craved from his stepfather. I don't think we'll ever know his motivations fully. But I do believe Kevin brutally murdered my Callum and four other men who didn't deserve his wrath. He has to be stopped."

Brent took a breath, fearing Mitch's reaction. Knowing that if Mitch didn't do something, he'd have to.

Mitch sat. His lip quivered. He wiped the remnants of his tears from his cheeks. He looked up, like he was praying. He looked all around, like he was searching for something. He stood.

"You need to change your major to Pre-Law, counselor." He spat those words. "You can make all the accusations you want. Back it all up with your own twisted ideas. But Kevin did not do this."

"Then ask him."

Mitch looked at him. He walked toward the door.

Worried, Brent asked, "Where ya goin'? What ya gonna do?"

"I have to see Kevin. Now."

Defeat.

"Lemme go with ya."

"No, this is something I have to do alone."

Kevin

Kevin hated that Mitch took off so quickly after the magic they made, right there in Kevin's own bed. He sighed as he remembered every delicious detail. He longed for Mitch to be there, wanted him to just hold him.

His life had changed so much since he'd met Mitch. He'd been lost. He knew that now. All that crap he'd done. Sloan didn't deserve it. He knew that now thanks to Mitch and his love. Kevin vowed to himself he would somehow make it up to Sloan as soon as he returned from his business trip. With his mother leaving for God knows how long, Sloan was the only parent he had left. And a parent he was. That was something Kevin had not believed or accepted for so long. But he knew with newfound certainty that Sloan cared about him.

He almost drifted off to sleep, thinking of his newly acquired appreciation of Sloan and of Mitch, the man who had turned him around.

All this shit will stop.

A sudden revelation. "Oh, crap! That research paper's due, and I haven't even started. Why can't my school have the day off like Mark's? His school makes their own rules, I guess. They're always giving those kids the day off. Damn! If I'm turning over a new leaf, I've gotta get my paper done on time. No more bullshit. Not for Sloan. Not for my teachers. Not for myself."

He leaped out of bed and went to his desk, not even stopping to pull on clothes. Using both his laptop and his desktop, he managed to cobble together fifteen hundred words on climate change. Thank God for his mind and the way it worked. He was able to instantly remember the stuff he found on the desktop while turning it into a credible thesis on the laptop. Finishing, he pushed *print.* Nothing.

He pushed *print* again, fully knowing if it didn't work the first time, it wasn't gonna work the second time. With the expected negative results, he mumbled, "Oh, shit," and decided to investigate. Out of paper.

The day before, Mark screamed at him for using up all the paper. He remembered that now. Fat lot that helped him. No printer paper, none, in the house.

He'd have to go get some. But where in the hell do you buy printer paper in the middle of the night? *Walgreens...they're open twenty-four hours.*

He pulled on some clothes, ran downstairs, jumped into the Spyder, revved it up, and headed out.

He parked and ran into the store. Passing the entrance, he noticed a guy about his age, standing, smoking a cigarette. The guy eyed him, but Kevin didn't think anything about him. He was always getting looks. A combo of his face and the Spyder. He smiled. The Spyder got 'em every time.

Looking for the aisle he needed, he saw the guy, who now had come into the store. But Kevin had Mitch. He didn't need to pick up a stranger to get his rocks off. Those rocks were very pleasingly gotten off earlier, thank you, ma'am, bam-bam. He giggled under his breath, wondering if Mitch would like his irreverent reaction. After all, what they did was an almost sacred act, Kevin felt.

He grabbed a ream of paper off the shelf, took it to checkout, pulled out a ten, and handed it to the cashier. Taking his change, he returned to his car.

In his own driveway, Kevin took his purchase and jogged toward the front door. He wanted to get this task over so he could get back under the covers to dream of Mitch.

Just as he entered the door lock code, he felt hot breath over his shoulder.

"What's that?"

Kevin didn't recognize the voice.

He felt a push. Stumbling into the foyer, he managed to look over his shoulder. The guy from Walgreens.

"Alone in this palace, pretty boy?"

The uninvited visitor used his foot to push the door closed. Kevin heard the lock click. *What's going on here?*

Kevin wanted to bluff his way out, hoping to convince the guy there were servants galore, ready to pounce on him. But his brilliant mind was not working. He couldn't think of anything that would make the guy think he was not alone. Then it came to him, and he hoped it worked.

"Hey, guy. I hoped it was you. But be quiet. Mom's upstairs, and she's a light sleeper. Let's go somewhere else where we can be alone. What say?"

"What did you have in mind, *girl*?" Utter contempt in the last word. "Maybe Mommy'd like to watch, huh?"

Kevin started to panic. The guy wasn't leaving, and it was obvious he wasn't buying Kevin's story.

"Mama, you up there?" the guy called loudly. "Come out, come out. Yer baby has somethin' to show ya."

The guy was brazen. Anybody could have been in the house. But Kevin figured this guy saw the fear in his eyes, heard in his voice the "mom is sleeping" was a lie. Kevin didn't know whether to try to overpower him or run.

But he didn't get the chance, either way. The musclebound goon grabbed him. Kevin tried to break away. But the predator was too strong.

"Oh, like it rough, do ya?" He pushed Kevin, binding his arms with his enormous biceps. "Where's yer bed? Upstairs? You're not my usual type, but I was at that fuckin' store for hours. You're the best choice to wander in. Let's go." Kevin dragged his feet. "March!"

As they went up the stairs, Kevin's mind wandered. *Okay. I can't get away, but if I let him take me, let him do what he wants with me, maybe he'll leave after. I just have to stay calm. Just lie there and let him do whatever he wants.*

"Which room?" The voice was sharp, stabbing.

Kevin stopped in front of his bedroom. He'd left the door open, so the rapist could see his bed, covers totally in disarray.

As the guy pushed him into the room and onto the bed, he said, "Looks like ya started the party 'thout me. Your boyfriend just leave? Or did ya have some very active solo action?" The guy was hovering so close over Kevin's face that he could smell the foul odor of his breath.

"My boyfriend left to get burgers for us, so he should be back any time now. I went for printer paper because I suddenly realized I had to print out some research. But I texted my boyfriend to let him know where I went. He'll be back any minute." Kevin babbled, hoping to stave off the inevitable.

"Then we better get at it, baby," the guy said. He pressed his forearm against Kevin to hold him down.

Oh, god, oh god, oh god—please forgive me for everything bad I've ever done. Let this be over quick.

Mitch

Mitch's hands shook as he pushed the key fob button. He got into his car. He sat, dreading. Even if Kevin was innocent—which he was sure of—Mitch's asking could destroy their lives forever.

I love Kevin. I'm supposed to trust him. Asking such a thing of the man I love. It's unthinkable.

But dammit. Brent made sense. The pieces fit. I don't want them to. But they do.

The sun peeked over the horizon. Mitch, wanting to delay this as long as possible, reached for his phone. He wanted to see what time it was. But he'd left his phone on Brent's coffee table. He couldn't call Kevin and warn him of the shitstorm he was about to face even if he wanted to.

He started the engine. He was low on gas. He had plenty to get back to Kevin's house, but stopping for fuel was a distraction. And God knows, it was a welcomed distraction—anything to delay.

He pulled into an Exxon station. He got out. Unscrewed the gas cap. Put the nozzle in. Stood as the pump clicked away, filling the tank. Tank full, he removed the nozzle. Hung it on its hook. Went to the window to pay. Returned to the car.

He pulled away from the station and entered the street.

How many minutes did that take? Whatever, they were precious minutes that Kevin could live peacefully before I destroy his life. He'll never forgive me. I should let it lay. I know he's not the killer. But Brent...

He drove toward the inevitable. Twenty miles an hour. Even at this ungodly hour, cars were passing him, honking, furious with him. But he needed delay. He was going to drop a bomb soon. The later, the better.

Look at that golden haze. It's gonna be a beautiful day. A day the woman there waiting for the bus may remember as a joyful one. A day the guy in the plumbing truck may remember as the day he made his biggest sale. A day that homeless man with the collection cup may get enough to eat for three days, maybe even find a place to take that shower he's wanted for the last week. A day the waitress in that diner may win the lottery.

A day my own life will end.

He pulled into the circular drive. Turned off the engine.

Dread made him shudder.

He got out of the car. He sighed. He plodded toward the front door. He punched in the code Kevin gave him.

He stepped inside. Quiet. He thought of the adage 'silent as a tomb.' No doubt because he felt he was entering his own tomb.

He looked upward. Kevin's room. Far end of the hallway.

The door was shut. He didn't remember shutting it when he left, but that was hours ago. Kevin might have gotten up for some reason and then closed the door when he came back.

Lord, don't make me do this. But he had to.

He gripped the banister. Put one foot on the first step. Paused. Took a deep breath. Step by creeping step, he climbed.

He turned the doorknob. Pushed the door open.

There was a guy on top of Kevin. His body blocked Kevin's.

Kevin! Cheating on him!

Mitch's dread morphed into anger, total fury.

"What the hell?" Mitch stood in the doorway, a statue. A statue of anger and distrust and disgust and incredulity. Mitch couldn't move.

The guy on top of Kevin jerked his head around. Mitch caught a glimpse of blood. Kevin's head oozed red. The heavy side table lamp lay on the floor.

Mitch leapt to the bed. Grabbed the predator's shoulder. Pulled and pulled. The guy held onto Kevin's neck, choking him. Kevin turned a purplish color. He was trying desperately to breathe.

Mitch put everything he had into yanking the guy away. Finally, with his arm around the guy's neck and the shit struggling for air himself, the man loosened his grip. Kevin gasped for air.

Mitch flung the guy across the room.

Wanting to hold Kevin, wanting to help him breathe, wanting to tell him he loved him, Mitch heard, "This is fun."

Kevin's attacker grabbed Mitch, forced him around. His face inches away from Mitch's. "Never got me two in one night. This'll be a personal best."

He slugged Mitch.

Mitch's heart pounded. It was like he felt the adrenaline racing through him. He knew the guy's fist hit his chin, but he didn't feel it. Not even thinking about himself, his mind on saving Kevin, Mitch head-butted the guy, making him lose his balance. His attacker, no, Kevin's attacker, tumbled over backward. Mitch kicked him in the groin, over and over.

This once-confident rapist, murderer, whatever, doubled over, clutching himself, screaming in pain.

Mitch got his belt off. Jerked the guy over. Forced his arms around behind him. He wound the belt around the guy's crossed wrists, pulling the belt as tight as he could. Semi-stunned from the head-butt and totally immobilized from the kicks, the intruder lay spent.

"What in holy hell?"

Mitch was startled by the voice coming from the doorway. Sloan.

"Call 911! Kevin. Needs help." Mitch gasped, finally trying to breathe from all he'd just done. He added, "The cops need to get here 'fore I kill this piece of shit!"

22
Brent

"How's Kevin?" Brent shouted, running toward Mitch in the waiting room.

Mitch said nothing. He looked frozen, collapsed in the chair.

Sloan intercepted. Quietly, he told Brent, "Kevin's in surgery. It may be hours before we know anything. Mitch is a wreck right now, after what he's gone through. After what Keven's gone through. He needs a friend, though, so I'm glad he called you. I'm Sloan, by the way, Kevin's dad."

"Good to meet you, Sloan. I'm Brent," Brent said automatically, his good upbringing kicking in despite his concern for Mitch at that moment.

Brent looked at Mitch. He was broken. But who wouldn't be broken at a time like this? Brent was still in the dark. Didn't know exactly what had happened, but it was painfully obvious he'd been wrong about Kevin. Mitch might make him pay for that the rest of his life. And maybe he deserved it. He was so desperate to find Callum's killer he jumped to the very wrong conclusions.

He walked over and sat in the chair next to Mitch. He leaned in and took his hand. "I know you don't want to talk right now, but I'm glad you called me. I'll be right here until we know something. And after that, I'll be here with you and Kevin as long as you want me here. And I hope that's a long, long time—for us all three.

Mitch was still catatonic. But Brent thought he felt some tension release in the hand he was holding.

Minutes turned into hours.

Eventually, a woman showed up, distraught. Brent overheard her conversation with Sloan.

"I got here as soon as I could. I was on a conference call with China, and you know how that goes."

"That's always the case with you, isn't it? A conference call takes precedence when your son is fighting for his life. Makes sense to me." Sloan's voice was acid.

"That's not fair, Sloan. You know how important my project is. These China connections could fund it entirely. You said Kevin was facing hours of surgery. I couldn't do anything here, but by completing that call, I could be saving a lot of other children's lives."

Now interested in this conversation, Brent looked up. He saw the expression on Sloan's face. It was utter contempt for this woman. That's how Brent thought of her. She may have given birth to Kevin, but she'd just proven she was nothing but some woman, some stranger, in her son's life.

"Look," Sloan said, "I'm not going to argue with you right now. I'm too busy worrying about my son. But, in case you forgot, we have another son. Mark has no idea what's going on. For whatever reason, he, unlike Kevin, seems to think you care about him. Call him to tell him you're picking him up. You tell him how his brother is on an operating table right now. But don't bring him here. Not until we know more. And not until I can stand seeing your face again."

And with that, Kevin's mom left.

Brent watched the clock on the wall as it ticked off each second. Another hour went by. He felt a stirring in the hand he was holding. He looked at Mitch.

"I never shoulda listened to you." Mitch's words were halting, like he was pulling them from the depths of his soul.

"I know. I know. I was dead wrong." Brent suddenly felt guilty for his choice of words. Dead was the last word Mitch needed to hear right then. "But I'm here now for you and for Kevin. Let me stay. Talk if you want. Don't if you want. But talking might help."

Mitch began to sob.

Brent put his arm around Mitch's shoulder and pulled him closer. He heard Sloan say, "I'm gonna get some coffee."

Brent looked up.

"No, Sloan, Kevin's your son. You don't have to leave."

Sloan gave an almost imperceptible smile, and he shook his head. "You guys need some alone time. I'm glad you're here for Mitch. Maybe he'll open up to you. The police got very little out of him. And I certainly didn't. I'm just glad I took the redeye home, or Mitch might have killed that asshole. And Kevin..." He didn't finish his sentence.

"Thanks, Sloan. I'll come get you if we hear anything."

Sloan left.

"Okay, Mitch. We can talk. If you want to."

Mitch raised his head and wiped his tears. "I can't believe I actually thought Kevin was capable of what you said he'd done." The words were measured. Quiet. Bitter.

"I know, I know, I know. From now on, I'll leave police work to the cops. I'm just glad you wanted me here now, after all I said and did."

"After they took Kevin from the ambulance here at the hospital, I was lost. Couldn't face this alone. Yeah, Sloan was here, but I needed a friend. And you're the only friend... "

He sobbed again.

"I *am* your friend. A shitty friend. But still a friend."

Mitch swiped his eyes with his sleeve. Sucked the snot back into his nose. Looked at Brent. "Don't be so hard on yourself. Everything you said made sense. I didn't wanna believe it, but it did make sense. *All* the signs pointed to him. And I know Kevin had proven he was a badass. But the more we fell in love, the deeper it got, he shed that skin. So I dreaded confronting him. Not believing, but believing. And not wanting to. The not knowing was killing me. I had to ask him and deal with it."

"But you *didn't* have to." *Why oh why did I say that? Now he'll just re-live the horror he experienced.*

Mitch became more animated.

"God, Brent, you can't imagine what I've gone through. We had the most amazing night last night before you called. Then I listened to you, and I knew I had to find out if what you'd said was true, all the while telling myself you had to be wrong. And believing you. All at the same time.

"Then I got to Kevin's house. All I could see from the door to his room was what looked like some guy and Kevin fuckin'. I went ballistic. But then that shit turned around, and I could see he bashed Kevin's head in and was chokin' 'im to death. I don't even remember what all went down after that. I just know I was not gonna let 'im do any more damage. So I lit into him. I swear, if Sloan hadn't shown up, I woulda killed the guy. I know I would."

"Anybody would've. He was trying to kill the love of your life. Don't even think your reaction was anything but loving and courageous, Mitch."

"Well," Mitch said, heaving a huge sigh. "I guess you're right. But that's to figure out another time. Right now, we have to get Kevin well."

Just then Sloan arrived, almost colliding with the doctor, still dressed in bloody scrubs.

"He lost a lot of blood, but we managed to repair the damage. And ex-rays show his throat is okay. It'll be sore for several days. The bruising'll be ugly. But he's gonna make it. The kid's a fighter. Don't expect his thought patterns to be normal, though. Takes a long time for the brain to heal from all this. May be days, even weeks, before he can put together what happened to him. Right now, though, he's safe, and he's in recovery. You can see him, Mr. Howell."

By this time, Mitch was standing beside Sloan. "This is Kevin's boyfriend, Doctor. Can he come with?"

"Certainly. But just the two of you. And only for a few minutes. He's still under sedation. We'll keep him there awhile as we let the brain heal."

"I'll be right here, Mitch," Brent said. "I'm not going anywhere."

✟✟✟

Brent punched Mitch's number on his phone.

"Hey, guy," Mitch said.

"How's Kev today?" Brent asked.

"Makin' a lotta progress since you were here last. They're sayin' he might be released soon. Till then, it's just wait. And waiting's not what I'm good at."

"Just hang in there."

"Ya hear? They finally confirmed Kevin's attacker is the serial killer. The DA charged him with five counts of murder and one count of attempted. They also attached special circumstances. So now they're hate crimes. Death penalty's on the table. Indiana rarely does an execution, Gordon said, but the DA's confident in this case she can win. And even if the punishment's never carried out, the shit hole will be in jail for the resta his life."

Brent listened, saying nothing. Mitch was repeating things they both already knew. But he let Mitch talk, knowing he was still processing everything.

"Yeah. I heard. But here's somethin' ya don't know. In fact, other than checkin' on Kevin, this is why I called ya."

"Spill."

"So, even though we know who did all this now, I'm still obsessin'. I was lookin' at the pic the news photographer shot the night this guy was arrested at Kevin's house. I dunno how they let him get s' close, and it's kinda gruesome. You really did a number on 'im, m' friend. And good for you, I say. Anyway, I noticed somethin'. His collar had some sort of pin stuck in it. You know, the kind people wear that show they belong to a group of some kind. I blew up the pic, and guess what I found?"

"What?"

"That pin had a crown of thorns with a W underneath and C superimposed on the W. Get it? Warriors for Christ. We were right. The killer was one of Fellows's people."

"Ya sure?"

"I've stared at a trillion of those Fellows videos. And all his followers wear a lapel pin. On their suits. On their collars. A pin exactly like the killer wore."

Mitch huffed a "Got him" under his breath. "Brent, can ya screenshot your blowup and email it to me?"

"Sure, but why?"

"Just do it. It'll become clear very soon. Watch Force Four news. Five o'clock."

Mitch

Mitch long ago forgave Brent's suspicions of Kevin. But Brent was not far off the mark. The *accused*—Mitch hated that they had to use that word 'cause the asshole was guilty as sin—did indeed drive a low-slung sports car, used a metal-alloy baseball bat for many of the crimes, and one look at the uncle who raised him told you why he chose victims who looked alike. The uncle, they said, was brutal in his parenting—which doesn't excuse the murders at all, but it does explain them somewhat—and, like many serial killers, the guy was obliterating his uncle over and over. Why he chose Kevin, who didn't fit his profile, was still a mystery.

In none of this was any mention of Spencer Fellows.

Brent's latest discovery was the icing on the cake.

When Brent called, Mitch was about to head to Channel Four to be interviewed by Marlon Gordon. Gordon begged for an exclusive as soon as he knew Mitch had taken down the killer. But Mitch held Gordon off. He wasn't ready to relive that night in public. After the District Attorney spoke to Mitch, though, he realized he had to go public. Telling his story to her, even more than telling it to the cops, was cleansing somehow. But the DA cautioned him not to blow the case by giving his testimony away to Gordon or any other reporter.

So when Gordon called for the twelve-hundredth time, Mitch made a deal with him. He'd speak to him as long as he didn't talk about the case but rather about the victim. He said he'd only talk if the interview was about Kevin and all the other gay victims of this guy.

And Gordon's response was exactly what Mitch expected: "Why don't I bring on Dr. Fellows as well? I know you *have* to take issue with his position. Maybe you could talk sense into the good doctor." Mitch heard Gordon, through the phone's cyberspace, trying to pile on contempt to those two words, but Mitch knew that ratings seeker Marlon Gordon only wanted Mitch's *daddy* on for the controversy he brings. That was okay, because Mitch *wanted* to share the screen with his father.

Marlon Gordon pounced on Mitch as soon as the receptionist put down her receiver, having announced his arrival.

"So glad you agreed to do this. Our viewers deserve to know everything about this case."

Yeah, and think of the ratings it will bring, Marlon. Visions of NYC dancing in your head?

As they walked, Gordon filled him in on what would happen on the broadcast. "Dr. Fellows is here. In the studio. I'll speak to him first. Then we'll have you on for the rebuttal."

Mitch could tell by the tone of Gordon's voice that he had it all planned.

Nothing's gonna screw up Marlon Gordon's chance at the big time.

The broadcast began with familiar talking heads doing breaking news. Then the ever-smiling, perfectly coiffed weatherman gave his forecast. Finally, the announcement came: "Here's Force Four's Marlon Gordon with an update on the story he's been following for months. Marlon?"

Mitch looked at the overhead monitor as Gordon began. "Our entire town's been abuzz with the news of the serial killer who had been terrorizing the gay community for several months. Thankfully, our district attorney has told us she's totally confident they have their man, and he'll be punished to the full extent of the law. But many of you have clamored for comment from the young man who brought this killer down. We'll hear from him, exclusively, in just a moment. But first, a familiar face is here with us now, Dr. Spencer Fellows."

On the monitor, the camera cut to a close-up of Mitch's father.

"Dr. Fellows, you wanted to speak?" Gordon's voice came from off-screen.

"Thank you, Marlon." That fake smile broke out on Mitch's father's face, the one he pasted on whenever he faced a camera. "It is a sad situation. This young man accused of these alleged crimes did God's work. Our Heavenly Father was, and still is, angry that homosexuals are invading our city and spreading their agenda. So the Lord chose this angel to avenge Him. And, mark my words, the Lord will indeed show His wrath if this man is executed."

Fellows opened his mouth to continue when Gordon abruptly cut him off.

"Thank *you*, Dr. Fellows. In our studio, we have someone close to Kevin Bland, the surviving victim of these heinous crimes. He'd like to speak, and then, Dr. Fellows, perhaps you will have further comment."

Mitch's heart pumped faster. Finally. His chance. He had to do this. For Kevin. And for every other gay, lesbian, bisexual, or transgender that had felt the wrath of not God, but Spencer Fellows, his own father.

He glanced at the monitor to see a split-screen image of his father on the right, himself on the left. So Marlon wants to see my daddy's face as I talk. Good. I want to see it too.

Mitch quickly smiled into the camera as he listened to Gordon's voiceover. "In our studio this evening is Mitchell Christman, a man who knows Kevin Bland extremely well and, in fact, is the man who saved him from death. He'd like to give his take on what happened."

Mitch took a short breath. He began to speak.

"As Marlon said, I know Kevin well. He and I are partners, deeply devoted to each other. Kevin's a brilliant young man. He's got a bright future ahead of him. He's witty. He's caring. He's loving. I'm not here to speak of my part in bringing down the man who almost killed someone I love very much. That, I'm told, could jeopardize the case. And, Dr. Fellows, even you, I would think, would not want to put this case in doubt in any way. Let's just say the killer seems to have harbored a deep-seated hatred for gay men, and my Kevin, unfortunately, got in his way. I thank God every moment that I was able to save Kevin. And not your God, Dr. Fellows, for I have no use for the deity you think is capable of such hate and anger."

His father was stoic. Not a trace of reaction.

Mitch smiled inside. The best was yet to come. He continued. "Christ taught us to love. Not just the people we think are worthy of our love. But each and every person we encounter. Kevin makes me feel I can rule the world. He supports me. He loves me. And love like that can only be a good thing."

He noticed a tiny sneer on his father's face. But the man still looked so smug. So sure of himself.

Mitch began to recite. He'd carefully constructed this speech for maximum impact.

"I came into this world as a child of a woman who'd been wronged, gravely wronged. I grew up never knowing who my father was. You know the term 'father issues?' Well, I had those big time. I thought a dad was the greatest gift any kid could have. I saw my classmates with their dads, dads who played catch with 'em, carried 'em on their backs, took 'em to football games. My heart ached. I had the kindest, most loving, most supportive mom anyone could ever have, but there was a giant gaping hole in my life. Where was my dad? Why didn't I have a dad like I saw all the time with the other kids?

"And then, when my mother was dying, she told me who my father was. It was a shocker. I knew the man. This man could not be my dad. No way. But mom had proof."

Was Dr. Spence starting to crack?

"I lived with my secret. I mighta wanted a dad, but I didn't want this one. There was no way I would admit to anyone *he* was my father. This man was the most hateful man on the planet. He proved it each and every day.

"He wanted the masses of the world—yeah, made a fortune off their backs—to think he was goodness personified. But instead, he spouts vicious and vile words, hate personified, begging anyone within the reach of his voice to praise a murderer. He claims God is so angry that he'd want people like me, his own son, a proud gay man, wiped off the face of the earth. Spencer Fellows, your God's indeed angry, but I'm not the one he's angry with."

Before Mitch finished, the camera cut to a full-screen image of the doctor. In the monitor, Mitch saw Fellows's composure slip, but his hubris, no doubt, allowed him to think he could salvage his reputation. Fellows stood, frozen, letting the camera take him in.

A soundbite started playing, accompanied by a scrawl at the bottom of the screen—subtitles making each word clear.

The voice of Spencer Fellows played as Mitch observed the takedown of his father. The man visibly cratered. "This is enough to set you up for life. Get rid of that thing inside you, move far away, and leave me alone. I've got plans for my life, and they don't include you."

When the voiceover finished, the camera once again showed a split screen image, Mitch on the left, Fellows on the right. Mitch said, "Dad, I not only have more on that tape, but I have my mother's journals. Plenty of proof, *Daddy*."

Dr. Spencer Fellows was still that frozen statue on the screen beside Mitch.

"Oh, and one more thing. Since I'm here to talk about Kevin and not myself, Dad, you have said repeatedly—we've all heard it in the countless interviews you love to give to Marlon, here—that you have never seen this vicious killer. Never knew him."

Mitch held up the picture Brent sent him.

"If that's true, then why is he wearing one of your lapel pins? My friend tells me, because he's done an awful lot of research about you and your followers, that you hand these out to your faithful all the time."

Suddenly, the face of Dr. Spencer Fellows disappeared from the screen as he walked away, a cameraman following his back all the way out of the studio.

Then Gordon reappeared. "Apparently, Dr. Fellows has nothing to add. This has been Marlon Gordon, Force Four News."

Mitch

Mitch went straight to the hospital after he left the elated Marlon Gordon. He had no idea if his words had crushed his father or not. He figured the weasel would find a way out of all of it. He always did. But this time, though, he was in deeper shit. And Mitch was glad.

When he bounded into Kevin's room, Kev was eating his dinner. The TV was off. Good. Mitch knew he'd eventually tell Kevin everything, but right now, he didn't need to know. He was recovering well, and tonight, he'd let Kev eat his Jello in peace.

"Tell me ya got a burger and fries with ya," Kevin said when he saw Mitch. "I'm starvin' to death, and this ain't cuttin' it." He pointed to his dinner tray.

"You'll be outta here 'fore ya know it. I'll take you for the best burger I can find. I'll do m' research, babe."

"Where ya been? Dad and Mark were here, but they left for the night. Mom. Well, you know mom. She's saving her African children and loses track of time. I don't like it one bit. But I'm dealin'. She comes 'round some. Not much. But some. We're not on a hug and kiss and make up track yet. She and Sloan are still on the outs too. Ya know what? That's their problem. And really, I think that'll work itself out. My point's I been all alone, pinin' away, waitin' for m' honey pot."

"They got you on that morphine drip again? You be crazy, babe."

Mitch laughed. Then he leaned over and kissed Kevin.

"Mm-m-m. You taste good, Mitchie. Climb up on this bed and make me feel better, better."

"No way. Nurse Ratched's on duty tonight. Talk about goin' ballistic. I don't wanna incur her wrath. And you're still too frail to be put through that."

Actually, the nurse they called Nurse Ratched—they'd both read the book and seen the movie *One Flew Over the Cuckoo's Nest*—was the best and nicest of all of the nurses. But she loved to play like she was easily riled.

"Okay, babe, time for ya to tell me all about your day. I hate havin' to go to classes. They take up my day, time when I could be here with you," Mitch said. "How they treatin' ya?"

"Fine, fine. Doc says every day is progress. Maybe five more days, and then I'll be ready to face the world. The psych's workin' with me to recall that night. I really don't wanna. But the DA thinks my testimony will be the cherry on top. They got a ton of evidence now they know who did it. They c'n tie it all to him. But she still wants me on the stand. So the mind doctor is tryin' to work with me. But you know all that."

"I know, but I just love hearin' you talk. Your throat was so fucked up for so long that I missed hearin' your voice. Anyway, you keep takin' baby steps with that memory thing. I don't want you freakin' out. You suffered enough, babe."

They spent the rest of the evening joking, playing gin, making plans for the future, and kissing. A lot of kissing.

Kevin

Kevin sat up in his hospital bed, watching the morning news. He felt good. The bandages on his head had gradually decreased in size until now he had little more than a Band-Aid. He soft-pedaled it to Mitch the night before, but the memories were coming back pretty fast. The psychiatrist who showed up like clockwork at his bedside every day cautioned him that the memories could be brutal. Kevin, though, found he wasn't haunted by what happened that night. He was too happy that his Mitch had shown up to save him.

And now his Mitch had saved himself. He saw the replay on the morning news. There he was. Mitch. In front of everybody. Keeping that secret had to be hard on him. Kevin wondered why Mitch locked up something like that inside him for so long. He could have helped him with it, just as Mitch helped him so much. All that hate he harbored for Sloan. What a waste of time it was. Mitch had made him see that.

And that lapel pin thing! Wow. Amazing. Not only did Mitch expose the good doctor for his dirty deeds, but he tied him to the murders. Sure, Fellows had nothing to do, really, with the murders, but he certainly was the one working the remote. He might have just come right out and told the guy, "Kill for me." Maybe this will end the reign of Dr. Spencer Fellows for good.

Suddenly, a burst of happiness came through the door like a hurricane. Mark.

"Kev! When you getting' outta here? I want some ice-cream, some batting practice. I miss my brother, yo!"

"Well, listen to you, you little gangsta—yo!" He repeated Mark's rap slang.

He leaned toward Mark while his little brother gave him a big, big hug.

"Careful, Markie. Your brother's still delicate." Sloan's voice filled the room.

"'S okay, Dad." Kevin loved the huge smile that broke out on Sloan's face as he called him Dad. "This little squirt can't do much damage."

Then the air in the room seemed to turn a little colder as a huge bouquet slowly made its way to the bed, borne by none other than Kevin's mother—he couldn't bring himself even to *think* her name, much less call her mother. She'd tried, but not even his being snatched from the jaws of death was bringing him closer to forgiving her.

"Kevin, dear, I hope you like roses." She placed the vase on the bed stand, and then leaned over for him to kiss her cheek. He declined.

Looking embarrassed, angry, or hurt—Kevin had long ago quit trying to read his mother's emotions as they were always fake anyway—his mother stood upright.

"She's tryin' to be nice, Kev. Can't you see that?" Mark had come to his mother's rescue.

"Kevin, dear," his mother said, "my heart broke and only started mending when I heard you were out of surgery."

Yeah, sure. Do you have a heart?

With a hesitance, a stitch in her voice, she continued. "Yes, I put far too much into my work. I was too wrapped up in it to even rush over here that morning, too caught up in an international call, as Sloan very pointedly made me realize. Thank God for that. That's right. I was angry at the way your father spoke to me until I realized his every word was true. Your workaholic mother could have done more for you."

Kevin saw the unexpected. His mother was fighting back tears over this revelation.

"Not just that night." She looked like she was trying to keep the tears from letting her say what she was determined to say. "But throughout your entire life." She began sobbing.

"I missed so much, baby. That little bundle of joy I once held so delicately I was afraid I would break him, became this strong, intelligent, beautiful young man. And I missed it all."

She held out her hand to him, and he took it. He didn't know why. Maybe he believed her. Maybe he thought he should play along with this.

Maybe what she said stirred up some emotions buried so deep he hadn't felt them for years.

She grasped his hand like she was hanging off a cliff and was pleading for him to pull her back.

"But that's over."

He looked at her. *What? What's over?*

"I wanted it all—career, marriage, family—and I thought I had it. But when it all started to slip away, I knew I was a failure." The sobbing started again. "With all of it."

She locked her eyes onto his.

"So I took these last weeks to do some reflection. I was afraid you didn't want me here. The few times I came, you wouldn't even look at me, much less talk to me. But that didn't deter me one bit. I kept up. I phoned the doctors and the nurses twice a day."

"Yes, I did continue with my work."

Of course. You say you've turned over a new leaf. But your work will always come first. His heart fell. He'd begun to believe her.

"I haven't given up my project, but I won't be flying anywhere. I handed over the heavy lifting. From now on, I only delegate. I told your Dad to have armed guards remove me from my office if I stay one moment after five pm each day. No more. I'm going to cook, clean, and love my two precious boys and my wonderful husband."

She stood. Silent. No one spoke. It was as if she had said nothing. She started to tear up again.

Kevin laughed.

His mother looked like he had hit her with a hot poker.

"You don't even know how to boil water, Mom. Cook doesn't want you anywhere near her kitchen. And we have a full-time live-in maid with two helpers who come three times a week, so cleaning's out."

He paused to let that sink in. Then, just as he saw his mother's tears starting to fall again, he spoke.

"But I'll let you keep one of your promises. You *can* love me."

The tears flowed freely at that. But Kevin could see they were tears of joy. Markie applauded. And Sloan grabbed his wife into a hug.

"Can I join the party?"

"Mitch!" Kevin yelped.

The Howell family moved out of the way so Mitch could give Kevin a hello kiss.

Wanting more and more and more, Kevin, nevertheless, pulled away after one kiss. "Mitch, I don't think you've met my mom Do—." He began to voice her name in introduction when Mitch grabbed her into a hug.

"Good to finally meet ya, Mom!" Kevin saw his mother beam. It felt good to see her so happy. And he did believe the speech she'd made. He knew it would take time to work everything out, to erase all the bad stuff and fill their lives with good, but he knew they'd work it out. If there was one thing his mother knew how to do, it was work.

Sloan spoke. "Saw the news last night, Mitch. Real sorry to hear your story. Took lots of courage for you to tell it."

Kevin added, "You did a brave thing, babe."

Mitch was uneasy at what Sloan had said because he still hadn't told Kevin. But it seems the beans were spilled. "You know?"

"Saw the replay this morning."

Kevin's mom added, "Mitch, you'll never be able to keep anything from this one. Never. I know." She smiled at Kevin.

"Well, as long as it's all out, let me clue you in on what I just saw. On the way over, I drove by daddy dear's compound. Deserted. It's like cobwebs grew on it overnight. Dr. Spencer Fellows musta made a fast retreat after he left that studio yesterday. Not only that, but the building's covered with graffiti. I saw "MURDERER" and "GET OUT OF TOWN" and "I LOVE MY GAY SON, YOU SCUM" and tons more. I think the good doctor's been run out of town on a rail. I may have seen some tar and feathers too."

"That's wonderful news," Kevin's mom said. "Good riddance."

"Yeah," Mitch said. "We're rid of him. And I hope this all follows him wherever he goes. People like him just set up shop in a new town, a new place. But if I know Marlon Gordon—and I do, ya know—I could get ya his autograph—he's takin' this story national. The man's nothin' if not ambitious with a capital A. Maybe m' friend Mar can keep my father from spreadin' any more hate."

"Come on, family," Sloan said. "Let's let these boys have some alone time." He ushered his wife and second son out of the room.

"Why didn't you ever share this with me? Especially now. You had to know I'd see it on TV."

"I guess I couldn't admit to the world that I was the progeny of such a hateful man. I was afraid people would judge *me* by my father's deeds."

Kevin took Mitch's hand. "Horse hockey. Most people know Spencer Fellows for what he is, and the others? His minions? Blind sheep. Who cares what they think? I only know if you'd told me, I would have thought no less of you." He picked up Mitch's hand and kissed it.

"So, it looks like you four are one big happy family again."

"Yeah, looks like it, don't it?" Kevin smiled and then paused. "Operative word *looks*. I know we got a rough road to travel, but it seems my mother has made a sea change in her attitude, and it only took the almost death of her eldest."

"Well, at least something good has come outta all this," Mitch said. "I was never much of a God person. But I think something out there is guidin' us. Something gave me the strength to fight that night. And I thank God or whatever for that."

"Well, if God *is* an angry God, let's hope He rains down his wrath on Spencer Fellows."

Acknowledgments

I've learned so much during my writing career, and I've been guided and taught by so many wonderful mentors. Once again, I want to give a shoutout to Kelly Bennett, for she is a tireless champion of my work and is always there to praise me and scold me. Kelly is a friend par excellence and an author beyond compare. And I also want to thank Ian Henzel and Rattling Good Yarns Press for believing in An Angry God when others turned away from it, declaring it too dark for young audiences.

About the Author

Russell J. Sanders writes because he's compelled to do so. It seems every time one of his books is published, there is a sigh of completion, and then a new idea crops up, propelling him to create a new world for characters that need guidance. Between these creative explosions, Russell travels—most of the US states, Jakarta, Bali, Tokyo, India, Trinidad and Tobago, London, Amsterdam, Paris, Italy, the Caribbean, and Canada are among the exotic locations he's visited. After living almost his entire life in Texas, he is now exploring his new home state Nevada and his new hometown Las Vegas. One thing is always assured during these journeys: Mexican food will be sought out. As a native Texan, Tex-Mex and related Mexican cuisines are Russell's passion. Whether the dishes turn out good or bad, he must try them. Some very good enchiladas have been had in Tokyo and Indonesia. The worst were in Wyoming, where you might expect better. In between bites, Russell wants to encourage all to read his novels. His deep desire is to entertain while promoting understanding through fiction. Mostly, he wants young persons who are LGBTQ to realize they are normal, deserving to love and be loved, and for those who know them, to realize that as well. He lives in Las Vegas with his husband, who is gamely trailing him in search of the next great enchilada.